MAGIC BOUND

The Haven Chronicles: Book 2

by

Fi Phillips

Burning Chair Limited, Trading As Burning Chair Publishing
61 Bridge Street, Kington HR5 3DJ

www.burningchairpublishing.com

By Fi Phillips
Edited by Simon Finnie and Peter Oxley
Cover by Burning Chair Publishing

First published by Burning Chair Publishing, 2022

ISBN: 978-1-912946-26-6

Also by Fi Phillips:

Haven Wakes – The Haven Chronicles: Book 1

To Dolly and Charlie, those wonderful souls who plied me
with books and tales of magic from the very beginning. This
fairy tale is for you.

Chapter One

The entrance hall of the Alastor Phobus Academy and the courtyard beyond were a bustle of boys and suitcases as the beginning of the school half term holiday beckoned. Three or four vehicles were already parked in the courtyard ready to collect their respective children. Service robots loaded cases and bags, passing them fluidly from limb to limb. A couple of the teachers waited with the boys, keeping them in line until their parents arrived.

Steve watched from a window that looked out onto the courtyard from the chequer-board tiled hallway. Part of him wished he were going home too, back to the safety and familiarity of his own bedroom, but of course that was not going to happen. His parents were still 'away' on the Continent. *Or missing*, his mind pushed in. *Shut up*, he thought back.

"At least you'll have the place to yourself." Jon's voice cut through Steve's mental wanderings. "No one to bother you."

"Yup. There's that," said Steve as he turned to his best friend at school—to be fair, his *only* friend at school, really.

Jon was dressed in his own clothes now, instead of the term-time school uniform. It was still a version of traditional smart—dark dress trousers, white polo shirt, and polished shoes. The only thing that set it apart from their uniform was the lack of a tie, no emblem, and the addition of a mustard duffle coat.

"I got you something." Jon held out a flat, haphazardly wrapped, package. "It's not much."

"What's this for?" said Steve.

"Your birthday." Jon waved the package in Steve's face.

A distinct, recognisable, and wonderful aroma wafted past Steve's nose. "Is that what I think it is?" Steve snatched the parcel from his friend and peeled back a corner to reveal a large chocolate bar, with raisins and popping candy buried in its milky goodness.

"Like I say, it's not much," said Jon with a shrug.

"It's perfect." Steve inhaled one last lungful of the sweet aroma and, fighting the urge to taste it straightaway, wrapped it up again. "Thanks, Jon."

"Happy birthday, Steve."

"Ooh, how romantic." One of Curtis' sidekicks smirked at the two of them. "Don't you make an adorable couple?"

"Shut up, Greig." Curtis, one-time bully and now Steve and Jon's reluctant protector, yanked his friend away. "I told you. We don't bother Haven or Shaw."

"I was only having a bit of fun," Greig moaned as Curtis dragged him through the door to the courtyard beyond.

"I almost like the new Curtis," Jon laughed.

"Yeah. Still, I won't miss having them around," said Steve.

"You'll still be here when we get back, won't you?" Jon looked suddenly worried. "I mean, you've only been back a few weeks."

"I'll be here," said Steve. "Where else would I go?"

Another vehicle pulled into the courtyard, not as shiny as the others. The moment it stopped, the rear passenger door was flung open and a woman dressed in a bright yellow dress spilled out. She wore enough cosmetics to make her age practically unguessable. Her posture gave the impression of someone awkwardly attempting grace and style but falling short of either.

"Jon, dear," she called in shrill tones. "Jon, where are you?"

"Good. Right then." Jon hoisted his bulging rucksack onto his back. "That's my stepmother. I'd better go. She'll only start shouting for me louder." He rolled his eyes.

Steve smiled and nodded as his friend charged out of the school. He watched Jon evade his stepmother's embrace, swinging his rucksack down and narrowly missing the woman's well-coiffed head.

That's that then, Steve thought as he watched his friend's car drive off. *Still, I've got this.* He looked at the wrapped bar of chocolate. It was an expensive brand, something Swiss; and if he was very careful, he could make it last the whole week.

As Steve walked back to his room, chocolate bar in hand, he thought about his friend's comment. *"You'll still be here when we get back, won't you? I mean, you've only been back a few weeks."*

The exact figure was one month, one week, and three days. Steve knew this because he'd been counting the days ever since he had said goodbye to Blessing and the other magicals, stepped through a door in Hartley Keg's shop in Darkacre, and been transported to the headmaster's office.

One month, one week, and three days since he had finally pushed back against Curtis and his cronies and put an end to their bullying.

And one month, one week, and three days since Eleanor Palmer, his late uncle's PA and more recently Steve's ally and friend, had stood up to the headmaster and his secretary Miss Scritch, wrapping up Steve's adventure in her professionally efficient way of getting things done.

All through that time, he had waited for a knock at a door, any door, to signal that Hartley and Blessing hadn't forgotten him. For all its dangers and lack of tech, Darkacre had grown on him. He missed his banter with the mischievous shopkeeper and his chats with Blessing. Life without them felt—he searched for the right word—'grey', he decided. Yes, life without them felt decidedly 'grey'.

*

Thirteen years old, Steve thought as he sat at the desk in his room, about twenty minutes later. *I'm a teenager now.* He wasn't sure exactly how he was expected to feel about that. Was he supposed to act in a more grown-up way, or was he still a kid?

The chocolate bar lay on the bed with the crumpled wrapping paper. He had allowed himself two squares of it, letting each one melt and pop slowly in his mouth. After all, it was the only birthday present he was likely to get this year, with his parents not being around. It was special. He didn't expect anyone else would give him a gift.

Still, his new room was *like* a gift. After Eleanor's meeting with the headmaster, Steve had been moved from his old cupboard of a room in the main school building. He knew it was partly to guard against him 'absconding' again. That was the word, Miss Scritch had used. He'd half expected to be placed in the dormitory, but instead he had been assigned one of the turret rooms.

Originally converted to be teacher accommodation, it had fallen out of use when the more modern staff block had been built. It was his new maths teacher, Mr Tobias, who had suggested Steve be given the room, which had been a surprise, but anything was better than the 'cupboard'.

The turret room was just as it sounded: roughly round with stone walls that revealed the construct of the original school building. The windows, although now bearing panes of glass, were three narrow slits in one section of the wall. The floor consisted of polished wooden boards, some of which creaked when you stood on them. There was a walk-in cupboard that acted as a wardrobe, sparse but comfortable furniture, and a door that locked with a keycard. That last detail was what pleased Steve the most. There was no chance of Miss Scritch, or anyone else, just barging in.

Confining himself to his room, however, was not the plan for the half-term holiday. That would become a bore in no time at all. Instead, he would investigate as much of the school as he could, barring locked doors and Miss Scritch, and take full advantage of the lack of a queue in the canteen. High on his list was a visit to the school library to scour the history books for anything that might hint at the existence of magic and the secret underground world that Hartley had introduced him to.

There was a knock at the door—*rap rap rap*—and a voice that he instantly recognised.

"Haven? Are you in there?"

"Yes, sir."

Steve went to the door and pressed the entry pad beside it. The door slid open to reveal Mr Tobias, the most recent addition to the teaching staff at the school. Compared to Mr Oxtoby and the other teachers, Mr Tobias was the youngest by about twenty years. To Steve's eyes, his teacher was still old; but not ancient like the other teachers.

"Ah, you are in," he said.

"Yes, sir."

"Mind if I come in?"

"Er, okay." Steve stepped back as the teacher took a couple of steps into the turret room.

"Hasn't changed much," said Mr Tobias, nodding his head as he looked around.

"Sir?"

"This used to be my room. Back when I was a student teacher. Is that a present?" Mr Tobias nodded to the chocolate bar and screwed up wrapping paper.

"Yes, sir. It's my birthday." Steve was beginning to feel uncomfortable. He wasn't sure he'd ever spoken to the teacher for this long, not on his own anyway. "Did you want something, sir?"

"Oh yes, of course." Mr Tobias returned to the door and stepped out into the corridor. "The Head wants to see you. In his office. He sent me to fetch you."

"Right," was all Steve said, but his mind raced through a hundred reasons the headmaster, Mr Hendrickson, would want to see him. Was he being moved to the dormitory? Was he being expelled? Had Miss Scritch designed a half-term study schedule to torture him? The only good reason he could think of was that his parents were back and he could go home. "Why?"

"You're asking the wrong person, I'm afraid," said the teacher. "I'm just the messenger. Ready?"

"Yes, sir." Steve pulled the keycard from the slot by the door, tucked it into his trouser pocket, and took a deep breath as he left his room.

*

Bad news it is then, thought Steve as he faced the headmaster and his secretary. Both adults looked furious. Miss Scritch's complexion was growing more purple by the minute, while if the headmaster clenched his jaw any tighter, he was likely to break a few teeth.

"We've had a communication—" Miss Scritch began before the headmaster raised a hand to stop her.

"We have had a communication, Haven," he said. "From Eleanor Palmer. It appears that she would like you to visit the Haven Robotics Corporation during the half-term break."

The headmaster glared at Steve expectantly.

"Thank you," was all Steve could think to say.

"As your interim guardian while your parents are away," said the headmaster, lending a tinge of contempt to the word 'away' as if he didn't really believe it, "Miss Palmer's request has been considered."

That doesn't sound good, thought Steve. He glanced over at his teacher. Mr Tobias made a subtle shrug.

"And while I am not completely comfortable with your being away from school, I feel that the visit would be educational," said the headmaster. "But you must be chaperoned by a member of staff."

"So that you don't abscond," said Miss Scritch.

"I think that was clear, Miss Scritch," said the headmaster. "Unfortunately, we only have a skeleton staff over the holiday—"

"I'd be happy to escort Haven," said Mr Tobias. He gave Steve a quick smile. "If that's acceptable, of course."

"Well, that would save me the time of speaking to the rest of the teaching staff. Thank you, Mr Tobias," said the headmaster.

"Sir?" Steve raised his hand. "When is the visit?"

"Didn't I mention that?" said the headmaster.

"No, Headmaster," said Mr Tobias. "I'm sure you were about to tell us though."

"Of course, I was," said the headmaster. "A car will be sent to collect you at 9am sharp tomorrow morning, Haven."

"Sharp," repeated Miss Scritch.

"Thank you, Headmaster. Miss Scritch." Mr Tobias laid a hand on Steve's shoulder. "We'll leave you in peace now. Won't we, Haven?"

"Yes, sir." Steve did his best not to smile as his teacher steered him out of the headmaster's office. "Thank you, sir."

"Well done, Haven," said his teacher as he closed the door behind them. "Ready for an adventure?"

"Yes, sir," said Steve and this time he couldn't restrain the smile that dashed across his face.

Chapter Two

When the headmaster had said that a car would collect him from school, even though Steve knew he would have a teacher to accompany him, it had filled him with dread. Given that his past two experiences with Haven Corporation automated vehicles had put his life in danger, he really didn't want to take a third chance on them. So when the vehicle that turned up was a long, midnight blue, antique car with a human driver, he was relieved, to say the least.

So far so good, Steve thought to himself as the driver opened the rear door on his side of the sleek vehicle.

"Don't take an eye off that boy, Mr Tobias." Miss Scritch stood at the entrance to the school, arms crossed and jaw set. "Haven has a history of troublesome behaviour."

"Of course, Miss Scritch," said the teacher. "I'll be sure to keep Haven in my sights at all times. Shall we?" He smiled at Steve and pointed to the open car door.

Steve climbed inside and breathed in the smell of the polished leather seats. He ran a hand over the smooth, wooden panel in the door, wondering if it was real, actual wood or synthetic. The wood was stained so dark it was almost black and burnished to a glossy sheen.

"I'm looking forward to this," said Mr Tobias as he climbed in on the other side of the car and closed his own door. "Exciting, isn't it?"

"Yes, sir," said Steve.

For the most part, Steve and his teacher sat in silence on the ride to the Haven Corporation. The window glass was so heavily shaded that the passing buildings were mere vague smudges. An opaque glass panel split the passengers from the front seats where the driver sat. Every time Steve looked at the panel, he caught his teacher's eye reflected in the glass and looked away again.

When they eventually arrived and climbed out of the car, all of the awkwardness of the ride fell away as Eleanor Palmer gracefully rushed to greet them.

"Steve, it's lovely to see you," she said, taking his hands in her own. He knew she wasn't the hugging type. "And this is?"

"Mr Tobias, he teaches me maths at school," said Steve as she released him.

"Leonard Tobias. Please call me Len." The teacher offered his hand to her.

"Eleanor Palmer, interim CEO here at Haven Corp," she said, taking his hand and shaking it once before releasing it. "Steve and I are old friends."

That's one way of putting it, Steve thought, *seeing as we only met a few days ago.* He had to admit though that it felt like longer, after all they'd been through together, so he nodded in agreement.

Steve was surprised to see that the lower levels of the Haven Corporation building were wrapped in scaffolding, and then wondered why he was surprised. Even with Blessing's containment magic, the ferocity of the explosion must have taken an immense toll on the building.

The surrounding plaza didn't look any different to Steve though. The neighbouring glass and steel towers that sat in the shadow of the Haven Robotics Corporation looked as pristine and gleaming as they always had. A stream of smartly dressed commuters departed an e-bus that had stopped on the other side of the travel-way that ran through the plaza. The commuters left through the front door of the e-bus, while their robots used a door towards the back of the vehicle. An advertisement that ran along the length of the bus read, *'30 years of global energy stability thanks to the Helios Project'.*

With the last commuters and robots departed, the doors closed, and the e-bus rose to its former level above the road. As it smoothly moved off, a single, hooded figure wearing sunglasses remained alone at the bus-stop. As she saw Steve, she jolted, almost standing.

The darkling, he thought. *What's she doing here?* He wanted to wave at his friend. If it had been just him and Eleanor, he would have done. Never mind waving, he would have rushed over to the bus-stop and hugged the shadowy fae. As it was, he did nothing.

"This is Mr Cady." Eleanor gestured to an older, spectacled man dressed in neat, white overalls who waited a couple of paces behind her. "Mr Cady is one our senior robotics engineers."

"Hello," said Mr Cady in a cheerful tone. "Good to meet you."

"We've a lot to catch up on," said Eleanor as she took Steve's arm and pulled him along with her. "So much to discuss. Come along now."

As the glass entrance doors slid apart, Steve stopped. It was a knee-jerk reaction, a sudden gut-realisation of where he was. His breathing raced as he remembered the last time he had crossed this threshold. He looked down at his feet, screwing his eyes shut.

"What's wrong, Steve?" Eleanor released his arm. "Are you unwell?"

"I just…" He opened his eyes and took a deep breath. "There used to be the Haven logo engraved in the floor here." He swallowed, hoping his teacher hadn't noticed his alarm.

"Oh, that," she said. "It was damaged in the explosion. We replaced it with plain tiles for now. Shall we?" she asked.

"Yeah, of course." Steve took another deep breath and followed her into the lobby with his teacher and Mr Cady close behind.

The interior of the Haven reception area was just as Steve

remembered it. A white robot receptionist waited behind a glass desk to the left of the entrance. Across the polished, marble floor and at the back of the area was the same lift door they had passed through on their way to meet with Winters. The only difference that Steve could see were the two grey-suited guards who stood on either side of the lift door.

"Now, Steve. We've got a lot to cover, so I've drawn up a schedule," said Eleanor. "Are you ready to get started?"

"Yes please," he said. "Can't wait."

"That's the spirit," she said, taking his arm again. "Come on."

"Excuse me, Miss Palmer." The robot receptionist spoke in a pleasant, measured voice, one limb raised in the air. "Mr Ledwitch has just arrived. He would like to speak with you. He is waiting in your office."

"Now?" said Eleanor with a note of annoyance. "I have a guest."

"That is what he said, Miss Palmer."

"I see." Eleanor took a moment to gather her thoughts, then said, "Please tell Mr Ledwitch that I will be with him shortly."

"Yes, Miss Palmer."

"It appears that I must leave you earlier than I had planned, Steve," said Eleanor. "However, Mr Cady is more than capable of showing you around and answering your questions." She nodded to the engineer. "Mr Tobias?"

"Yes, Miss Palmer?" said the teacher.

"I realise that you have been assigned to chaperone Steve while he is away from school, but I would appreciate a word with him before you leave. In private."

"As you pointed out, I'm Steve's chaperone away from school." Steve felt Mr Tobias lightly grasp his shoulder. "I can't leave him alone."

"He won't be alone," said Eleanor. "He'll be with me and, as I'm sure the headmaster has informed you, while Steve's parents are away the boy is my responsibility."

"The headmaster won't be happy. Or Miss Scritch," said

Mr Tobias. He removed his hand from Steve's shoulder. "But I suppose what they don't know can't harm them."

"Thank you, Mr Tobias." She took a deep breath, releasing it slowly through her lips. "I do hate impromptu meetings." She gave Steve a final smile, turned and left them, her high heels tapping on the polished floor.

"Just the boys then." Mr Cady rubbed his hands together. "Shall we make a start?"

"Sounds good," said Steve with a smile but as he followed the engineer, he couldn't help but wonder about the darkling outside.

*

Eleanor had been true to her word when she said that there was 'a lot to cover'. The tour she had arranged around the robot works was extensive. What struck Steve the most was how quiet the establishment was, except for the piped, harmonious, instrumental music that followed them from room to room. The place was exceptionally clean too. Every surface was polished and dust-free.

Each of the rooms handled the construction and testing of different parts of the robots. The first few involved the assembly of the spherical-shaped bodies. Almost silently, bar the odd click of one component marrying up to another, dozens of arms pulled together the chassis, power supply, patented Haven intelligence processors, and all the servos and motors you'd ever need within the central processing orb.

Steve was fascinated by the design of the processors. He'd always imagined they would be based on the shape of the human brain, but nothing could be further from the truth. They consisted of two black, metal, rectangular slabs which measured about ten centimetres long, eight wide, and a centimetre thick. The slabs sat parallel, a thumb's width apart, their flat sides facing each other. Between the blocks arced a vibrant stream of multi-coloured plasma, which grew in intensity at the centre. Steve thought it looked like a cross between a sandwich and a squished hourglass.

The next room added all the sensors, communication devices, and cameras into what looked little more than large metal footballs. Tracking lasers bounced off and from the robot bodies chasing moving targets which flew around the room. A faint beep sounded as each tracking was confirmed.

"Is it safe for us to be in here?" Steve asked. "We might get hit by one of the lasers."

"Not a problem," said Mr Cady. He reached out a hand towards the barrage of flying lasers and tapped his knuckles on what seemed like thin air but sounded unbelievably solid. "We're stood behind a wall of transparent Kevlar. It's impenetrable to laser beams."

"Impressive," said Mr Tobias.

The third room, which Steve liked the best so far, saw robot limbs putting other robot limbs onto the spherical bodies. Each limb added seemed to have a different attachment at the end, many with grabbing abilities while others had more specialised uses. Every one of them was being tested. A smudged pane of glass was presented to an arm with a smooth rubber, cleaning blade on it, while another arm rapidly rotated a screw into a worn-out block of wood. Another vigorously shook a cocktail shaker so fast that the glass container became a blur. Yet another arm cut through a sheet of metal with an intense bright white light.

The robot limbs were tested for their use as legs too, switching between eight-legged transport, to four, to finally three with the five remaining limbs acting as arms to carry out various cooking tasks all at the same time.

"We've kept the best for last," announced Mr Cady as he led them into a large, open, and empty area.

"What happens here?" said Steve seeing nothing of interest.

"I think you'll like this," said Mr Cady as a door slid aside at the other end of the space. "Normally, only our top customers get this kind of display."

"We're honoured," said Mr Tobias. "Aren't we, Haven?"

"Yes, sir," said Steve.

A parade of robots—all different models of varying sizes—marched into the room. At the head of the parade, three tall robots like the ones that the school used for security strode on four limbs, displaying a variety of weaponised options. Behind them, the smaller domestic and cleaning robots travelled on all eight of their limbs. Two military robots stomped into the space next, travelling on four splayed feet that reminded Steve of the taloned claws of birds of prey. Their limbs were heavily armoured and thicker than those of the security robots to carry a central body that was the largest Steve had seen. It didn't stop there as an example of every Haven robot Steve had ever come across joined the line.

"And finally," said Mr Cady as three retail robots entered the room, each holding a small robot no bigger than the size of a grapefruit. "Meet DTM 1.0. Your uncle's last design."

"Isn't it a little small to be of any use?" asked Mr Tobias.

"Too small for lifting and carrying, yes," said Mr Cady. "DTM was designed to be a companion robot. Beyond the basic bonding process that all our robots possess, DTM can build a lasting connection with its owner. It can hold genuine conversations, play games and in the case of its owner being in danger or incapacitated, DTM can alert the relevant emergency service. We're just about to roll out production. Steve, you and your teacher are the first people outside the Corporation to even see it. What do you think about that?"

"That's brilliant," said Steve. "Can teenagers own them?" He could already imagine how the small robots might over-run the school—something else to annoy Miss Scritch.

"Unfortunately, not," said Mr Cady. "Even with the possible applications in the classroom, we can't get past the Government's eighteen-year minimum age limit for users. Maybe one day."

As the parade of robots returned to where they had come from, including the retail robots carrying the DTM models, Mr Cady manoeuvred Steve and his teacher back to the door they had entered through.

"This has been great," said Steve as he followed Mr Cady out of the space.

"I've enjoyed it too," said the engineer. "It isn't often I get to actually talk about what we do here to anyone. Professional discretion and all that. But then I suppose you *are* a Haven after all. It's the family business."

"It is, isn't it?" said Steve. "I hadn't thought of it in that way."

"Best get used to it," said Mr Cady. "Haven Robotics isn't going anywhere any time soon. Not if Miss Palmer has anything to do with it," he finished with a smile.

*

The two grey-suited guards who had stood either side of the lift doors in the reception area were nowhere to be seen as Mr Cady pressed the button.

"Here we are," he said as the doors opened. "Miss Palmer took over your uncle's penthouse office. She hasn't changed a thing though. You'll need to press the top-most button. Got it?"

"Got it," said Steve as he stepped into the lift.

"Miss Palmer did say she wanted to speak to Steve in private," said Mr Cady as Steve's teacher joined him in the lift. "She was quite adamant about it."

"Of course," said Mr Tobias. "I forgot about that."

"Not a problem," said Mr Cady as the teacher left the lift with a frown. "I'm sure Miss Palmer won't keep him long. You can wait in the car, if you like."

The lift doors closed between Steve and the two men. Something felt off but he couldn't put his finger on exactly what it was. Dismissing the thought, he pressed the button to the penthouse office.

Chapter Three

"This is unacceptable, Mr Ledwitch. I won't have it! I just won't have it!"

When the lift doors opened, Steve had assumed that Eleanor would be there with her polite affection and that her visitor would be gone. The worst scenario he had imagined was that this Mr Ledwitch, whoever he was, would still be in Eleanor's office and that he would be forced to make small talk with the man and behave. What he didn't expect to see was a full-on, noisy confrontation between the two adults.

"Miss Palmer, you do not have the right to decide what is acceptable, and what is not."

Mr Ledwitch was tall; far taller than anyone Steve had seen before, and thin to the point that his cheekbones seemed to jut out too far from his face. He wore a dark red suit, so deep in colour that it seemed black until the light caught the sheen of the weave. His slicked-back auburn hair was pulled into a tight pigtail. He towered over Eleanor like a cobra rearing over its prey.

The two grey-suited guards who stood behind the man turned as one when the lift doors opened. Eleanor and her visitor, however, continued to argue.

"As CEO of the Haven Corp—" Eleanor began.

"*Interim* CEO," snapped Mr Ledwitch. "And only because we allow it."

"Allow?" She took a short, sharp sniff as if the scent of the man offended her nose. "I am—"

"Redundant," he said.

"Hi." Steve took a slow step out of the lift, the doors closing behind him. "You said I should come up, Eleanor."

"Steve." Eleanor was red in the face as she turned to him, like his mum got when she was angry. "I'm sorry—"

"I'm Steve Haven." Steve held out his hand as he marched between the guards and across the room to Eleanor's visitor. He did his best to smile in a way that he hoped didn't look like he was gritting his teeth. "How do you do?"

"Haven." The man looked Steve up and down as if he were something dirty and unpleasant, then he folded his hands behind his back. "What are you doing here?"

"Steve is my guest." Eleanor took Steve's arm. "He's here for a tour of the business: his family's business. I asked him to drop in on me before he left. Did you enjoy yourself, Steve?" she asked. He could tell that she was doing her best to sound calm, but her fixed smile gave her away.

"I really did," said Steve. His face was beginning to hurt from his own forced smile. "The robot display at the end was the best."

"I've heard a lot about you, Master Haven." Mr Ledwitch stepped closer, bending a little as he stared down at Steve. "Have you been contacted by your parents? I wondered when they might return home."

"No." The question was so unexpected that Steve couldn't think of anything else to say for a moment. "I don't know where they are."

"I find that difficult to believe," said Mr Ledwitch. "What parents would go off without informing their only child where they were going? Are you sure they haven't contacted you?"

"Don't badger the boy." Eleanor tightened her grip on Steve. "If he says he hasn't heard from his parents, then he hasn't."

"I see." Ledwitch's eyes narrowed as he continued to stare at Steve. "You were there, weren't you?"

"Where?" said Steve.

"When Winters and the…" He paused. "You were there. I've

been told what happened. I've seen the aftermath for myself." He slowly shook his head. "Stupid little boy."

"Yes, I was there," said Steve. He could feel the anger burbling up from his stomach. "But I'm not stupid. I knew what I was doing."

"It's this." Mr Ledwitch jerked his head to glare at Eleanor. "This reckless petulance that has forced our hand. How can we trust the workaday world when your actions threaten our privacy? Our way of life?"

"When the Council put me in charge of the Haven Corporation—" Eleanor began.

"They were unaware of the full extent of what had happened," Mr Ledwitch snapped. "It was a misguided decision made out a sense of loyalty to the Haven family. It won't happen again." He gestured to the two guards. "Escort Miss Palmer and Master Haven out of here."

"You can't do that!" said Eleanor, retreating a step and taking Steve with her. "You don't have the authority."

"The Haven Corporation is under new management. My people will take over the roles of your workforce." He nodded to the guards. "Take them."

"You can't take over Haven Robotics," said Steve as one of the guards reached for him. "It's mine. Well, it's my parents'. And they're not here to agree to this."

"Typical Haven privilege," sneered Mr Ledwitch. "You remind me of your uncle."

As Steve grappled to find a sarcastic response, the lift doors opened again and three smartly dressed individuals stepped out, followed by two robots that were nothing like Steve had ever seen before.

"Sorry we're late," said one of the men. "We got here as quickly as we could."

The man who had spoken wore a brown suit that, although smart and well-kept, wouldn't have stood out in a crowd. His dark blonde hair was neither overly short nor incredibly fashionable, giving the impression that he'd styled it with a sweep of his hand and little thought.

Behind him two smartly dressed individuals, a heavily muscled woman with brutally short fair hair and a slim, dark-haired man with deep, intense eyes, waited between the two robots that were definitely not a Haven design. In fact, the only thing they seemed to have in common with any Haven model was their spherical body. That was where the similarity ended though.

Standing about waist-height to the man and the woman and made from black metal covered in studs, each robot bore a blue-lit line running vertically around their bodies. They moved back and forth a little, twisting to take in their surroundings.

"What are you doing here?" Mr Ledwitch appeared to shrink a little at the sight of the man and his colleagues. "Your involvement hasn't been sanctioned."

"To the contrary," said the man. "My superior's agreement with your people provides us with more than sufficient sanction to be here. Miss Palmer." He held out his hand to her as he crossed the room. "Apologies for the intrusion."

"I don't know who you are," she said. "So I've no idea whether an apology is necessary."

"And another apology," he said. "I should have introduced myself sooner. My name is Elrick Olen. These are my colleagues, Andra and Will."

Steve could see that Elrick Olen was considerably shorter than Mr Ledwitch, but his quiet confidence more than made up for that. Elrick refused to look up at the Council member, concentrating his easy smile on Eleanor instead.

"Mr Olen." Eleanor eyed the hand that he still held out to her. "You seem to have me at a disadvantage."

"Never my intention, Miss Palmer." Elrick dropped his hand and casually pushed it into his trouser pocket. "Quite the contrary in fact. I'm here to help."

"Under whose authority?" snarled Mr Ledwitch. "The

Council—"

"Oh, they've no say in this matter," said Elrick. "The Auditor made that quite clear. I can make a phone call if you like."

"This is preposterous," blustered Mr Ledwitch. "Your people's job is simply—"

"To clean up the Council's mess. Yes, I know that," said Elrick. "And after seeing what a dog's dinner *your* people made in response to the Winters incident, the Auditor has decided that we should have complete jurisdiction on this matter."

"You can't do that. I'll speak to Blaike Harn about this."

"You do," said Elrick, finally looking up at his opponent. "And she will tell you to keep out of this, Jonah. You and yours had your chance to examine the basement. Now it is our turn. Once we've finished our survey of what's down there, we'll let you have anything that we feel is yours. The rest remains with us."

"For what purpose?" Mr Ledwitch jabbed a finger at Elrick. "This is not what the Council agreed."

"While you're on your way out, Jonah, don't forget to take your people here with you." He gestured to the guards with his thumb. "My team will root out the rest. Sorry," he said with a tut. "I mean, show them the way out."

"You haven't heard the last of this," said Mr Ledwitch as he strode across the room in long, angry strides. "There will be repercussions."

"One last thing, Jonah," said Elrick with a click of his fingers as if he'd just remembered something. "Don't try to come back. Our robots will be posted at the doors. You know they can see your kind."

"Damn you and your robots."

"Lovely to see you again, Jonah," Elrick called after him. "Give my regards to your comrades."

"What just happened?" said Eleanor as the grey-suited guards joined Mr Ledwitch in the lift and the doors slid shut.

"Miss Palmer." Elrick held out his hand to her again. "We

have a lot to discuss. I can explain everything, in private."

"I see." Eleanor stared at his hand for a moment, and then she shook it once and released it again. "I would be very interested to hear that."

"Me too," said Steve.

"And you are?" said Elrick.

"This is Steve Haven," said Eleanor. "Heir to the Haven Robotics Corporation."

Heir? Steve thought. He liked the idea of being an 'heir'. "That's right."

"So you're Rex's nephew," said Elrick, offering Steve his hand. "How do you do?"

With the cuff drawn back on the man's outheld hand, Steve noticed a tattoo inked on the inside of his wrist: two triangles intersected by a horizontal line.

"Good." Steve shook Elrick's hand with what he hoped was a firm grasp.

"You arrived at an opportune time, Steve," said Elrick. "My people have an agreement with the Council. All very boring, business stuff. Nothing that would interest you."

"I don't mind," said Steve. "It's half-term, so I don't have lessons."

"He's right, Steve. Whatever *this* is," said Eleanor, looking at Elrick and his companions, "I need to get it straight before I involve you."

"But—"

"No buts, please." She took his arm and led him back to the lift doors, only pausing to wait for Elrick's companions to move aside. "I'll be in touch," she told him quietly as she pressed the button. "Soon," she added as he reluctantly stepped into the lift.

"Nice to meet you, Steve Haven," said Elrick as the doors began to close. "There's nothing to worry about now. Everything is just as it should be."

Chapter Four

Steve sat at the desk in his room. It faced one of the slit windows and, through the glass, he could see the shadowy blue of the twilight beyond.

It had been great to meet up with Eleanor again, one of the few people who he could be completely honest around because she knew all about the secret, magical world he had encountered. It should have been great to meet up with the darkling too but of course with his teacher in tow, that was always going to be a challenge. Seeing all those robots, how they were made, the new DTM model, all of that had been a jaw-dropping delight. Even the thought of putting Miss Scritch's nose out of joint to have time away from school would have previously made Steve's day.

But the presence of Mr Ledwitch, his demands to take over the Haven Corporation on behalf of the magical Council, and then what appeared to be a rescue by Elrick Olen and his people, had Steve on edge.

The drive back to school had been odd too. His teacher, usually affable and joking, had been in a definite bad mood. He'd hardly said a word to Steve and had stalked off as soon as the car had arrived back.

I wish I could speak to Hartley, Steve thought as he stood up and began to pace. *He'd know what to do.*

He thought about using the purple travelling chalk that would allow him to travel to Hartley, wherever he was. It sat snug in the back of the desk drawer, ready for the next time he needed to see his friend. But was this really a 'needed' situation?

He stopped at one of the windows. From there, he could see across the empty courtyard to the artificially grassed surround and the city lights beyond. The twilight dulled the edges of the courtyard wall and the two gates, merging the shadows into pools of black. Everything was still and quiet, and it was easy to imagine he was the only person left in the school.

He found himself shuddering, whether at the cold coming off the glass or the thought of being alone. A movement caught his attention amongst the courtyard shadows. He moved closer to the window and narrowed his eyes to make out what it was.

A single figure stood in the courtyard, staring up at the school. Their face was concealed by a hood and the lack of light, but as they raised a hand to push back their hood Steve already knew who it was.

"What's she doing here?" Steve knocked on the window glass. It was cold against his knuckles. "Hey, I'm up here," he said, slapping his hand on the glass.

The darkling looked up at his window, nodded once, and then she beckoned him with a sweep of her hand.

"Right," he said, nodding as he stepped away from the window. He grabbed his jacket from where he had flung it onto his bed and pulled it on. "Right." He took the key-card from the slot in the wall, punched his hand on the door-pad, and charged out through the opening door with his heart beating fast.

*

The twilight air chilled Steve's face as he trotted down the steps from the front entrance of the school.

"What are you doing here?" he said as he joined the darkling in the courtyard. He crossed his arms, partly against the cold but mostly to stop himself from hugging her. He wasn't sure she'd appreciate it.

"It is good to see you too," she said.

"Sorry. I just didn't expect to see you here. How are you?"

"I am well." The darkling shrugged. "I am always well."

"I saw you outside the Haven building. I wanted to talk to you, but I don't think my teacher would have liked it."

"That was your teacher?" The darkling shifted uncomfortably.

"Eleanor showed me around the Haven Robotics. Well, this man called Mr Cady did. It was really cool. But I saw Eleanor later and she was in this big row with a man called Ledwitch." Now that he had the darkling there, all the things he had wanted to say for ages erupted in a non-stop deluge. "Don't worry though. That's all sorted. How's Hartley and Blessing? Will I see them soon? It seems like ages since I was in Darkacre. I've been waiting for—"

"Steve." The darkling grabbed his shoulders. "Stop."

"Sorry," he said as she released him. "I haven't had anyone to talk to. Well, not anyone who knows about, you know."

"I understand," she said. "But I did not come here to exchange pleasantries. This is serious."

"What's wrong? Has something happened to Blessing? Is Hartley in trouble? He's always in trouble but—"

"Stop, please." The darkling released an impatient sigh. "I have been watching the Haven building to ensure that Winters is gone and the Reactor destroyed."

"And is it?" said Steve. "I mean, are they? Gone and destroyed?"

"The matter is unclear. The Council's involvement is puzzling. The situation would be easier if I could enter the building. But that is not the reason I am here." The darkling looked down at her feet for what seemed like a very long moment. When she spoke again, it was without her usual directness. "Hartley and Blessing have disappeared."

"What do you mean disappeared?" Steve felt his heart lurch into a gallop. "Disappear like magic—poof!—or disappear like missing?" *Like Mum and Dad.*

"No one knows where they are," said the darkling. "Not for the past week. James thinks Braeden Kendra's men may be involved. Frobisher says they have just gone off on an adventure using the door in Hartley's shop."

"What do you think?" said Steve.

"Haven? Is that you?"

Steve jumped as his teacher's voice rang out across the courtyard. "Yes, sir?" he said, spinning around.

"What are you doing out there?" Mr Tobias stood in the open door to the school, his figure silhouetted against the light from the hallway. "Who are you talking to?"

"Nobody, sir. Just getting a breath of air."

"You don't want to set one of the guard robots off," said his teacher. "Best come inside."

"Yes, sir." Steve looked around but the darkling had melted into the shadows. "Right away, sir," he said, and then he started up the steps.

*

"Goodnight, Haven."

"Yes, sir. I mean, goodnight, sir."

"Well?" said his teacher as Steve remained outside the open door to his room.

"Sir?"

"Aren't you going to go in?"

"Yes, sir. Of course, sir." Steve stepped into his room, pushed the door-pad on the wall and watched as his teacher disappeared behind the closing door. He pressed his ear to the door and listened. After a moment, he heard Mr Tobias's footsteps head off down the hallway. "I think he's gone," he whispered.

He turned around, staring into the shadowed corners of his room. "Hello? Are you there?"

Or am I just talking to myself?

A hand touched his shoulder and he all but fainted, staggering away from the grasp.

"Don't creep up on me like that," he said, holding a hand to his thumping heart. "It's not right."

"Apologies." The darkling clasped her hands, then sank onto the bed. "I am unaccustomed to…"

All of a sudden, she looked like a normal teenage girl, scared and worried about her friends. There was no sign of the warrior spirit he'd come to know.

"It's okay," he said. "You just made me jump." He dropped the key-card onto his desk and sat down on the chair. "So what now? Do we go looking for Hartley and Blessing? We could ask around Darkacre. Maybe if I speak to Eleanor, she can ask the Council to look into it, although I'm not sure she's on friendly terms with them after today."

"Enquiries in Darkacre is one option." The darkling sighed, hands unclasping. "Did you know that your teacher is a magical?"

"No, he's not," said Steve. "He's a maths teacher."

"And a magical," said the darkling. "He has a particularly disciplined aura. Military, almost."

"He's new," said Steve. "He arrived while I was away with you and the others."

"Before or after the explosion?"

"I don't know," said Steve. "Could it be a coincidence? Is that possible? Could he be an innocent magical trying to make a living from teaching?"

"Perhaps," said the darkling with a frown. "But in the circumstances…"

"What would Hartley do?" said Steve, more to himself than the darkling. He pulled open the drawer in his desk. The piece of purple chalk sat just where he'd left it. "Maybe…"

"Enchanted chalk?" said the darkling, suddenly at his shoulder. "I can see the magic ingrained in it."

"Travelling chalk," said Steve. "Hartley gave it to me."

"Where does it travel you to?"

"Hartley. Wherever he is."

"Do you know what to do with it?"

"Of course," he said, realising that for once he was a step ahead of the darkling. "I saw Abel use it. I'll show you."

He crouched down in front of the walk-in cupboard and began to draw a line from the floor up one side of the door frame. *I hope this is as easy as it seemed when Abel did it*, he thought. *Or I'm just going to look stupid.*

"I see it," said the darkling as he reached the top of the door frame. "The magic from the chalk is activating the door."

"Of course, it is," he said, beginning across the top of the door and hoping his words sounded more convinced than he felt. "Hartley made it."

"Is that it?" said the darkling when Steve stepped back a moment later. The line of purple chalk ran up one side of the cupboard door across the top and down the other side.

"One more thing to do," he said. Taking a deep breath, Steve knocked three times on the door.

Please be there, please be there, please be there, he thought as the door remained firmly closed. *Please, please, please, Hartley. I'll never complain about your cooking again.*

"What is supposed to happen next?" asked the darkling.

"Hartley," said Steve. "That's what." He pulled the cupboard door open. It was still a cupboard. There were his clothes all hung up, with his school shoes on the floor.

"It did not work," said the darkling. "But…" She closed the door and examined the chalk line. "There is definite magic here."

"But no Hartley there." He pocketed the chalk and threw himself down on the chair at his desk. "That's it then, unless you're any good at fighting robots."

"Why would I fight robots?" said the darkling. "What would be the purpose?"

"The only way I can leave school is to get past the robots that guard the site. It's all right for you. You can just shadow your way out."

"Then it is fortunate that I have a back-up plan," said the darkling. She closed the fingers of one hand and when she opened them again, she held what looked like a small picture frame. "When James found out that I was coming here, he gave me this. I believe he borrowed it from Hartley's stock."

"What is it?" said Steve.

"A means of escaping your school without the need to fight robots."

Grasping it with both hands, the darkling pulled the frame apart. It grew quickly, doubling its size as it pushed out in all directions. Now, each side of the square wooden frame was about a foot in length and in the place of a picture or back-board was a flat plane of swirling, grey smoke. On one side of the frame there was a slider bar with digits, running from 0 to 5.

"We'll never fit through there," said Steve.

"You may not," said the darkling. "But I have a remedy for that."

She pulled the frame sides further apart until the structure had more than doubled in size again, and then she laid it on the floor.

"Where does it go?" said Steve, kneeling down beside the frame to take a closer look.

"Where we ask it to go," she said. "One last thing." She crouched down and pushed the slider to two. "You first, Steve. Just tell it where you want to go. The frame will do the rest."

"Okay." Steve stood up, got ready to jump, and said, "I want to go to Hartley Keg's shop in Darkacre."

He heard the darkling gasp and the slap of footsteps landing on the floorboards behind him.

"Get away from there," rasped a voice that was half familiar and half strange.

In the middle of the room, Mr Tobias stood with his hand raised towards them. He was dressed in the clothes Steve had seen him in just a few minutes ago, but now he wore a pair of grey gloves which were edged with metal. Steve had seen gloves like that before, worn by the magical Council's army of agents.

"You're a Hidden," he said, feeling his heart begin to thunder in his chest.

"I won't tell you again," said Mr Tobias. The teacher's usual cheerful demeanour had been replaced by a predatory stance and stare. "I don't want to hurt you. This is for your own good."

"Keep going, Steve." The darkling prowled towards the Hidden. "I'll handle this."

"Very well." Mr Tobias turned his attention to the darkling with a cold switch of his head. "Take your chance, fae."

"Steve, get out of here!" she snapped as she pounced at the Hidden.

"Too slow," the Hidden sneered as he easily dodged her attack. "You'll have to do better than that."

Steve took a deep breath, dragging his eyes away from the fight as he turned back to the frame, or window, or trap door at his feet.

"I didn't want to do this but if it's the only way…" Mr Tobias thrust his outheld hands in Steve's direction, sending a shimmering mist spraying towards him.

With a final glance at the darkling as she advanced on his teacher, Steve took a deep breath and jumped into the swirling smoke.

Chapter Five

Steve forgot to brace himself for landing, so when he hit the floor his feet slipped out from beneath him. He slapped down onto a cold, tiled floor, coming to rest with his head against a table leg.

"What the—? What are you doing here?" said a familiar voice.

Steve raised himself up, then screwed his eyes shut as a flare of pain in the back of his head made his stomach churn. "Lying down," he said as he slowly returned his head to the floor.

There was a sharp 'snap' above him, followed by a clatter as the frame, now back to its original size, dropped onto the floor.

"Mate, what have you done to yourself?" James, the teenage magical that Steve had met a few weeks before in Darkacre, knelt down beside him. "Where did you come from?"

"Hello James," said the darkling as she emerged from shadow form and picked up the frame. "You were right. This was very useful but…" She held a piece of the frame in each hand. "I do not think we will be able to use it again."

From Steve's vantage point on the floor, Hartley Keg's kitchen looked much the same as when he had last seen it. The floor was unswept. The ceiling was home to a healthy community of cobwebs. The sink was full of pots to be washed. The smell of old cabbage and burnt porridge hung in the air. It was good to be back.

"I think I may need…" Steve tried not to yelp as he touched a hand to the back of his head. When he looked at his fingers, they were smeared in blood. "Oh," he said. "Right." Then, he passed out.

*

"Hold still. Stop being a baby." James dabbed a dampened wad of fabric on the wound in the back of Steve's head. "I need to clear the blood away so I can see how bad it is."

"Do I need stitches?" Steve winced each time the wad touched his injured scalp. "There was so much blood."

"Nah, head injuries always look worse than they are," said James. "It's 'cos they bleed so much."

"It sounds as if you have a lot of experience," said the darkling. After a few minutes in shadow form recovering from her fight with Steve's teacher, she had returned to help James deal with Steve's injury. She held a tin of bandages, or rather what looked to Steve like strips of an old, ripped-up sheet. There was a bowl of water on the table, next to a pile of wet, bloodied strips.

"I've patched up my brother more times than I can count." James leant back, squinting at the wound. "Michael has a habit of getting into scrapes. Give me another bandage."

"I'm glad you were here." She took a strip from the tin and handed it to him.

"Ta." He grinned at her as he took the bandage. "Good to see you too."

"Has it stopped bleeding?" Steve felt dizzy and was doing his best to keep his last meal down. "We need to get on."

"Pretty much." James folded the bandage into a wad and pressed it onto Steve's head. "Hold this," he said, taking Steve's hand and pressing it over the bandage. "Look at me."

"Why?" Steve turned around.

"How many fingers am I holding up?" James put up a 'V' with his index and middle finger.

"Two," said Steve with a scowl.

"That's good. Feel sick?"

"A bit."

"You might be concussed." James stood up. "Best get you to Frobisher's."

"Why were you here?" said Steve as James pulled an over-sized hoodie onto his scrawny frame.

"I was waiting for that to open." James nodded to the door at the back of the kitchen. "I thought Hartley and Blessing were sure to be back soon, after some adventure." He sighed. "Something like that."

"You got us instead," said Steve. "Sorry."

"Give over." James looked around, then clicked his fingers. "Wait here," he said as he marched through the door that Steve knew would lead to the shop at the front of the building.

"What are you doing?" called Steve.

"Finding you a woollen hat from Hartley's stock," James called back. "To keep that bandage in place. We can't have you alarming people in the street."

"Frobisher will know what to do," said the darkling. "He may be bad-tempered, but he can be relied on."

"Hope so," said Steve. "Because at the moment, I have no idea what to do next."

"Here we go!" Steve heard James call out. "Perfect. As long as you don't mind pom-poms. And glitter."

*

Steve crushed the pom-pom-ed hat in his hands as Frobisher worked on the wound in the back of his head. He sat in an armchair by the fireplace in the gatekeeper's parlour, gritting his teeth and doing his best not to yelp every time Frobisher poked his finger into the wound.

"How is it you always bring trouble to my door?" Frobisher put the top on the jar of salve he'd been applying to Steve's wound and slapped it down on the dresser. "Steven Haven, you are a bother and a worry."

"Sorry, but—"

"And you." Frobisher cut Steve off as he turned his frown on the darkling. "You should know better than to tangle with a Hidden. What were you thinking?"

"That I should protect my friend." She glared back at Frobisher. "Is that not what we all should do?"

"All right, all right." James raised his hands. "Let's not get into any aggro. Fro', mate, we came here 'cos we trust you. These two need your help and let's face it, we're all worried about Blessing and Hartley."

Frobisher made a grunting noise and crossed his arms. "Not all of us," he said.

"Frobisher?" said Steve. "What did you put on my head? It smells funny. Kind of… off."

"It's a healing salve," said Frobisher. "Blessing invented it. Don't ask what's in it. You don't want to know."

"Right." Steve sat awkwardly upright, aware that if he leant back the wound would brush against the high top of Frobisher's chair. He didn't think the gatekeeper would want a mixture of blood and stinky salve on his furniture.

"I'll get a clean bandage," said James.

"And tea," said Frobisher as James opened the door. "Strong, sweet tea. Best thing for shock."

"I don't think I'm in shock," said Steve. "Just bashed about."

"Bully for you," said Frobisher. "The tea is for me."

*

"Well, what did you expect would happen?" Frobisher dithered around his parlour, his long, thin hands clasped before him. "Of course the Council would step in and help out the Haven Corporation."

"I do not understand," said the darkling, growing increasingly annoyed with the old man's pacing. "Why would the Council care about the Haven Robotics Corporation?"

"They're all messed up. The Havens, the Council, and the magical community, all entangled all the way back to when we first came here. It makes sense that the Council would caretake the Havens' company until they return. And Miss Palmer is a lovely lady. Very professional. It's hardly a surprise that they put her in charge."

"But they tried to take it away from her," said Steve. "A man called Ledwitch. He was ready to throw her out, and everyone who works there."

"Jonah Ledwitch," said Frobisher. "Ledwitch is a Council member, and the Council's trouble shooter. Makes sense they'd send him to deliver the bad news."

"Ledwitch knew I was there when Winters died. He said so. If it hadn't been for Elrick Olen, I don't know what would have happened."

"Who is this Olen?" asked the darkling. "Is he a magical?"

"Doesn't matter," said Frobisher. "It's not our concern."

"It's my concern," said Steve. "My parents own the Haven Corporation."

The darkling watched the gatekeeper shrug his bony shoulders. The old man's now oily aura crawled with anxiety. Something was wrong.

"How did the Council find out what happened at the Haven building?" she asked. "The explosion appeared to the workaday world as something that could be easily explained. Why would the Council get involved?"

"The Hidden must have sensed Blessing's magic," said James. "It's what they do."

"No, that cannot be it," said the darkling. "The Haven building is shielded against magical surveillance."

"How else would they find out?" said James. "There's not much damage on the outside. It's nearly all fixed already. Someone must've told them."

The old man tensed, looking anywhere except at any of them.

"Frobisher?" She tilted her head to look at him. "Do you

know?"

"All right, enough of the interrogation. I told them." He crossed his arms tightly over his chest and jutted his chin into the air. "It's my duty to watch out for this community."

"Frobisher!" James spread his hands palm up. "What'd you do that for?"

"They needed to know." Frobisher returned to his pacing. "Hartley Keg may think he's above the law, but he put this community in danger, angering Locke or Winters or whatever he called himself. Even venturing into Braeden Kendra's fortress too!"

"Yeah, to rescue Michael!" snapped James. "Or did you forget that?"

"Of course not." Frobisher's arms worked their way loose. "But still." He shrugged and dropped into the armchair opposite Steve's. "And I thought the place might need cleaning up after the explosion. The last thing we needed was a nosey workaday finding something incriminating."

"You told them about Winters?" said the darkling. "And the Reactor?"

"I had to," said Frobisher. "The Hidden are very thorough in their questioning."

"Have they contacted you since?"

"Not contacted, exactly. No."

"What's that mean?" said James. "Frobisher?"

"I didn't say any more, but I did let Ledwitch and a couple of Hidden through the gate into Darkacre."

"When?" said Steve.

"Just before Hartley and Blessing disappeared." He clasped his hands on his lap. "I know how that looks." He shook his head, eyes on the fire. "I thought I was doing the right thing."

"On the bright side, we know where they are now," said James.

"We have to go." Steve stood up suddenly, then flailed back down into the armchair as a wave of pain in the back of his head made his stomach turn over.

"You are in no state to travel," said the darkling.

"But—"

"You can rest up here," said Frobisher, climbing to his feet. "No sense in making yourself ill before you're recovered. I'll make up a couple of beds."

The darkling watched the old man's aura as he crossed the room. The crawling anxiety had gone, replaced by a heavy regret.

Chapter Six

Steve woke the next morning to the sound of thundering footsteps as James' little brother, Michael, slammed the bedroom door and charged down the stairs. Steve sat up in bed and felt a click in his back. The mattress he had slept on was little more than a big pillow stuffed with… well, Steve had no idea what it was stuffed with. Whatever it was, it had shifted and sagged during the night until he could feel the slats of the bed under his back.

In the end, Frobisher had realised that the darkling didn't need a place to sleep, so he had just thrown a patchwork eiderdown onto the spare bed in Michael's room for Steve. The boy had chattered for most of the night, asking Steve all kind of questions, and lighting the darkness with intermittent sparks from his fingers. Steve had no idea what time he had dozed off, but it felt as if he'd only slept for a couple of hours.

Pulling back the covers, Steve swung his legs over the side of the bed, found his trainers and quickly pulled them on. Aside from the two beds, the room looked as if it hadn't been touched for decades. The carpet was a faded shade of pink with the odd patch of threadbare. The walls were plastered but that was it—no wallpaper or paint. A bare lightbulb hung from the ceiling. The only vivid colour in the room were the garish, yellow curtains that hung at the window.

He stood up and went to a small mirror that dangled at an angle from a nail on the wall. The reflection that stared back looked sleepy but otherwise normal. Wincing with the expectation of pain, he touched the back of his head. He found the place where the wound should have been, but the only trace that he had been injured was a patch of hair that was flattened and a little greasy. Nothing hurt at all.

"Breakfast!" Steve heard Frobisher shout up the stairs. "Get it before it's gone."

Steve's stomach gurgled in response, and suddenly breakfast seemed like a very good idea.

*

"…and the next thing I knew, I was lying on the floor in Hartley's kitchen." Steve talked around a mouthful of eggy bread.

"That is so rad." Michael balanced the travelling chalk between his thumb and finger. "Why didn't the chalk work, then?"

"Travelling chalk. Stupid idea, if you ask me." Frobisher sat on the opposite side of the table to Steve, a delicate cup and saucer on the table before him. "Who knows where it might take you to? What if Hartley has fallen into a volcano or the ocean? What if he was being eaten by sharks? What then?"

"Unlikely," said the darkling. "But you do have a point."

"I suppose," said Steve. "But it didn't work. Not this time. Maybe I did something wrong."

"Hang on." James leant against the tall dresser that dominated one wall of the gatekeeper's dining room, a mug of tea in his hand. "If I understand this right, the chalk should have made Hartley open a door wherever he is."

"That's right," said Steve.

"But what if where he is doesn't allow that kind of thing?" James left the sentence hanging.

"What are you getting at?" said Michael.

"If Hartley is in the Confluence, that travelling chalk wouldn't work," said James. "That place is well warded against unauthorised entry."

"What's the Confluence?" said Steve.

"It's the Council-controlled area of the city," said Frobisher.

"If Jonah Ledwitch has Hartley and Blessing, that's where they'll be."

"Can I keep this?" said Michael. "Seeing as it doesn't work?"

"No, you cannot." Frobisher snatched the chalk from his grasp. "It's dangerous."

"Why does he have it then?" grumped Michael, slumping back in his seat. "He's a workaday. He can't defend himself, not like me. I can—"

"Yeah, Glitch. We know what you can do, but that's not the point." James raised an eyebrow at him.

"I'm just saying." Michael snatched the last piece of eggy bread from the plate in the middle of the table and stuffed it into his mouth. His cheeks bulged like a hoarding hamster.

"Here." Frobisher jabbed the chalk at Steve. "Take it. I'm not happy that you have it though."

"Thanks." Steve pocketed the chalk. "So what next?"

"It's obvious, isn't it?" said James as he pulled out a chair from the table, flipped it round, and sat on it with his arms rested on the back. "We go to the Confluence and find Blessing and Hartley."

"Is that possible?" said the darkling. "Can we just walk in?"

"The Confluence is open to all magicals," said James. "Plus those workadays in the know."

"I hope you're not proposing that the boy goes there," said Frobisher. "Hartley Keg is a grown man. He can look after himself."

"And what about Blessing?" said James. "Can she look after herself? She's just a kid."

"Don't you think I know that?" Frobisher gave a long, tortured sigh. "I never imagined they'd take her, too. I thought it would fall on Keg's shoulders. It's all a terrible mess."

"A mess is as good a place as any to start, "said Steve. "It can only get tidier from there."

"What are you talking about?" said the gatekeeper.

"It's something Hartley said to me once. And he's right.

Frobisher, we caused this mess. Me by setting off the Reactor and you by telling the Council. We have to tidy it up."

"Keg's got inside your head." Frobisher clamped his arms crossed. "You sound just like him. If you want to galivant off to the Confluence, I won't stand in your way but—"

"Will you come with us, Frobisher?" said Steve.

"I will not," said the gatekeeper. "I'm keeping my head down and out of the way of harm, thank you very much. I have this one to look out for." He nodded at Michael who rolled his eyes in response. "And the gate of course. I am the gatekeeper after all."

"I can look after Michael," said James. "He's *my* little brother."

"I don't need looking after," sulked Michael.

"And Pete Dunstan can oversee the gate while you're gone. I know you've been training him up."

"He's not ready," snapped Frobisher.

"He's ready enough," said James. "It'll only be for a short while. A couple of hours, tops."

"But…" Frobisher's brow drew down into a deep frown over his sizeable nose as he looked from James to Steve and back again. "You have all the answers, don't you? I bet you're pleased with yourself."

"Does that mean you'll take us to the Confluence?" said Steve.

"Well, I can't have you marching in and upsetting the Council now, can I?" said Frobisher.

"That's the man," said James. "I knew you'd see sense."

"So what do we do when we get there?" said Steve. "Do we just knock on the door and say, can we have our Hartley back?"

"I was going to say that the Council won't like you interfering but, truth be told, that would only be the feelings of part of the Council." Frobisher picked up his cup and saucer and took a noisy slurp. "Kiri Ema is our best bet."

"Who's that?" said Steve.

"She's one of the Council members. The best of the lot, if you ask me," said Frobisher. "She's fair. She'll listen to you."

"So we are agreed," said the darkling. "We go to the Confluence, speak to this Kiri Ema, and bring our friends home."

"You make it sound so simple," said Steve. "Things are never simple with Hartley around."

"Never a truer word spoken," said Frobisher. "There's hope for you yet, boy."

*

Steve stood at the gateway between Darkacre and the city beyond. The last time he had left this way had been in an attempt to rescue Hartley. That time, it had been from Thomas Winters. This time, it was from the Council. He wondered if rescuing Hartley Keg was beginning to be a habit.

"Don't forget to fetch Pete Dunstan the minute I leave," Frobisher told James for the third time since they had stepped out onto the street.

"I know, I know, Fro'." James tutted. "I'm not deaf. I'll get him. Chill."

"And Michael, you listen to James," said Frobisher. "He may be a clever Alec, but he's canny."

"Clever Alec," Michael smirked.

"Thanks, Fro'," said James. "I think."

"Best hand over your travelling chalk to me for now." Frobisher held out his hand. "You'll never get it past security yourself."

"And you can?" Steve pulled the chalk out of his pocket.

"I have my ways." Frobisher grabbed the chalk, turned his back on them all, and hunched over.

"Where are you hiding my chalk?" said Steve.

"Mate, don't ask." James shuddered. "Trust me, you don't want to know."

"Right," said Frobisher as he turned back to face them all. "That'll do."

"And you are sure that Kiri Ema will help us?" said the

darkling.

"Not sure about anything," said Frobisher. "But she's your best bet."

"Is it a long way from here?" said Steve.

"The entrance to the Confluence is on the outskirts of the city," said Frobisher. "Where Darkacre used to be."

"It's a fair hike," said James.

"But just this once," said Frobisher as he opened a door beside the main gateway. "I'll let you use the official door."

"Was that…?" Steve was convinced that the door hadn't been there before. "What do you mean 'official'?"

"The Council installed it so they can come and go at ease," said Frobisher. "It opens into the Confluence. Of course, we'll have to get you through Security."

"No bother," said James. "I've done it. Even got workadays in there before now." He elbowed Steve.

"Just behave," said Frobisher as he led the way through the open door. "Button your lip. Stay calm. That way they're less likely to detain you."

"Detain?" said Steve as the darkling pushed him through the door. "What do you mean, detain?"

*

Steve stepped out into bright, white, unnatural light. The area they stood in was long and narrow. It seemed altogether workaday with its polished floors and frosted glass walls, except for a couple of things.

The first were the three stone archways that three queues of visitors filed through. The archways were made from a pale, marble-like stone into which had been carved a range of symbols that shone with a pale blue light.

The second thing were the guards. Each archway had an identical pair. The first was a tall, broad mountain of a man with sandy hair, dressed in overalls that were the same colour as his skin. He towered over the passing people. The other was exactly what Steve imagined a storybook werewolf to look like. It had a wolf's head, stood on two feet—paws?—and had arms instead of front legs. It wore loosely fitting trousers that stopped mid-calf; or whatever the wolf equivalent was of mid-calf.

"Word of warning before we go in." Frobisher beckoned Steve and the darkling to join him at the end of one of the queues. "Let me do the talking."

"I don't have a problem with that," said Steve.

"Don't make any sudden moves," said Frobisher. "And don't, under any circumstance, look the lycan guard in the eye. They'll take it as a challenge, 'specially if they're hungry."

"I can do that," said Steve. "Or not do it."

"Good, good." Frobisher lowered his voice as he continued. "The Council uses golem guards for their interpersonal skills and strength."

"And the lycans?" asked the darkling.

"Mainly for their noses," said Frobisher. "They can sniff out most concealed items, 'specially magical contraband. It doesn't do any harm that they scare the life out of most people either."

Almost on cue, there was a scream as one of the lycan guards snarled and snapped at a visitor. The target of its aggression was a small woman dressed in a woollen, pea green coat and a floral head scarf. She pleaded with the accompanying golem in a high-pitched squeal, her hands clasped in a praying gesture.

"That's odd," said Frobisher. "The lycan must have sniffed out something the archway missed."

The archway that the woman had passed through looked identical to its neighbours. The light from the carved symbols shone the same calm shade of blue.

The lycan thumped its chest with a clawed fist, then twisted its hands in a gesture to the golem. The golem nodded and grabbed the woman by the scruff of her trembling neck.

"Show yourself," he said. "And do it quickly."

The woman carried on in her pleading for a second more and

then, with a shudder, she collapsed in on herself, devolving to a pile of padded rags.

"That explains it," said Frobisher. "The archway wouldn't pick up on a shapeshifter."

The pile of rags shook and rearranged itself into something that looked like a ragdoll, if ragdolls were human-sized and had no hair or face. It gave a shrug and held up its hands which looked to Steve like a pair of oven mitts.

The golem clamped a giant hand around the shapeshifter's arm, nodded to the lycan, and then marched his prisoner through a side door. A moment later, a golem walked back in and took a place at the archway. Steve had no idea whether it was the same one or an identical replacement. All of the golems in the room looked exactly the same.

The lycan shook itself and gestured for the next person in the line to approach.

"What'll happen to the shapeshifter?" asked Steve.

"Best not to think about that," said Frobisher. "It's just lucky that the golem took him out there, and not the lycan."

*

The queue moved more quickly than Steve would have liked and in no time at all, they faced the scrutiny of the golem and lycan guards at one of the arches.

"What is your business in the Confluence?" said the golem in a deep but not unkind voice. Close up, he was even taller than Steve had first thought.

"Visit to see an official," said Frobisher.

"Which official?" said the golem.

"Council member Kiri Ema."

"You are in luck," said the golem. "Council member Ema is on site today. Do you have any goods to declare?"

"Hang on." Frobisher patted his jacket, smiled uncomfortably at the golem, and began to pull things from his pockets.

"Is this all?" said the golem as Frobisher handed him a fob-watch that wasn't ticking, a piece torn from a paper map, a smoker's pipe, a red ribbon, an acorn, a rubber band, a comb, and finally a curled-up sleeping mouse.

"Almost." Frobisher reached inside his jacket and pulled out a roughly woven corn dolly. "For luck," he said as he popped it onto the pile of items that the golem held.

The lycan took a sniff at Frobisher's belongings, and then shook its head.

"That's fine," said the golem as he handed Frobisher's things back and the gatekeeper put them away. "What about the rest of your party?"

"Nothing else," said Frobisher.

"What about the boy and the darkling?" said the golem, looking to his companion guard.

The lycan growled and took a long sniff at Steve's shoulder.

Don't look at the lycan, don't look at the lycan, Steve thought. He gritted his teeth as the lycan's whiskers tickled his neck.

"They're not carrying," said Frobisher. "I made sure."

"Is that right?" The golem looked at the lycan. Steve heard the creature snort and felt its breath on the back of his neck. "All good then." The golem pulled a ticket from a device on his belt and handed it to Frobisher. "Lift One. Move along. Next."

Chapter Seven

The interior of Lift One was neat and polished, with lacquered wooden walls, floor and ceiling, and gleaming golden trims. On the far wall was a round, wooden device that matched the finish of the rest of the lift. It had a polished metal crank on one side, the kind you might find on an old-fashioned pulley, and a gold trimmed slot. Stretched across the device was an oval-shaped screen that currently bore the word *'Arrival'*.

"Here we go." Frobisher pushed the ticket into the slot. With a *snap*, the ticket disappeared inside. The letters displayed on the screen flickered and changed to *'Concourse'*. Frobisher grabbed the crank and pushed it around in one rapid cycle.

When the door closed behind them, Steve expected to feel a slight judder to indicate that the lift was moving. No such judder came, and the doors instantly opened.

"Where are we?" he asked as first Frobisher and then the darkling exited the lift.

"The Concourse," said the gatekeeper. "How else do you expect to get to Kiri Ema's office?"

Steve stepped out of the lift into what appeared to be an immense frosted glass box—glass walls, glass floor, even glass overhead. A line of symbols, like the ones Steve had seen carved into the security archways, ran along each wall just below the ceiling. The symbols shone with a pulsing light that changed shade from red, to yellow, to green, then blue, and finally a cold white light before changing back to red again. Beneath the symbols, four tall archways led off each side of the space.

Suspended in mid-air were what appeared to be crystal

chandeliers, but on closer inspection Steve decided they looked more like ornately carved chunks of ice. A cold, steady light sat at the core of each. There were ten or more of the light sources, all floating in a circuit around the space through which a steady stream of people flowed: people with their families, people leading animals—Steve recognised most of the beasts, except for a couple that looked like a hybrid between a snake and a chicken—and many, many people walking with the look of boredom that comes from simply going about your normal life. It took Steve a moment to figure out what was missing. Not a single robot travelled through the Concourse.

When Steve turned around to look at the closing lift door, he found that it was white, arched in shape, and adorned with silver studs and a crystal doorknob.

"Here's the plan," said Frobisher. "I'll take you to see Kiri Ema. If she turns us away, we'll head back to Darkacre, no arguments. If she offers to help… well, I haven't thought that far ahead yet."

"The two of you should do that," said the darkling.

"What are you going to do?" said Steve.

"Something else," she said, backing away. "I will find you."

"Well, that's downright mysterious," said Frobisher as the darkling disappeared through one of the archways. "Looks like it's just us two. Now, then. Kiri Ema."

"What about her?" said Steve as he followed Frobisher along the Concourse.

"A word of warning."

"Is she a lycan?" said Steve.

"No, no, no," said Frobisher. "Nothing like that. She's lovely. That's the problem. She puts people at ease and then you find yourself telling her everything. She's canny, see?" Frobisher tapped the side of his sizable nose. "Clever. So just watch what you say."

"I can do that," said Steve.

"I hope so, for both our sakes." Frobisher nodded towards

one of the archways. "It isn't far."

*

Each holding cell was a cube of clear glass, piled one on top of the other, each pile stacked up next to another pile. There must have been twenty piles of twenty cells and the darkling could see that there were more cells piled up behind those at the front.

Each cell held a single occupant. From time to time, there would be a high-pitched note like a fingernail tapped on a crystal glass, and the cells would move around like pieces in a puzzle, sliding down, up, back, or aside.

"Does Daddy dream?" said a small child, round face framed with black curls, who stared up at the golem guard.

"Come on, Carl." His mother took his hand. "It's time to go."

"But does he?" Carl pulled his little body as far from his mother as he could, eyes intent on the golem who towered over him.

"Yes," said the golem.

"Does he dream of me?"

"Of course," said the golem. "Happy dreams of his family."

"That's good." Carl nodded, letting his mother draw him closer. "I dream of him too."

The golem watched the boy and his mother leave the holding cell area and then he turned to the cell they had visited. Inside a man lay on the floor, eyes closed, hands folded on his chest.

"You can come out now," said the golem. "I know you're there."

The darkling took solid form from the golem's own shadow. "Do they dream?" she asked, staring at the prisoner.

"No," said the golem. "The Council make them sleep but there are no dreams."

"You lied to the boy."

"I gave him the answer he needed." He smacked a hand on the glass wall and pushed the cell into motion up and away out

48

of sight.

"That was kind," she said.

"Why are you here?" the golem asked.

"I came for my friends. A man called Hartley Keg and a young girl called Blessing."

"You're too late," said the golem. "The Hidden took them to be prepared for the intervention."

"Took them where?"

"Council chambers," he said.

"Will they be returned here?"

"Unlikely. Would you try to rescue them, if they were?" The golem smiled. "The clay remembers the way you think, darkling."

"He would have disapproved," she said. "He would have told me not to involve myself in the lives of people."

"He would have expressed that sentiment. That does not mean he would have believed it."

"Would you stop me?" she asked.

"I would try," he said. "But it might be difficult to stop a darkling, a traveller, and a being so powerful in magic. But that notion is moot. You must direct your efforts to a different location."

"Thank you," she said as she reached the arched doorway. "I am glad the clay remembers me."

"Always," said the golem. "Go well."

*

The smooth glass floor of the Concourse gave way to worn but unpolished wooden floorboards as Frobisher led Steve into the waiting area for Kiri Ema's office. A cushioned wooden bench ran the length of the wall to the right. In front of them, there was a vibrant-green painted door. To one side of the door, words that floated a few inches off the ochre-painted walls read, *'Do not knock. Wait to be called'*.

On a whim, Steve reached out a hand to touch the writing.

With a tiny squeal, the writing jumped away from his grasp. It reformed itself higher up the wall, well out of Steve's reach.

"Suppose we'd better sit," said Frobisher.

"But this is urgent," said Steve. "We need to see Kiri Ema right now."

"You'd be surprised how many of my visitors say that to me." In the now open doorway stood a small, elderly woman in green robes that engulfed her. Her white hair was drawn back into an untidy bun and secured with a pointed rod. An ornate black tattoo ran across her chin. She looked from Steve to Frobisher and back again with a wide smile. "Shall we?"

She left the door open, scooped up armfuls of her robes, and headed back into her office. Frobisher nudged Steve and pushed him through the doorway.

Kiri Ema's office wasn't so much a room, as a garden. Winding, rough branches spotted with moss burst from walls that were all the colours of the forest. The ground underfoot was short grass, patched with daisies and buttercups. Overhead, what seemed to be a real, blue sky rolled above a panoply of blossom-laden twigs.

Kiri Ema sat on a bench that appeared to be part of the trees that surrounded it. Her green robes pooled on the grass around her feet. She gestured to a series of wooden stools that formed a circle with the bench.

"Sit, sit," she said. "Tell me how I can help."

"Hi." Steve sat down, then looked to the gatekeeper, unsure of what to say.

"Madam Council member," Frobisher began as he too sat.

"None of that, Stan," she said with a smile. "We're old friends. Now, what ails you?"

"Go on." Frobisher nodded to Steve to speak. "Tell Kiri Ema what the problem is."

"Our friends are missing," said Steve. "Someone told us they were here."

"In the Confluence?" she asked. "What are they called, these friends of yours?"

"Hartley Keg and Blessing." Kiri's smile didn't waiver, but Steve was sure he saw her eyes widen a little.

"What's your name?"

"Steve Haven," he said.

"I thought so." She chuckled, a deep throaty sound that somehow put Steve at ease. "You have your father's look. Those gorgeous blue eyes. Quite the stunner."

"Thank you," he said, feeling his cheeks burn a little. "But—"

"Your friends, yes." She nodded. "It's a difficult matter, isn't it?"

"Is it?" said Steve. "All anyone knows is that they've disappeared, and the Council might be involved." He shrugged. "Are you?"

"Oh dear." Her smile dimmed a little. "My fellow Council members can be a little guarded in making announcements. Still, I thought they'd have told Darkacre." She shook her head. "Here's the way of it," she said. "Hartley and Blessing have been called in to answer questions on their actions at the Haven Corporation building. You know about that?"

"I was there," he said.

"But you're not a magical, Steve. The Council—well, the others—felt that this intervention didn't concern you."

"But it was me who—"

"Steve." Frobisher nudged him. "Let Kiri Ema speak."

"No, no, he's allowed to express himself. I know what happened there, Steve. Hartley filled me in. You want to own your part in it. I understand that. But this isn't so much about what happened as to whether it threatened the safety of the magical community. If it was up to me, I'd be applauding you all."

"Can we appeal?" said Steve. "Or can I be a witness? Say what happened?"

"Possibly, possibly. The intervention will begin this afternoon. I can arrange for you to be there. But Steve, you must be aware that the Council may point the finger at you too."

"That's fine," he said. "I don't mind. I was part of it." But even as the words left his mouth, he was wondering what he was letting himself in for now.

"That's agreed then." Kiri Ema stood up and grabbed the lengths of her robe in her arms. "Be at the Council chambers at the strike of three, and we shall see what we shall see."

"Thank you, Kiri Ema." Frobisher stood up, gave a deep, back-clicking bow, and then raised an eyebrow at Steve.

"Thank you, Kiri Ema." Steve stood up too.

"No problem at all, boys," she said. "Now, best be off. I have Council members to convince."

"Can we see them?" said Steve as Frobisher headed for the door. "Hartley and Blessing? I want them to know I'm here."

"Not before the intervention, I'm afraid, no." Kiri Ema patted his hand. "I'm sorry."

"We won't take up any more of your time, Kiri Ema." Frobisher grabbed Steve by the collar. "The boy will be at the Council chambers at three. I'll make sure."

"I'll look forward to it."

Kiri Ema gave Steve the brightest of smiles as Frobisher dragged him from the room, but as the door closed behind them, he saw the smile drop from her face.

Chapter Eight

"What are we going to do now? We've got hours to kill until three."

"I'm not exactly chuffed about being away from the gate for so long." Frobisher looked up and down the Concourse as crowds of chattering people moved around the two of them. "I need a cup of tea," he said. "Come on."

"Halt." A Hidden stepped in front of the old gatekeeper, bringing him to such an unexpected and sudden stop that Frobisher almost bumped into him. Dressed in a grey hooded uniform with metal trimmed gloves, the mirrored mask of the Hidden provided no hint of the person behind it. "Council member Ledwitch has requested your company." He said 'requested', but it sounded more like an order to Steve. "The boy must come too."

"Of course," said Frobisher, placing his hand on Steve's shoulder. "We'll be more than happy to attend, won't we, Steve?"

"Yes?" said Steve, remembering his first encounter with Jonah Ledwitch at the Haven Corporation building.

"Follow me." The Hidden turned on his heel and started off at speed towards one of the archways.

"Same rules as security," Frobisher whispered to Steve as they followed. "Button your lip, stay calm, and let me do the talking."

"How did they find out we're here?" Steve whispered back. "Are there cameras?"

"No need for cameras when there are Hidden around." Frobisher tapped a finger to his lips as the Hidden looked back at them. "We're coming," he said with an uncharacteristic smile and a hand on Steve's shoulder. "Lead on."

*

If Kiri Ema's office was a garden, Jonah Ledwitch's was a dungeon.

In comparison to the sparkling, well-lit concourse, the office of Jonah Ledwitch seemed dark and closed in. To Steve, it felt as if the ceiling hovered somewhere close in the shadows overhead but the echoes of their footfalls on the stone floor betrayed the fact that this room was larger than it looked with a high, unseen ceiling.

Flame-shaped lanterns fixed on stone posts created a circle of light around a heavy, wooden desk and a black leather chair.

The Hidden who had led them there stepped back into the shadowed edges of the space and disappeared from view, leaving Steve and Frobisher under Jonah Ledwitch's unblinking stare.

"Council member Ledwitch." Frobisher made a brief bow.

"Frobisher." Jonah Ledwitch remained sat at his desk. "Thank you for answering my summons."

"Of course," said Frobisher. "This is the Haven boy. Steve, this is Council member Ledwitch." Frobisher nudged Steve.

"Hi," said Steve. "Again."

"Again?" said Frobisher.

"We briefly met at the Haven Corporation," said Ledwitch as he stood and stalked around to the front of his desk. "Master Haven was an annoyance then, also."

In the dark room, the Council member seemed even taller than when Steve had met him for the first time. His smart suit was gone. In its place, he wore red robes which were probably supposed to reach the floor but instead hovered at ankle height, showing the base of the trousers Ledwitch wore beneath.

"How can we help you, Council member Ledwitch?" said Frobisher.

"I was wondering, Frobisher, why you have brought a

workaday into the Confluence? Would you care to explain your actions?"

"Well." Frobisher looked at Steve. "You see…" His words tailed off.

"I'm here for the intervention," said Steve. "I'm a witness."

"A witness?" said Ledwitch. "Interventions do not call for witnesses."

"The boy was worried for his friends," said Frobisher. "Council member Ema said he could attend."

"Council member Ema is not in charge." He looked Steve up and down. "The boy's attendance should have been discussed by the entire Council, not decided upon by one. I suggest you take him home."

"But Council member Ema is expecting us," Frobisher blustered. "It's arranged."

"It can be unarranged." Ledwitch returned to his chair. "You may depart now."

"Hang on." Steve stepped forward, ignoring the fact that Frobisher was shaking his head at him. "You can't investigate what happened at the Haven Corporation without me. I was there. I saw it all. I—"

Steve stood his ground as Ledwitch banged his fist on the desk.

"You are as outspoken as the rest of the men in your family, Master Haven. Somebody should teach you manners. Frobisher, remove him from my sight while I still have control of my temper."

"Yes, Council member." Frobisher took Steve by the shoulder. "Come on, lad. We tried."

"Frobisher," came a gruff but not unfriendly voice. "How are you, gatekeeper?"

The speaker was a giant of a man. That was the first impression that Steve got of the white-robed man who strode towards them with a grin. When he took a good look at him though, he realised that it wasn't that the man was overly tall. He just moved like he expected to take up a lot of space, as if he were really a polar bear walking on his hind paws. The man's blonde hair was pale to the point that it was almost white, cropped short and bristling. The sleeves of his white robes were pushed back to reveal muscular arms.

"I am well, Council member Wolff," said Frobisher as the man squeezed him in a bear hug. "Thank you," he wheezed as he was released.

"I've told you before, Frobisher. Call me Volund. And who is this?" Volund Wolff stared down at Steve. "Your apprentice?"

"An unpleasant annoyance," bristled Jonah Ledwitch. "One that is just leaving."

"Steve Haven," said Steve. "And I'm not leaving."

"Do I sense a disagreement?" said Volund with a lop-sided smile. "Pray, do tell."

"The boy is here for the intervention," said Frobisher nervously.

"Ah, of course. The Haven boy. You were there," said Volund. "You saw it all with your own eyes. Jonah, he must attend. He will add some meat to the bones of the intervention. I insist."

"Thank you, Council member..." Frobisher coughed. "Volund. Steve is very grateful."

"Yes," said Steve as Frobisher elbowed him. "Really grateful. Thank you."

"That's decided then." Volund slapped a hand on Steve's shoulder. "We shall see you there, won't we, Jonah?"

"Frobisher!" was all that Jonah said in response.

"Yes, Council member Ledwitch?" Frobisher turned to the Council member with eyes so wide it looked as if they might pop out of his skull.

"You will keep the boy out of trouble until the time is right. Do you understand?"

"Of course, Council member Ledwitch," said Frobisher. "Come on, Steve." He placed a bony hand on Steve's arm. "We don't want to inconvenience the Council members any longer."

As Steve let Frobisher pull him away, Ledwitch clicked the fingers of one hand and the Hidden who had escorted them there stepped out of the shadows.

"Right then," said Frobisher, still holding onto Steve as he marched them both down a narrow corridor. "If ever there was a trial by fire…" He left the sentence unfinished.

"You can let go now." Steve struggled free. "I'm not a kid, you know."

"No, children can be controlled." Frobisher shook his head. "You played a dangerous game there, Steve. Challenging Jonah Ledwitch like that. I'm surprised you didn't get burnt."

"It worked, didn't it?" said Steve. "We're still going to the intervention."

"That may be, but there are ways of doing things," said the gatekeeper. "And then, there's your way." He tutted. "Trust a Haven to get results, no matter the consequences."

"Cup of tea?" said Steve.

"Absolutely."

*

Dong, dong, dong. The sound of a clock chiming three rang out so loudly it caused the floor beneath Steve's feet to vibrate. Strangely, there was no clock visible anywhere nearby. As the last chime faded away, the ornately carved and crystal-studded wooden doors that led to the Council chambers swung open.

"That's it then," said Frobisher. "In you go."

"But the darkling isn't here yet," said Steve. "We can't go in without her."

"She hasn't been called," said the gatekeeper. "She won't be allowed to attend the intervention. Anyway, she wasn't there so she's no good as a witness. I'll say my goodbyes now." He offered his hand to Steve.

"Aren't you coming with me?" said Steve. "I don't know what to do or where to go."

"You go in there." Frobisher nodded to the open doorway. "You answer the Council's questions and you be polite. Simple."

"Not simple," said Steve. "Not simple at all."

"I've done my bit." Frobisher clamped his arms crossed. "I didn't want to come here, but I did. Got you through security. Took you to Kiri Ema. You should be grateful."

"I am grateful. Honest." Steve tucked his hands into his pockets. "I'm just a bit scared."

"Scared is good," said Frobisher. "Scared keeps you from doing something stupid. Now, you go in there and you defend your friends. I may not approve of Hartley Keg, but Blessing doesn't deserve any of this. You speak up for her, you hear?"

"Yes, Frobisher."

"And you look after yourself," the gatekeeper said in a kinder tone. "You hear?"

"Yes, Frobisher. Thank you."

"Good." Frobisher nodded. "Off you go." He pushed Steve towards the doorway. "Don't keep them waiting."

*

A shiver ran through Steve's body the minute that he stepped into the Council chambers. The warmth of the concourse fell away to the kind of chill you might feel in the middle of the night when there's nowhere to shelter or not enough sheets on the bed.

The glass floor ended at the doorway behind him and was replaced by well-trodden, stone paving slabs. The large space was round; at least, the stone floor that he could see was round but the walls themselves were simple darkness. Steve wondered what would happen if he touched the unseen wall. Would his hand simply disappear into nothing? Above, the ceiling was equally dark and yet the room was well-lit from an invisible source.

The only things that signified the existence of any boundaries at all were three stone framed doorways, the one behind him that he had entered through, a matching one on the other side of the room and a third, larger set of doors to his left.

Where a fourth door might have been, to his right, seven thrones surveyed the room. The thrones were approached by three stone steps. Each throne was carved from deeply stained wood and strewn with furs. Five thrones were topped by a glowing, painted symbol: a white square, blue spiral, red upward pointing triangle, a green oval that lay on its side, and on the central throne, a yellow circle.

The thrones were empty but, in the centre of the room, two Hidden stood on either side of a round, raised, stone platform, their hands folded before them and their masked heads down.

"Er." Steve hovered just inside the doorway, not knowing where to go. Should he wait there to be called or announced? There wasn't anywhere to sit other than the thrones.

"Who are you?"

The little man who appeared at Steve's side glared up at him. He was dressed in a black suit and top hat. His ginger hair had been slicked back behind his ears and his beard was waxed into a point. He held a clipboard in one hand and a quill in the other.

"Steve," said Steve. "Haven. I'm a witness."

"You're not on the list," said the little man without checking it.

"It was a last-minute arrangement." Kiri Ema stood in the doorway opposite, holding up lengths of her green robe.

"Arranged by whom?" said the little man.

"Arranged by me," Kiri said in a sterner voice. "Do you have a problem with that, Clerk?"

"No," said the little man, shrinking a little more. "Thank you, Council member Ema." He made a deep bow, clicked his heels, and disappeared.

"Gnomes." She rolled her eyes as she walked over to Steve. "So pedantic."

"Hi," he said. "Frobisher had to go."

"Quite right," she said. "He wasn't there. He has nothing of any use to say. All right?"

"Yeah," he said, nodding. "Er, where do I go?"

"Oh dear." She looked around. "I suppose it is a bit sparse. Petitioners usually stand before us or kneel. Always seems a bit archaic to me. I think we can do better than that."

Releasing the folds of her robe, she grabbed the pointed rod that secured her bun and tugged it free. Steve expected her white hair to fall down but it stayed exactly where it was. With the most subtle of moves, she pointed the rod—which Steve now realised was a wand—at the paving slabs in front of the thrones and drew a tight circle in the air.

Two side-by-side paving slabs shook themselves free, opened outwards onto their edges, and fell flat on the neighbouring slabs. The gritty earth that was revealed trembled as first one and then another green shooter burst up into the room. For a moment, they twitched and turned as if seeking a route, and then each went in a different direction—one left, one right.

As Steve watched, the shooters—now thick stems—laced back and forth, crossing each other, tangling, weaving, creating a mass that bit by bit took the form of a bench. By the time the process had finished, only a couple of minutes later, the stems had thickened into twigs and branches and a long, high-backed, wooden bench waited before the thrones.

"Wow." Steve was aware that he was staring and that his mouth had dropped open. "That was…"

"Sufficient," said Kiri, popping her wand back into her bun. "Now, best wait here while the others arrive and then you can take a seat. And Steve?"

"Yeah?" he said.

"Don't worry. We'll get this sorted. You'll be out of here in no time at all. Promise."

"Right," he said as she smiled up at him. "No time at all."

"Deep breath," she said as the large set of doors to his left creaked open. "Here comes the pomp and circumstance."

Chapter Nine

The first person to appear was a very normal looking, young woman. She had long, straight, dark hair and equally dark eyes, and she was of an average height. In fact, other than the long, yellow robes she wore, there was nothing out of the ordinary about her appearance at all. Behind her and hand in hand, walked an elderly woman and a young boy, both dressed in black. They looked so like the woman that Steve assumed they were all related. The boy appeared as 'normal' as the young woman, but Steve noticed ornate tattoos peeking out where the elderly woman's sleeves met her hands.

"The woman in yellow, that's Blaike Harn," whispered Kiri. "Head of the Council."

Next came Volund Wolff, his sleeves still pushed back and a broad grin lighting his face. After that were two faces that Steve also recognised. Naomi Onai appeared as Steve had seen her at the Gathering in Darkacre, dressed in blue robes and with her black braids elegantly arranged high on her head around a silver tiara. Her hand rested on the arm of Jonah Ledwitch who towered above her in his red robes.

Blaike Harn went to the middle throne, the one marked with a glowing, yellow circle, and when the old woman and the boy stood before the unmarked thrones on either side, Blaike Harn sat down. The elderly woman nodded to the boy, and they too sat.

Volund Wolff went to the throne marked with the white square and collapsed onto it as if it were a comfy chair, sitting aslant with his legs crossed at the ankles.

Naomi Onai took the throne between Volund and the elderly woman, the one marked with a blue spiral. Unlike Volund, she sat elegantly upright, her hands resting on the arms of the throne.

"What is this monstrosity?" Jonah Ledwitch halted at the newly created bench. "Who did this?" he snapped.

"That's my monstrosity, thank you very much." Kiri crossed her arms. "Somewhere for our guests to sit. This is an intervention after all. Not a trial."

"Thank you, Kiri." Blaike Harn spoke before Jonah Ledwitch could continue. "That was very thoughtful of you."

"Thank you, Blaike." Kiri took Steve's arm and pulled him a step forward with her. "This is Steve Haven. He would like to speak up for Hartley and Blessing."

"I know who he is," said Blaike. She stared at him in a way that, while not obviously aggressive, made Steve feel that he wasn't welcome there. "I hope you will be able to help us clear up this matter, Master Haven."

"I'll try," he said. "Can I see them?"

"They will arrive shortly," said Blaike. "Kiri? If you wouldn't mind."

"Of course, Blaike." With a final smile to Steve, Kiri hauled up the lengths of her robe and went to the throne marked with the green symbol.

"Jonah, are you joining us?" Blaike stared at Ledwitch blankly, neither hostile nor welcoming.

With a snort at Steve and a curt nod to Blaike, Jonah Ledwitch strode to the empty throne and threw himself into it.

The two Hidden who stood at the central platform raised their heads as another of their kind stepped through the open doorway. Behind the Hidden, Hartley and Blessing walked hand in hand. Aside from a metal collar that each wore around their necks, they looked exactly as Steve remembered them. Hartley wore his patched, tweed jacket and his flowing hair and beard were as messy as always. Blessing walked with her head down, her face shielded by her long, blonde hair.

"Hi." The barely audible word stuck in Steve's throat. He took a step towards his friends, and then stopped as one of the Hidden at the platform snapped its mirrored head to face him.

When Hartley saw Steve, he frowned—an expression that Steve rarely saw on the shopkeeper's face—and then he elbowed Blessing and whispered something to her. Her head bobbed up and a surprised smile spread across her face as she locked eyes with Steve.

"Hartley. Blessing," said Blaike as the doors closed behind them. "It appears that seating has been provided for you. Please." She gestured to the bench. "You also, Master Haven."

"Are these contraptions really necessary?" Hartley tapped the metal collar around his neck. "How much harm do you think we can do against the five of you and your Hidden contingent? We're a little outnumbered."

"Quite right," said Kiri. "This isn't a trial. We're all fr—"

"They stay," said Blaike in a calm but firm voice. "For now. Please take the seat that my colleague has so kindly provided for you all." She looked at Steve on the final word.

"As you wish." Hartley drew Blessing with him to the bench and sat down.

"Hi." Steve rushed to sit beside them. "It's good t—"

"Hello Steve," Hartley said solemnly and then he pressed a finger to his lips with a wink.

"You understand why you are here, Hartley Keg?" said Blaike after a moment of watching the three. "And you, Blessing?"

"I don't," said Steve.

"I suppose not." Blaike released a sigh. "Very well. I'll make it clear then. This intervention has been called as a result of the incident at the Haven Corporation site. You were not called." Blaike raised a hand as Steve opened his mouth to speak. "Because you are not one of our community. You have no magic and therefore you could not be at fault for what happened."

"I agree with you wholeheartedly, Blaike," said Hartley. "Steve was just a harmless bystander. He bears no fault in this matter."

"But—" Steve piped up.

"However, shouldn't it be the late Thomas Winters, or would you rather call him Jared Locke, who is on trial here? He was the villain of this incident."

"This isn't a trial, Hartley," said Blaike with a twitch of her lips. "This is an intervention."

"And yet, we are treated like prisoners." He jiggled the collar around his neck. "It certainly feels like a trial."

"How dare you speak to the Head of the Council in that way?" Jonah Ledwitch balanced on the edge of his seat, looking as if he was coiled to strike. "Show some respect."

"I have plenty of respect for the Council, Jonah," said Hartley. "I simply ask for an explanation of our treatment."

"An explanation." Blaike brought her hands together, fingers arched as if she were about to pray, and touched them to her lips. Her eyes, however, remained on Hartley all the time. "Here is your explanation," she finally said. "You and the girl endangered the privacy of the magical community. First, you failed to report the actions of Jared Locke. Second, you used magic out in the workaday world and sought to evade capture by the Hidden. Finally, your actions resulted in the devastation at the Haven Robotics Corporation."

"And which of those is your real concern, Blaike?" said Hartley. "The fact that we used magic outside Darkacre or that the Council can no longer get their hands on the Reactor?"

"All of it," said Blaike, again with that twitch of her lips. "That and the fact that Blessing demonstrated elevated magical powers far beyond her age and ability. All of it must be addressed."

"Shall we begin?" Jonah Ledwitch still hovered on the edge of his seat.

"Please do," said Blaike. "The floor is yours."

"Thank you, Blaike." Jonah climbed to his feet in a swift, smooth motion and looked down on Hartley, Blessing and Steve with a smirk. "I have so many questions to be answered," he said.

"Let's get on with it shall, we?"

*

Twenty minutes later, Jonah Ledwitch still hadn't exhausted his seemingly endless list of questions.

"So you admit to transporting yourself and your companions into the middle of the city where any passing workaday could have seen you?" He didn't look at Blessing as he questioned her, walking up and down with his hands folded behind his back.

"Yes, but I didn't have a choice. I had to get us away from the explosion." Blessing's voice wobbled as she spoke. "It was instinct."

"Instinct?" Jonah stopped and now he did look at her, fixing her with an intense stare. "Or perhaps you just did not care if you were seen."

"It wasn't like that," she said. "I'd never transported people before. I didn't know what I was doing. It just happened."

"It just happened." Jonah repeated her words. "How convenient for you." He looked her up and down before returning to his leisurely stroll. "And were you seen?"

"I don't know. I don't think so."

"But you don't know. She doesn't know," he announced to the Council members. "She has no idea whether she revealed the existence of magic to the workaday world."

"I didn't see anyone."

"But you can't be sure, can you?"

"No," she said.

"So, as far as you are concerned, there may well have been a crowd of workadays there to see you magically appear. You just didn't see them."

"It was night-time. Dark," she said.

"Hardly dark," said Jonah. "The city is well-lit. Anyone could have looked out of a window at the exact time that you appeared. Isn't that so?"

"Yes," she said in a quiet voice, looking down at her clasped hands.

"Even if your actions were accidental, instinctual, you obviously are not in control of your magic."

"I am normally. This was an emergency."

"So you're saying that you can be trusted to behave in normal circumstances, but not when you are in danger?"

"No, that isn't it. You're twisting my words."

"Leave her alone, Jonah." Hartley took her hand. "This is bullying, not questioning. Why don't you ask me one of your questions? I have plenty of things to say to you."

"I'll come to you in time." Jonah looked at Steve. "What about you, Master Haven? Do you think mistakes were made?"

"I…" Steve looked at Hartley. "Blessing saved us. That wasn't a mistake."

"But if we…" Jonah spread his arms wide in a gesture that suggested 'we' was the Council. "If we had been told about Locke's actions, there would have been no reason for Blessing or you to be involved. We would have handled the situation in an efficient and concealed manner."

"Handled?" Hartley snorted. "Taken the Reactor for yourself, you mean. Blessing did what she thought was right. No, let me correct that statement. Blessing did the right thing. She's a hero. All this pontificating is nothing more than a cover for your anger at the destruction of something you wanted for yourself."

"I am simply stating a fact," said Jonah. "She is a young girl who acted carelessly in expressing her magic. In most circumstances that could be excused, but these are not 'most circumstances'. She exhibited an alarming strength of magic."

"It just happened," she sobbed. "I was trying to help."

"So you keep saying, girl, but—"

"This is getting us nowhere," said Kiri, as she slapped her hand on the arm of her throne. "All Jonah is doing is taunting the girl."

"I agree," said Volund. "It seems to me that we know what

happened. The workadays are none the wiser. Why are we still talking about this?"

"It seems obvious to me," said Jonah. "The girl is a danger to our community and should be removed."

Removed? thought Steve. *What does that mean?*

"There's no obvious about it." Kiri glared at Jonah, her small hands clamped into fists. "She's only a child. Stands to reason her skills are still developing. Isn't that so, Hartley Keg?" she called across to him.

"Absolutely, Kiri." Hartley stood and made a small bow to her. "Blessing is constantly learning about her magic; just as we all did when we were young."

"I agree with Jonah," said Naomi Onai. "Her recent display of increasing magical powers would indicate that the girl is a threat."

"There is a fine line between threat and asset," said Volund. "I say the girl could prove a benefit as part of our community. She has shown great power: power that may become useful in future."

"Hold on." It was Steve's turn to stand up now. "Blessing isn't an asset, and she isn't a threat. You can't remove her or use her. She's a human being."

"Steve." Hartley touched his arm.

"No." Steve pushed him away and stepped closer to the Council members. He noticed the Hidden take a step towards him, but that was all. Their hands remained at their sides. "Blessing is my friend. She saved me, saved a lot of us. If she hadn't done what she did, Winters would have had no worries revealing magic to the world. Then you really would have had a problem on your hands."

"As I said, if we had been informed of the Winters situation first, we would have handled it properly," sneered Jonah. "Instead of having to tidy up your mess."

"Exactly! My mess!" snapped Steve. "I removed the bars from the Reactor, not Blessing. It was me."

"Do you want to take her place?" said Jonah. "Because it can be easily arranged."

"Stop trying to scare the boy," said Kiri. "He's just standing up for his friend."

"That's right," said Steve. "I am."

The boy in black tugged on the arm of Blaike Harn, and then whispered to her. She nodded in response.

"There is merit to what the Haven boy says," she said. "But there are still questions to be answered."

"Such as?" said Volund. "We know what she is capable of."

"Do we?" said Naomi. "She not only teleported through impenetrable protective barriers; she took passengers along with her. All whilst casting an orb that contained a city flattening explosion. She did all of those things at the same time and half of it from a distance. I say we test her."

"What do you mean: test me?" said Blessing, eyes wide. "Hartley, I want to go home."

"It's all right, Blessing." He took her hand. "I'll be here."

"Testing the girl's powers would be informative," said Blaike.

"It is decided then." Jonah nodded to the two Hidden. "Take the girl."

"None of that." Kiri jumped down from her throne, hoisted up her robe, and trotted down the steps. "Blessing, come with me," she said, holding out a hand. "Please."

"Okay." Blessing took Kiri's hand and allowed herself to be drawn to the platform in the middle of the room.

Steve dodged around Hartley and the Hidden to stand by Blessing's other side, sliding his hand into hers. "Hey there."

She smiled weakly. "You shouldn't be here," she said, almost apologetically.

He shrugged. "I had nowhere better to be." Then he smiled, hoping it would comfort her. He felt a hand on his shoulder and found that Hartley had joined them.

As the other Council members left their seats, there was a small clinking sound as if a metal spoon had been tapped on a glass bottle and the raised platform in the centre of the room slowly began to rotate.

Chapter Ten

Matching the speed of the turning platform, two stone columns rose up out of it. When they eventually stopped, one stood taller than Jonah Ledwitch, while the other had halted at table-top level. The Council members—other than Kiri Ema—watched from the other side of the platform.

The tall column was carved from a dark grey stone with veins of white that reached from its base to the very top. As Steve watched, the veins close to the floor began to glow, spreading a warm yellow a couple of inches up around the column.

The shorter column was formed from black, smooth stone inlaid with symbols and letters. On its flat top, a golden orb floated above a polished silver base. Three rings spun around the orb, each of them moving on an ever-changing axis.

"Blessing, all you have to do is place your hands around it," said Kiri. "And it will show us the power of your magic."

Blessing stepped back, pulling Steve with her. "Will it hurt?"

"Not at all," said Kiri. "Look, I'll show you."

Stepping forward, the Council member placed her small hands on either side of the orb. Almost immediately the yellow glow spread up through the veins of the taller column, climbing steadily and changing to a fresh green. When it finally came to a halt, the green illumination had reached about two thirds of the way up the column.

"There." Kiri stepped away from the orb and the coloured light dropped again, returning to its original yellow glow around the base of the column. "See? It doesn't hurt at all."

"Why is it still lit when nobody's near it?" said Steve.

"The Omnometer picks up on the ambient magic in the room," said Volund. "The magic we all emit. Even you, Steve Haven, a workaday, carry a tiny fraction of magic around with you."

"Blaike, it won't work while Blessing is restrained by a collar," said Kiri. "May I?"

"Of course," said Blaike. "But just the girl. Hartley Keg must remain collared."

"As you wish." Kiri reached up to place a hand on the side of Blessing's collar. Almost immediately, there was a delicate rattle and the collar dropped away into Kiri's grasp. "All right?" she said to Blessing.

"Thank you." Blessing rubbed her neck. "That's much better."

"We are trusting that you will behave," said Blaike. "Do not betray that sentiment, Blessing."

"Of course, she won't," said Kiri. "Now then. Are you ready?"

"I think so," said Blessing. "So, I just place my hands near it? That's all?"

"That's all," said Kiri.

Blessing nodded, slowly walking to the spinning orb with Steve at her side. As she released his hand, she looked at Hartley with wide eyes. He nodded to her with a smile.

When she placed her hands on either side of the orb, the response was instant and intense. The yellow glow shot upwards, paling in colour until it was almost bright white. Steve heard her catch her breath in fright, so he stepped closer.

"It's okay, Blessing," he said.

Almost immediately, the racing light hesitated, rising and falling a little until it came to a stop halfway up the column.

"What is this trickery?" said Jonah. "That cannot be right. She must be repressing her power."

"Can I stop now?" said Blessing.

"Not yet," said Naomi. "Not until we have a definite measure."

"She's done what you asked," said Steve. "Leave her alone."

"Steve Haven, step back." Blaike Harn's voice was calm but firm.

"Why?"

"Just do as I ask," she said. "Please," she added as Steve scowled at her.

"Fine." He did as he was told, backing away to stand beside Kiri.

The light in the column pulsed even brighter than before, now so white that it was hard to look at, and with a spark it shot upwards, hitting the top of the column with a sound like shattering glass.

"No!" Blessing staggered back, hands clasped to her face.

The light receded at speed, dropping down through the white veins until it returned to its modest, yellow glow at the base of the column. Smoke ran down the sides of the column and a smell of ozone hung in the air.

"Impressive," grinned Volund. "I've never seen anything like it. I think she's actually broken the Omnometer."

"Impressive?" snapped Jonah. "This is outrageous. The girl is out of control. She is dangerous."

"Just because she is powerful, does not mean she is out of control," said Volund. "I question the motivation for your opinion, Jonah. Where does it come from? Fear? Envy?"

"Blessing is not out of control," said Hartley, speeding to her side. "She might be powerful, yes, but since when was that a bad thing? Tell me that."

"I'm with you, Hartley," said Kiri. "The girl isn't a threat to us just because she's powerful. Her intent is good. That's what matters most here."

"I agree," said Volund.

"Volund Wolff—always the gallant. Are you so blinded by her power, that you can't see the danger here?" snapped Naomi Onai. "And as for you, Kiri Ema—"

"Enough. Enough." Blaike Harn's voice cut into the squabbling, raised but calm. "There is much to discuss, but please a little decorum. This is an intervention, not a playground."

"Apologies, Blaike," simpered Jonah. "It is sometimes difficult to contain oneself in the pursuit of justice."

"Justice." Kiri tutted but said no more.

"I don't feel…" Blessing's knees buckled, and she staggered onto Hartley. "I…"

"What's wrong?" said Steve, going to her side.

"She's exhausted by the testing." Hartley supported her with an arm around her waist. "Plus the effect of wearing that damn collar for so long, and the unnecessary upset caused by the intervention."

"Perhaps they can rest in the antechamber," said Kiri. "Just while we talk."

"And let Hartley Keg travel them out through whatever door is to hand?" snapped Jonah. "Is that your plan?"

"Don't be stupid, Jonah. He's obviously hampered." Kiri tapped her neck. "By the collar? Hartley can't use his travelling magic. We can send a Hidden with them, if it puts a stop to your paranoia."

"Preposterous," said Jonah. "They must remain here and—"

"Kiri is right." Blaike cut off Jonah's rant. "Wearing the collar will inhibit Hartley Keg's ability to travel. The girl may be exhausted but she must also be restrained. Replace her collar, then let them wait in the antechamber while we discuss the matter in private." She nodded to one of the Hidden.

"Don't worry." Kiri took Blessing's hand as the Hidden replaced the collar around the girl's neck. "It won't be for long."

"Of course not, dear girl. Just a little while more and then it'll be removed for good," said Hartley, but his usual good humour had been replaced by an expression that looked worryingly like… well… worry, to Steve.

As the Hidden opened the stone framed doors that the Council members had entered through, Steve had one hopeful thought that maybe Hartley would save the day, throw off his collar, and travel them all out of there. But instead, Hartley and

Blessing followed the Hidden through into the antechamber beyond.

*

"With all due respect, Blaike," said Kiri as soon as the doors to the antechamber closed. "Could you please tell me what this is really about? I know the death of Locke is a serious matter, and the loss of the Reactor too, but serious enough to place Hartley Keg and Blessing in holding cells? You act as if they're a threat. Collars? Is that really the answer?"

From the shadow cast by the bench that Kiri Ema had created, the darkling watched as the short Council member hoisted her robes and strode around the platform.

"How dare you speak to Council Leader Harn in that tone." Jonah Ledwitch pointed a long finger at Kiri but didn't approach her. "Show some respect."

"Kiri makes a valid observation," said Volund who had returned to his throne. "I, too, would be interested to hear the true motivation for the imprisonment and restraint of Keg and the girl."

"This is an outrage," said Jonah. "You should be—"

"The truth, Kiri." Blaike arched her fingers together, pointing the tips to the ceiling. "The truth is that the incident with Jared Locke was less a threat, than a wake-up call."

"How so?" Volund sat forward in his seat, intent on her.

"We have let the magical community operate with too little restraint over recent years," she said. "And there have been dire consequences."

"You mean, Xav Mallorick," said Volund.

"Mallorick, the sealing of Myrkhof, and now the incident at the Haven Corporation." She shook her head. "We have allowed too much leniency, allowed our community to decide how best to follow the rules we set. Our agreement with the workaday authorities is on the verge of collapse. It is only with their goodwill that we can continue to conceal the existence of magic. Jonah tells me that the Auditor has sanctioned Parity to investigate the incident with Winters. In short, we are losing control."

"So what are you saying?" asked Kiri.

"We need to show the community that they are still answerable to the Council. The girl must be made an example of. Her powers will be hampered permanently, and she will be imprisoned."

"You can't do that." Kiri dropped the lengths of her robe. "Blessing's actions had the best motivations behind them. If she hadn't done what she did—"

"There is no sense in arguing, Kiri. It's one against three," said Blaike as she returned to her throne. "I have discussed this matter with Naomi and Jonah, and they agree with me. I believe that's a majority."

"Four," said Volund. "I say we hang onto the girl, but only because I believe her power could be useful. I do not agree with hampering her magic."

"That's decided then," said Blaike, nodding to one of the Hidden. "Let's bring them back in."

As Kiri Ema began to shout, the darkling attached herself to the shadow of the instructed Hidden.

Chapter Eleven

The antechamber had the same stone floor as the Council chamber but with actual, physical stones walls too. There were two worn, wooden benches that faced each other on an immense rectangular rug bearing an intertwining tree design. Steve sat next to Blessing on one bench, while Hartley sat on the bench opposite staring down at his hands. One sole Hidden guarded the doors back into the Council chamber.

"There has to be something we can do," said Steve quietly. "Something we can say to persuade the Council."

"Perhaps," said Hartley. "If I'm reading the situation correctly, the Council is split in their decision. Volund and Kiri are on our side. Nothing more than I'd expect. Naomi and Jonah oppose. The deciding factor will be Blaike Harn. She is the one we need to win over."

"Volund sounds like he wants to control Blessing's power, instead of help," said Steve.

"There is that, true. Very true," said Hartley. "He does tend to take a military viewpoint on things."

"Who's the boy in black?" asked Steve. "And the old woman?"

"The boy is Blaike's son, Sora," said Hartley. "I've never seen him talk to anyone other than Blaike or his grandmother, Hisa. That's the old woman. The two of them act as Blaike's advisors. Hisa is a traditionalist, very much tied to the old ways. Unfortunately, she's likely to side with Naomi and Jonah."

"And the boy?" said Steve.

"Sora is a complete mystery to me. I have absolutely no idea what he will advise."

There was the sound of shouting in the Council chamber. Steve recognised Jonah Ledwitch's voice as the loudest.

"Sounds like it's getting heated in there," said Hartley. "I think we're best out of it."

"Me too." Blessing pulled at the collar around her neck. "I don't like this place."

"How are you feeling?" said Steve.

"I wish this collar was off. It makes me feel sick." She rubbed her neck. "What if we have to…?" She nodded to the Hidden standing guard. "You know."

"Don't worry about that, my dear," said Hartley with a wink. "I'm sure Steve and I can manage, if it comes to that."

There was a knock at the doors to the Council chamber. The Hidden opened them and listened to the speaker on the other side.

"Are we going back in?" said Blessing. "Hartley, what do we do?"

A shadow reached its way over the threshold into the antechamber and resolved itself into solid form. The darkling shoved the Hidden through the open doors and slammed them shut behind him.

"You have to go. Now," she said, straining to keep the doors closed against whoever was pushing on the other side. "I heard the Council's decision. It is not good. Not good at all."

"I'm sure we can talk our way out of this," said Hartley. "Blaike Harn is a reasonable woman. She—"

"They want to take Blessing's power away," said the darkling. "And imprison her. As an example to the magical community."

"Kiri Ema would never allow that." Hartley darted to his feet and added his weight to hers in keeping the doors shut. "You must be mistaken."

"Kiri Ema has been overruled. The decision is made."

"But that means…" Hartley stared open-mouthed at the darkling. "That changes things completely."

"I'll hold off the Hidden," she said. "Get yourselves out of here."

"But we can't," said Steve. "Hartley can't travel while he's wearing that collar."

"I'm afraid that the boy's right." Hartley grunted as whoever was pushing on the other side managed to shove the doors open a fraction. With a roar, Hartley pushed back and the doors slammed shut again. "I'm of little use with this monstrosity around my neck."

"What about this?" Steve pulled the travelling chalk out of his pocket. "Frobisher managed to smuggle it in."

"That's no good. It will only work to find me. Oh." Hartley gave a loud chuckle. "Of course. Do it, Steve. Do it."

"It'll work?" said Steve as he raced to the other door and chalked a line up one side of the stone frame.

"Not how it's supposed to work," said Hartley. "It will find me here, but it can't come from and to the same place. With any luck, it'll default back to the last location it travelled you to or from."

"Luck?" said Steve as he drew the chalk down the other side of the doorframe. "Is that all we've got?"

"As always," said Hartley. "For instance, we are lucky that the Hidden cannot travel themselves in here."

"They can't?" asked Blessing. "Why not?"

"It's banned in the Council chambers for security reasons. If one of them tried to travel in here… Well, let's just say it would be decidedly unpleasant for them. Ready yet, Steve?"

"Give me a chance." Steve knocked on the door three times. *Please work, please work*, he thought as he pressed down on the handle. With a click, the door mechanism engaged, and the door swung open.

"You did it," said Blessing, clapping her hands with glee. "Come on, Hartley."

"Ready?" Hartley raised his eyebrows at the darkling. "We'll let go and run after three. One, two…"

Before he could finish his count, the doors lurched open and one of the Hidden fell through, dropping onto the floor at their feet.

"Run!" shouted the darkling. "Get out of here!"

"I couldn't agree more," said Hartley as he galloped towards Steve and Blessing. "Go, go, go. This is terribly exciting, but we really do need to get on."

Exciting? thought Steve as he pulled Blessing through the door. *More like terrifying.* But deep down he had to agree that his friend was right.

*

"Yes, yes, yeeeeeessss." Hartley ran a heavy-footed victory lap of his kitchen. "I knew it would work. Didn't I tell you it would work?" He slapped Steve on the arm. "Marvellous." The darkling stood by the iron door at the back of the kitchen, their recent route there from the Confluence. To Steve, she looked ready to push it shut, should there be the need.

"I hardly think this is the time to celebrate," she said as Hartley did a little skip. "Will this not be the first place the Hidden look for us?"

"If I have learned one thing in this lifetime, Miss darkling, it's that there is always time to celebrate," said Hartley. "Not much, I grant you. Now then, first step—get rid of these collars."

"That would be good." Blessing sat at the table. She was pale, with dark shadows under her eyes. "I feel awful."

"Won't they come after us?" said Steve. He was too nervous to sit down and hovered by the table instead.

"Of course they will." Hartley pulled open a kitchen drawer. "Which makes it even more important that we get these collars off immediately."

"We may not have long," said the darkling.

"But as I didn't use my own magic, it'll take them a little while to track us from the Confluence," said Hartley, shutting the drawer. "And a little while is more than sufficient for our purposes. Aha!" He picked up a tin from the shelf above the loaded sink. "Now I remember. There was just enough time to hide it when Jonah Ledwitch arrived." He opened the tin and pulled out a bunch of keys. "Remember these?" he said to Steve, jangling them.

"Are those the keys you used in the underground to free the animals?" said Steve.

"The very ones. Now then, come here and tell me what the keyhole looks like on this collar." Hartley pulled his hair and beard free on one side of his neck. "It closed at this point so that must be where it opens too."

"I can't see a keyhole," said Steve, straining on tiptoes. "Are you sure it fastens here?"

"Absolutely. I remember it catching on my beard. The pain was excruciating."

"This is taking too long," said the darkling. "Even if there was a keyhole, your magic is restrained. You cannot use those keys to open the collar."

"I hadn't thought of that." Hartley dropped the keys into his jacket pocket. "It appears that we need assistance."

"Would a magical who can teleport things help?" said Steve as he remembered something.

"Well, of course, that would help," said Hartley. "That would be ideal but who—?"

"James." Steve and the darkling said at the same time.

"James, of course." Hartley slapped his hands together. "Just the man we need. I'll gather a few supplies first. Miss darkling, could you scout ahead? Your shadow form can move much quicker than we can run. Ask James if…"

But already the darkling was gone.

*

"That's a nice bit of gear." James turned Hartley's head back and forth while Hartley himself held his beard out of the way. "I may know a man who'd be interested in obtaining this."

"Wonderful to hear," said Hartley. "But more importantly, can you remove it?"

"Shouldn't be a problem." James pushed up his hoodie sleeves and flexed his fingers. "I'm a little out of practice though."

"Stop teasing him," said the darkling from her spot by the door in Frobisher's parlour. "This is serious."

"Spoilsport." James tilted his head for a moment, then gave a quick nod. The collar disappeared from Hartley's neck and clattered at the shopkeeper's feet. "Can I keep this?" James asked as he stooped to pick it up.

"If it was my decision, my dear boy, I would say indefatigably 'yes'. However, as you and Michael are living under Frobisher's roof, you might like to ask him that question."

"Fair do's," said James. "You next, Blessing."

"Thank you, James." Her voice was quiet and slurred. She leant against Steve on the armchair by the fire with her eyes closed.

"Oh that's so much better." Hartley bent his head from side to side, clicking his neck alarmingly. "I feel more like myself now," he said, giving himself a shake like a huge, shaggy hound. "Once Blessing is free, we'll need a door."

"Well, we've got plenty," said James as he crouched down in front of Blessing and took her hand. With another nod, the collar disappeared from her neck and reappeared in James' grasp.

"No, no, no. We can't use a door in this house. That would incriminate you all. We'll have to find one elsewhere."

"What about the gate to the city?" said Steve. "Frobisher left someone in charge."

"Excellent idea, Steve," said Hartley. "Blessing?" He bent down to look at her. "Do you think you can walk?"

"I can walk," she said, climbing to her feet and then dropping back down. "In a minute."

"At the intervention, when you were out of the room, I heard

Blaike Harn mention someone called Parity," said the darkling. "Who is Parity?"

"Parity isn't a person," said Hartley. "It's a clandestine team of workaday operatives. Above the law and below the radar. It's a very long and complex story that we don't have time for right now, I'm afraid."

"The Auditor has sanctioned Parity to investigate the incident with Winters," said the darkling. "Those were Blaike Harn's exact words."

"Like the men at the Haven Corporation," said Steve.

"What men?" asked Hartley. "When did this happen? Why didn't you tell me?"

"I haven't had the time. There's been too much running," said Steve. "Eleanor invited me for a tour of the Haven robotics factory. At the end, Jonah Ledwitch was there. He told Eleanor that the Council would take over the business. Then a man called Elrick Olen arrived. He said the Auditor had put him in charge. Who's the Auditor?"

"Think of them as an impartial referee," said Hartley. "Neutral. Attempting to maintain balance in the world. When certain workaday governmental individuals became aware of our magical community, the Auditor was put in place to make sure that neither side interfered with the other and that the general public were kept unaware of the existence of magic. Parity is their toolkit."

"They're looking at what's in the basement," said Steve. "What if the Reactor survived the blast?"

"Oh, that's bad," said Hartley. "No wonder the Council are acting in such an extreme fashion."

"I have to get in there," said the darkling. "Hartley, can you travel me in?"

"Not with the Hidden on our trail," he said. "They'd pick up my travelling magic in an instant. I can't take that risk. I have the children to think of."

"But the place is shielded from my kind. There's a guard-stone at the entrance that prevents me from entering. I need you—"

"The stone with the Haven logo on?" said Steve. "That's gone. It was broken in the explosion."

"There's no time for this discussion right now," said Hartley. "We need to depart. Steve, are you ready?"

"Yeah, of course," said Steve. *As ready as I ever am when Hartley Keg asks if I'm ready.* Which of course meant not ready at all.

"My eternal thanks, James," said Hartley as Steve helped Blessing to her feet. "I'd like to say that I'll see you soon, but you know how it is."

"I do." James grabbed his hand and shook it. "Keep lucky," he said with a wink.

"Always," said Hartley.

*

Their way out of Darkacre was in sight when Steve heard the Hidden arrive. If there had been a clear path to the gate to the city, they could have made a run for it. Unfortunately, the two Hidden blocked that path and were rapidly closing in on the friends.

"This way." Hartley turned on his heel. "Ah," he said as a third Hidden appeared just a few feet in that direction. "That's a problem."

"What do we do?" said Steve.

"Well, we can't go back. Can't go forward. So it'll have to be down," said Hartley as he dropped to his knees.

"Down?" said Steve. The Hidden were almost within reaching distance now.

Hartley levered up the heavy manhole lid that sat in the middle of the cobbled road. "Down!" he shouted.

"But—"

"No time to argue," said Hartley. "Trust me on this. There's no other way."

Taking a last look at the Hidden, Steve mentally crossed his fingers that he wasn't about to end up in the Darkacre drains, and then he jumped into the manhole.

Chapter Twelve

Steve landed on a threadbare carpet that did nothing helpful to break his fall. The darkling dropped lightly onto her feet at his side, then she reached to catch Blessing as she too fell from a square hatch in the ceiling.

Hartley came last, knees buckling so he landed heavily on his face. The hatch in the ceiling snapped shut and Hartley moaned something into the carpet.

"Are you all right, Hartley?" The darkling lowered Blessing to her feet, propping her against a chest of drawers, and then she rolled the shopkeeper over onto his back. "Can you continue?"

"My nose." He grasped it with one hand. "Is there blood?" When the darkling shook her head, he loosened his grasp and sat up. "Is everyone accounted for?"

"I'm good." Blessing nodded. The colour was coming back into her face, and she didn't look so sleepy now.

"Where are we?" Steve rubbed at his elbow which had taken the brunt of his landing.

The room was a cacophony of floral images, from the sunflower wallpaper to the rosebud bedding on the rickety, wrought iron bed, to the garish orange tulips on the curtains.

"We're in Elsie's bedroom. You remember Elsie, Steve? She sold us some rather delicious mead at the Gathering." Hartley staggered to his feet and pointed to the one door in the room. "That way out. Quickly now."

Before they could react, the three Hidden appeared between them and the bedroom door, each raising a gloved hand towards

Hartley and the others.

"Ah. Not that way out, in that case. Follow me, people," said Hartley as he took Blessing's hand.

"Where?" said Steve. "There aren't any more doors."

"Well, there aren't in the literal sense." Hartley backed up, drawing Blessing along with him. "But who wants to be literal?"

He dashed his free hand into the full-length mirror that leant against the wall behind them. Steve waited for the mirror to smash but Hartley's hand passed into and through the glass as he pulled Blessing with him.

That's a new one, thought Steve as the darkling pushed him into the mirror.

*

Steve cringed, shielding his eyes, as he emerged into a room of the brightest white. When he looked around, he realised that this was more than simply a room. It was as he imagined the size and shape of the inside of one of the terrace houses in Darkacre to be, if someone had removed all the walls and floors inside one of those houses. The remaining surfaces were spotlessly white.

Looking up, Steve saw that there was no ceiling above, just more white surfaces matching the pitch of the roof. There were no doors or windows either. In fact, the only feature, high up above them, was a man playing at a drum kit which was suspended from—well, more sat *on*—the pitched ceiling. From their perspective he was upside-down, but his lengthy, brown hair sat snug against his skull.

"Hello, Hartley," he said, staring down—or was it up?—at them. "Time for a cup of tea and a slice of Battenberg?"

The wall in front of them squealed slightly as a white table, laid with a steaming teapot, cups and saucers, plates, and a slab of cake, slid out followed by four chairs.

"Please accept my profuse apologies, Phil." Hartley marched past the table. "That Battenberg does look delicious, but it'll have to be a definitive rain check."

"That's a shame," said Phil. "I have cheese."

"Sorry my friend, but it'll have to keep. I could do with a random exit however."

"No worries," said Phil. "One of those days?"

"One of those days would be an understatement," said Hartley.

"Happens to the best of us," said Phil with a nod. "Have a good one." The table and chairs disappeared back into the wall. In their place, a wooden door sprang up from the floor and opened outwards.

"Marvellous," said Hartley. "Phil, you are an absolute joy. Apologies for the intrusion that may follow us. Three of them to be exact."

"Not a problem," said Phil.

To the sound of drumming overhead, Steve followed Hartley and the others through the door.

*

Steve's feet skidded in mud. The air felt cold and damp. The friends stood in between two dug-over soil channels in a patchwork of flower and vegetable beds.

"Where are we now?" asked Steve.

"Darkacre community garden. Don't you remember it?" Hartley dashed to the left-most building in a row of mismatched sheds surrounded by all manner of fruit bushes. "You really must keep up, dear boy."

He yanked the shed door open, and then dodged as a clatter of tools—spades, a gardening fork, and a rusty rake—fell through the open door.

"Darn things." Hartley kicked the tools away as he ran a hand over the wooden door frame. "The Hidden are too close for comfort. We need to hurry. Quick sharp."

A sound that was now all-too-familiar to Steve, announced

the arrival of their pursuers. The Hidden stood a few feet away.

"Come on." Steve pushed Blessing onwards as the Hidden started towards them.

"One-two, one-two," said Hartley as they reached him. He pushed Blessing through the doorway and nodded for Steve to follow. "Miss darkling, no time for tarrying."

"I am not coming with you," she said. "I will hold off the Hidden for as long as I can, and then I must take up the reins of my old mission."

"But how will you find us?" Steve hesitated between the darkling and the open door. "You don't know where we're going."

"Come on." Hartley tugged at Steve's arm. "The Hidden are closing in. We must depart."

"Here." Steve pulled the travelling chalk from his pocket and held it out to her. "You know what to do with this."

"Very well." She snatched it from his grasp with a nod. "Now go."

"Find us," Steve called as Hartley dragged him into the shed. "We need you."

As the door swung shut, Steve glimpsed the three Hidden encircle the darkling.

*

A breeze blew across his skin and gravel rattled under his feet. They stood on a path that ran up to a large, old, timber-framed house which sat in the middle of a circular garden surrounded with hedges. Behind them, a honeysuckle-nestled archway marked their point of arrival.

"Jeannie," said Hartley as an elderly woman stood up from her gardening. She wiped her hands down the apron she wore, pushing back her grey curls.

"Time for a coffee?" she asked with a smile.

"We can't stop, I'm afraid," he said. "Sorry, my dear."

"Next time then," she said.

"You can count on it. Oh, you may have visitors." He shrugged. "Again, I'm sorry."

"Visitors or the other?"

"Most definitely the other," he said. "I don't suppose you could delay them, could you? If it isn't too much trouble?"

"Anything for you." She picked up the handles of the wheelbarrow by her side and manoeuvred it towards them. "Off you go then."

"You've always been my favourite relative, Jeannie." He blew her a kiss. "Give my love to the Ways," he called back to her as he staggered one or two steps along the path.

"What's wrong?" said Steve as Hartley buckled at the knees.

"Too much travelling in one go," said the shopkeeper, clambering back up. "But I can't rest yet."

"Don't worry. I'll see to this," Jeannie called as she pushed the wheelbarrow along the gravel path towards the archway. "You just concentrate on keeping him on his feet."

"What we really need is somewhere the Hidden can't follow us," huffed Hartley. He leant heavily on Steve as the two of them moved as quickly as the shopkeeper could manage along the path. Blessing ran ahead to the house. "I can't keep this up forever."

Steve looked back at the sound of clanging metal and crunching gravel. Two Hidden lay on the path. Another lay across the wheelbarrow, his face in its contents. Jeannie fussed around them apologetically, attempting to help them up but 'accidentally' tripping them back over with the handle of the spade she carried.

"Good girl," said Hartley as he ran his hand over the frame of the old, studded, timber front door of the house. "You can always count on the Kegs to get in the way."

*

Steve was hit by the stink of damp soil as he charged through the doorway. His feet slipped away from beneath him and he landed on his bottom.

"What is this?" he said, rising to his knees and wiping green slime from his hands.

"Just wet moss, that's all." Hartley tried to pull him to his feet but gave up, puffing and wheezing. "Sorry. Don't have the strength."

"Where now?" said Steve as he clambered to his feet.

"Onwards," Hartley wheezed pointing a wavering hand across a clearing in a forest of thick, heavy, high-reaching trees. "Not far. That-a-ways."

Steve looked back as he followed his two friends. There was no actual doorway, only a long dead, wrecked old tree. Sunk into the centre of a small forest clearing, the tree's centre had been hollowed out, although it was impossible to tell whether the space had been created intentionally or by rot.

Kind of a door, he thought.

"Where are we going?" He reached the edge of the clearing and dodged into the forest. "Hartley?"

"Sanctuary," Hartley wheezed. "Where the Hidden and the Council can't follow." The shopkeeper had lost his usual enthusiasm and plodded along, staggering from tree to tree. Blessing matched Hartley's faltering speed and caught his arm every time he stumbled.

The trees they ran amongst were much larger than anything Steve had seen before. They stretched ragged, heavy branches around and above him, interlinking so closely that the light filtered dimly through the green leaves, with only the occasional glint of sunlight peering through.

A flicker of white caught his eye, dashing between the trees to his right, but when he looked to see what it was, he couldn't see anything other than the trees. When he fixed his eyes on the route ahead again, the flicker was back in the corner of his eye and matching their pace.

"He can't keep this up," said Blessing as Hartley stumbled

into a tree and almost slipped to his knees. "We have to stop."

Steve heard that all-too-familiar and now dreaded sound. He didn't have to look back to know that the Hidden had found them.

"They're here," he shouted. "We can't stop. Keep going."

Steve burst from the forest into a wide clearing filled with bright sunlight that blinded him for a moment. His brain didn't connect with his feet straightaway, so he kept running.

"Ow! Mind yourself," Hartley grumbled as Steve bumped into him.

"Sorry." Steve blinked as his eyes became accustomed to the light. "Where are we?"

Hartley leant against a worn, stone column, his chest rising and falling rapidly as he caught his breath. Blessing stood at his side, her hand on the shopkeeper's arm.

Around them and lining most of the forest clearing were small, knee-high rocks. On the other side of the clearing, a sheer face of rock opened into a carved-out doorway.

"Sanctuary. We're safe," wheezed Hartley. "For now."

"No, we're not," said Steve as three Hidden appeared at the edge of the clearing.

As he had seen them do too many times before, the Hidden each raised a hand flat-palmed towards Steve and his friends as they moved as one into the ring of stones.

As Steve prepared himself to fight, two things happened so quickly that it took a moment for him to realise what they were.

A sleek, white hound, teeth bared and snapping, leapt from the forest and knocked one of the Hidden to the ground. Face down, they were helpless as the hound sank its teeth into the Hidden's shoulder and restrained them on the ground. An arrow sped past Steve's head and buried itself in the leg of the second Hidden, felling them to the ground where they moaned and struggled. The third Hidden skidded to a halt at the attack.

Steve staggered aside as a strong hand pushed him out of the way. A woman, tall and dressed in a long, green dress, strode past him. She wore a battered, leather quiver of arrows on her back, and a long, slender bow was slung over her shoulder. A well-worn, leather gauntlet extended over one sleeve, tied off just below her elbow. She whistled to the hound which relinquished its hold on its squirming prey and dashed to her side.

"None may harm those who seek sanctuary," the woman snarled at the Hidden. "That is the rule, as it has always been. Get up, you poor brainwashed creatures." With a swift movement of her foot, she nudged the Hidden who had been pinned by the hound. "Help your companions to leave this place," she snapped at the third.

Both felled Hidden struggled to their feet with the help of their unharmed companion, one with a hand clamped to their shoulder, and the other grasping their leg where the arrow still protruded. With a last look at Steve and the others, the Hidden came together, and then they disappeared.

"Ana, always a pleasure," said Hartley as he slipped to the ground and landed on his bottom, comfortably propped against the central standing stone.

"Hartley Keg, if only I could say the same." Ana rolled her eyes. "If you think I'm carrying you indoors, you're greatly mistaken."

"I can do that," said Blessing, crouching down beside Hartley.

"I'll help," said Steve, joining them. "Come on, Hartley."

"Let me be." Hartley batted away their hands. "I just need a nap and then..." His eyes closed and his mouth widened into a throaty snore.

"Leave him there," said Ana.

"Are you sure?" said Steve, looking back at the forest. "What if they come back?"

"He'll come to no harm with Moon on guard." She whistled to the hound, which settled at Hartley's side with its muzzle across the shopkeeper's legs. "Come on." She started across the clearing at speed. "Selene and Cate will want to see you," she said.

"Who are Selene and Cate?" asked Steve as Blessing took his arm.

"No idea," she said. "But they sound nice."

"Do they?" he asked as Blessing pulled him with her. *Because this one just took out three Hidden without breaking a sweat.*

Chapter Thirteen

The home of the three sisters was actually more comfortable than Steve had thought it would be. It wasn't so much a cave as a cave-house carved into the rock side. The ceiling was low, but the uneven, whitewashed walls gave the impression that the space was much larger than it actually was.

There were no windows, but the golden light from the fire flickering in a corner fireplace perfectly illuminated a room which was festooned with furs: furs on the floor, furs across armchairs, even a fur on one of the walls. The room was filled with the scent of the crackling fire, a sweet, smoky smell that instantly relaxed Steve.

Ana, Selene, and Cate couldn't have been more different from each other, and yet strangely alike. To Steve's eyes, it was as if they were the same person but at different stages in their lives. Each wore a long green dress, high at the neck and long in the sleeve. Each had jet-black hair and eyes to match.

Ana, who had protected them from the Hidden, looked the youngest by far, maybe in her early twenties. She was fresh-faced with hair drawn tightly into a long, low-slung plait. After the introductions, she stood by the cave-house entrance, keeping an eye on the sleeping Hartley.

Compared to Ana, Selene was a bundle of joy and warmth. She looked to be the age of Steve's mum. In fact the more she talked, the more Steve thought of his mum. Selene constantly pushed stray hairs away from her face, tucking them behind her ears or back into the loose bunch that wobbled at the back of her head. Wrapped in a white, woollen shawl trimmed with matching, round beads, she was the only one of the sisters to sit and talk with Steve and the others.

The third sister, Cate, was obviously the eldest. Her face was lined with age and her black hair was streaked with threads of silver. It hung loose around her frail shoulders, merging with a black shawl that appeared to be woven from dark, silky feathers. She hunched over a black, polished staff, listening to her sister chat and nodding from time to time.

"You've had quite an adventure then." Selene poured from an earthenware teapot into three small cups which sat on a table made from a thick slice of tree trunk fixed on stumpy legs. "How exciting."

You could call it that, thought Steve. *I'd call it the 'worst day ever'.* He accepted one of the cups. The tea smelt sweet and herby.

"He's up," called Ana from the door. "Best lock the pantry, Selene. He always eats us out of house and home."

"You exaggerate," said Cate. "A little," she added with a faint smile.

"Speaking of food has made me hungry," said Selene. "I'll serve."

"Ladies! How are you? Wonderful to be in your company again." Hartley stood at the cave-house doorway, the white hound by his side. "Long time, no see."

"Not long enough," said Ana. "I'll help Selene." The two younger sisters left the room, disappearing through a door that Steve hadn't noticed before.

"Hartley Keg, why can't you ever visit without bringing trouble to our doorstep?" said Cate, shaking her head. "I know, I know, it's not in your nature," she added as he opened his mouth to speak.

"You know me too well, Cate," he said, striding across the room to kiss her cheek. "It is wonderful to see you, dear lady."

"And you know the rules while you are here: no unnecessary magic." She wagged a finger at him as she spoke. "Agreed?"

"Agreed," he said. "Now, do you think your sisters will take long to prepare the food? After all that travelling, I'm absolutely ravenous."

"Always the same," said Cate, clicking her fingers at the hound, who came to her immediately. "Well, make yourself useful and set the table." She nodded her head towards a roughly hewn wooden table, which sat close to the front doorway.

I'm sure that wasn't there before, thought Steve as Hartley began to convey the teacups to the table. *Or those,* as he suddenly noticed the seven chairs arranged around the table, where a moment ago he could have sworn that there were none. *What is this place?*

He caught Blessing's eye. She looked tired and a little puzzled, but there was no mistaking the relaxed smile on her face. She looked completely at home in the sisters' cave-house.

"Joining us, Steve?" Hartley pulled out a chair.

"Yeah, sure." *It's just more magic,* he thought as he sat at the table. *Nothing to worry about.* He pushed away the niggling sense that there was plenty to worry about, and that their worries had only just begun.

*

Steve watched the forest, with the standing stone at his back. Above him, the night sky was a perfect black, interrupted only by a scattering of stars and a bright, generous full moon. His hands were dug into his jacket pockets, partly to guard against the chill evening air, but also as a way to hide his fidgeting. Despite the warmth of the sisters' welcome, he couldn't settle or relax.

"They can't get in." The younger sister, Ana, stepped out from the cave-house. "The Hidden, or the Council. You are safe in Sanctuary."

"I know," he said. "It's not that."

"Then, what?" Ana joined him. Her bow and arrows were nowhere to be seen but she still wore the leather gauntlet.

"Planning an escape?"

"No, not that either." He shook his head. "One of my friends had to leave us. I hoped she might meet us here."

"It would be difficult for her to find this place. Unless she has a traveller like Hartley Keg."

"Come on! Nobody is like Hartley Keg," Steve joked.

"True," said Ana with the slightest of smiles.

"But she has a way of finding us—well, finding Hartley— wherever we are." Steve shrugged. "I thought she might turn up."

"You're worried about her."

"Of course. She's my friend and she put herself in danger for us," said Steve. "She does that. And now she's gone off on her own, to take up the reins of her old mission again. Those were her words. And…" He stopped, taking a deep breath to calm himself.

"You miss her," said Ana.

"You know, I had forgotten how beautiful the night skies are here." Hartley Keg stood in the entrance to the cave-house, a bowl of something tasty-smelling steaming in his hand. "They are a marvellous sight."

"How long have you been there?" said Steve.

"Only a moment." Hartley grinned, then slurped from the bowl, before smacking his lips in satisfaction. "I had also forgotten about Selene's cooking. Delicious."

"Always with the flattery." Ana folded her arms loosely. "We do have spoons, you know."

"This is sufficient," he said, wiping a hand across his dripping beard. "Cutlery just gets in the way."

"Don't make yourself too at home," said Ana. "Sanctuary is not a hotel."

"Of course not." Hartley stepped out of the cave-house, the bowl still nestled in his hand. "But it is a most welcome wayside for a weary traveller like me."

"So you ran from the Council and this is the first place you thought of?" said Ana.

"Oh my dear, not by a long mile," said Hartley. "I wanted to put as much distance between ourselves and the Council as possible, and put the Hidden off the trail too. Your door was, I believe, number four."

"Five," said Steve.

"Only if you count the brief visit to my shop."

"Five?" she said, raising an eyebrow. "We're honoured."

"Don't be like that, Ana," said Hartley. "I didn't want to bring trouble to your door, again, but I was exhausted after so much travelling. Despite appearances to the contrary, I'm not as young or sprightly as I used to be. I knew that we would all be safe here."

"But are we really safe here?" said Steve. "The Council probably have an army of Hidden that they can throw at Sanctuary."

"This is consecrated ground," said Hartley. "In a manner of speaking. There are rules that govern what happens in this space. Those who seek sanctuary cannot be harmed here or removed against their will."

"Because Ana and her sisters would stop them?"

"Yes," said Ana. "The three of us and our home."

"The cave-house?"

"The house. The cliff. This circle of stones. The forest. All of this."

"The Council know they would be fighting a losing battle," said Hartley. "So they won't cross that particular line. They respect this place. For now."

"If you think respect keeps them away, then you are deluded, Hartley. They fear this place," said Ana. "Let's be honest."

"Fear? Respect? It all comes down to the same thing in the end," said Hartley. "However, the Hidden did track us here before you and Moon saw them off. The Council know where we are. It won't be long before they arrive with their demands."

"Then what do we do?" said Steve. "Hide? Run?"

"I abhor the idea of hiding," said Hartley. "But for now, I

fear that may be our best option." He took another slurp from his bowl and let out a loud belch that reverberated around the space. "Pardon me." He wiped the back of his hand across his soupy mouth. "First, however, we catch our breath here. If that's acceptable to you, Ana?"

"You've claimed sanctuary," said Ana with a shrug. "It isn't up to me."

"It is acceptable to me," said a voice that Steve had not heard much since their arrival.

The eldest sister, Cate, stood with one hand on the standing stone and the other on her staff. Steve hadn't seen her walk out of the cave-house. It was as if she had simply appeared.

"Hartley Keg, you are an annoyance and a bad influence on occasion, but you will always be welcome in our home. Let the Council and the Hidden come. We will hear what they have to say, as a courtesy, but it is your and your friends' decision on whether you leave here with them."

"Thank you, Cate," said Hartley. "As ever, I am honoured by your support."

"But, Hartley Keg, you know full well you cannot stay here forever."

"Absolutely, Cate," he said. "Even you can't magic up enough food to satisfy this appetite for that long." He slapped his free hand on his belly with a grin.

"Incorrigible, as ever," said Cate with a slow shake of her head. "Now, come inside. Selene has provided a platter of sweet things. Hurry, or the girl may eat them all up."

Steve watched Hartley and Cate go inside, the eldest sister leaning her free arm on Hartley's shoulder. Ana walked behind them, slowing her pace to match her elders.

"There is no need to stand guard." The youngest sister called back from the doorway. "We will know if your friend arrives."

"You will?" he said.

"Of course," said Ana. "Now come, please, don't offend my sister. Eat her food. Or at least, join us in the cave-house." She breathed in the night air, looking up at the moon. "Let tomorrow worry about itself. Take tonight as an opportunity to rest."

"Right." Steve took one last look at the wall of forest. "Rest sounds good," he said, and then he followed her indoors.

*

"You must try this." Selene held out a plate of sticky pastries. "Gastrin," she said, taking one for herself. "They're delicious."

The table was spread with all kinds of niceties: pastries, orange slices, jars of honey and jam, thin slices of cake fried in egg, piles of pancakes, and small golden-brown sweets shaped into crescents.

"Maybe when I've finished this," Steve slurped around a mouthful of honey-soaked orange slices. He did his best to keep the excess of citrus-sweet saliva from escaping his mouth.

"I'll take one." Blessing accepted one of the gastrin and took a careful bite. "So good," she said, her face warming with pleasure.

"And there's loukoumades and honey candy. I do like having guests." Selene settled down at the table and breathed in the scent of the gastrin she held in her fingers. "As you say, so good."

"Selene, anyone would think you were trying to make our guests fat." Cate was suddenly at her sister's shoulder. Steve was getting used to the way the eldest sister seemed to just appear like that.

"Everyone likes a treat." Selene took a small bite of gastrin. "Besides, they've had a terrible time. Honey always sweetens a mood."

"It really does," said Steve as he helped himself to one of the loukoumades which he found to be some kind of doughnut when he bit into it.

"If my mum was here, she'd want to know the recipes for all of this." The words moved so quickly from his mind to his lips that he didn't have time to consider what effect they would have. Suddenly, no amount of loukoumades or honey could take away just how much he missed his parents.

"Then I shall give you the recipe so you can pass it on to her," said Selene.

"I don't know when I'll see her." He shrugged, putting the half-finished doughnut back on his plate. "If—"

"Sleep," said Hartley, patting his stomach. "I could do with a good night's sleep after all that excitement. I'm sure I'm not the only one."

"I don't think I could sleep," said Blessing, licking her fingers.

"Me neither," said Steve.

"I have just the thing," said Selene. "A cup of rose tea. Yes?"

"Sounds like just the tonic we need," said Hartley. "I can't remember the last time I had rose tea."

"The children can sleep by the fire," said Cate as Selene left the room. "Moon will keep them safe." She looked pointedly at Ana.

"I'll go and help Selene." Moon the hound stirred as Ana stood and went to the door in one seamless movement. He watched her leave, and then he rolled onto his back, blinking one eye open to watch them all.

"And I think I might go for a stroll," said Hartley. "Consider the stars for a while. Cate, mind joining me?"

"Of course," she replied with a quick nod.

As the adults left the room, Steve noticed that the armchairs on either side of the fire had been replaced by sofas, each of which held a folded-up fur and a pillow. The sight of them made him want to curl up on one straightaway.

"Sticky fingers," he said with a yawn. "I need to wash my hands."

And almost as if he had willed it into existence, a bowl of hot water and a small towel appeared on the table.

I could get used to this, he thought, dipping his fingers into the bowl to wash away the honey and sugar. *Think it and it appears.*

"Hey, Blessing," he said, wanting to let her in on his thoughts. But when he looked around, she was already asleep on one of the sofas, her hand trailing down to rest on the hound.

Chapter Fourteen

Once the darkling had seen the door close on her friends, she had delayed the three Hidden in the only way she knew how. She had fought them, with fists and with feet, in the full knowledge that she could not defeat them. But after what seemed like only a minute or two of combat, they had regrouped and disappeared.

The following early morning found her at her previous vantage point, sat at the e-bus stop outside the Haven Robotics Corporation. Her first instinct, knowing that the magically imbued guard-stone had been removed from the entrance to the building, had been to travel inside in shadow-form. That had been the plan, at least, until she discovered that the glass sliding doors prevented her from doing so. Just like the walls, the doors contained a sliver of water between two sheets of reinforced glass. She couldn't pass through water in shadow-form.

So she waited for the next person who would walk into the building. If she was quick enough, she could attach herself to their shadow.

An e-bus rolled to a stop in front of her. The doors slid open, obscuring an advertisement selling commercial space on the Janus Orbital Station. The advert adapted to swim leisurely across the external side of the still visible windows.

An elderly man, who had stood at the other end of the bus stop with audio-buds in his ears, waited patiently as the bus lowered. A repeated beeping marked the vehicle's descent until it finally reached ground level.

The man stepped into the front of the vehicle as those disembarking climbed down from the middle section. Two of these, a stylishly dressed couple, waited for their robot to untangle itself from the limbs of the many other robots crammed into the partitioned-off rear section of the bus.

A man dressed in a coat that, while still smart, had obviously seen better days, dodged around the couple. His coat fell open and the darkling caught a glimpse of the Haven Robotics staff badge that he wore.

As the low beeping returned and the e-bus rose to its former level above the road, the darkling fell in pace behind him. Taking advantage of the vehicle to hide her from the travel-way traffic, she melted into shadow.

*

"Good morning," said the man as he reached the Haven Corporation reception desk. "Any messages for me?" he asked the robot who sat there.

"Good morning, Mr Cady," it replied in a measured but pleasant tone. "Yes, Miss Palmer has asked that you meet with her as soon as you arrive."

"That sounds a bit urgent for this early in the morning," he said. "Is she in her office?"

"Yes, Mr Cady. Shall I inform her that you are on your way up?"

"I suppose you'd better," he said.

Hanging tightly to the man's shadow, the darkling travelled with him to the lift at the back of the space.

"Do you mind?" Mr Cady said to the two large, black, spherical robots that guarded the lift. Unlike the robots the darkling had seen before, these two had no limbs and balanced uneasily in place. "I'm just..." He pointed to the lift, then pointed up. "Okay?" he said as he pressed the lift button.

The lift doors slid open and he hurriedly stepped inside,

jabbing his finger on the button for the penthouse office. The robots watched him, or rather what the darkling took to be 'watching', turning the blue lights that ran up and down each robotic sphere towards the lift.

Mr Cady leant back against the wall as the lift doors closed, releasing a sigh that sounded a lot like relief to the darkling. His aura, though shades of grey like that of most workaday adults, flickered with spots of coloured light, brightest red for the stirrings of anger and sickly yellow that showed how nervous he was. As the lift progressed, the darkling watched the red dissipate, but the man remained nervous.

When Mr Cady, with the darkling in shadow tow, walked into the penthouse office, Eleanor Palmer greeted him in a polite but familiar fashion.

"Mr Cady, thank you for seeing me at such an early hour. I'm sure you have lots to attend to, but I wondered if I could borrow your judgement for a short while."

"Of course, Miss Palmer. Is there anything wrong?"

"Wrong?" she said. "I hope not. Please." She invited him to sit on the chair in front of her desk with a sweep of her hand. "I feel I am in need of a second mind to assess my predicament."

"I'm always at your service," he said as he sat. He watched Miss Palmer pace for a moment before asking, "Are you all right?"

"I'm fine. Just rather distracted." She took a seat at her desk, sitting uncomfortably upright. "Where to begin." She tapped her polished nails in a rapid rhythm on the tabletop. "The guard robots," she finally said. "I noticed that they're stationed quite extensively throughout the building. Even in the basement. Thankfully not in here."

"That's right," said Mr Cady. "They're all over the place, and always in pairs. I must admit that I'm rather curious about the design. Unlike our own models that make it very clear what they're about, the guard robots' functionality is entirely concealed. I'd be very interested to take one apart and find out just how close their processing units are to Haven tech."

"Do you think they're armed?" she asked.

"It's possible."

"I feared you might say that. It's one thing being surveilled, but…" She left the statement unfinished.

"They're obviously designed to intimidate," he said. "If I could examine one, I could tell you for sure. I don't suppose you could ask?"

"I already did. The answer was 'no'. They mentioned something about national security."

"I see," he said. "In that case, I can only observe the robots and surmise what they can do."

"That would be something," she said. "Thank you. I fear the Corporation may have jumped out of one fire and into—"

Before she could finish, the lift doors opened. The man who entered the room wore the warmest of smiles and walked with one hand casually tucked into the pocket of his suit trousers.

"Miss Palmer," he said. "I didn't realise that you had a visitor. Elrick Olen." He held out his other hand as he advanced on Mr Cady.

"Mr Olen," said the robotics engineer, standing to shake the other man's hand. "Norman Cady."

"Mr Cady is one of our senior robotics engineers," said Eleanor.

"Pleased to meet you, Mr Cady," said Elrick. "Unfortunately, I must interrupt your meeting. I need to speak to Miss Palmer, in private."

"Of course," said Mr Cady. "Miss Palmer, I'll get on it straightaway."

"Thank you, Mr Cady," she said. "That would be appreciated."

"Keep up the good work," said Elrick as Mr Cady returned to the lift.

"Will do," said Mr Cady, with a smile.

When the doors closed and the lift began to move, however, the darkling saw the smile drop from his face. The anger in his aura returned, but this time it was accompanied by deeply-felt concern.

*

Having left Mr Cady's shadow when he stepped out into the reception, the darkling took solid form in the lift and pressed the button to descend to the basement. By the time the doors opened again, she had reverted to shadow.

After the well-lit interior of the Haven Corporation building, she had expected the same down there, but instead the doors opened onto near darkness. The way out of the room was marked by the barest touch of illumination from a light source somewhere deeper in the basement. Stationed on either side of the lift doors were two more of the black guard-robots she had seen upstairs. At the movement of the doors, each swivelled towards the open lift, their blue lighted panels bright in the dim room. Seeing nobody, the robots turned away from the lift. The darkling took her chance and flowed out into the shadows beyond.

One of the many benefits of shadow-form was the sight it provided in complete or near darkness. Maybe 'sight' was the wrong word. It was more a perception of how things were. She had expected the basement to show signs of the explosion, however contained, that had happened there only weeks before. Instead, the construct of the basement was as complete and undamaged as if no such incident had occurred there. To the darkling's eyes, however, each wall, the floor below, and the low ceiling overhead shone with the magic that had been used to repair them.

After flowing through a number of empty rooms, all pristine and undamaged, she found the thing she had been looking for. Or rather she found the thing that she had hoped would be gone.

Steve had told her about Winters' laboratory, how it had

appeared as a smooth white wall blocking their way, with no apparent door. He had also told her about how the activated Reactor had torn the laboratory apart in the build-up to the explosion. And yet there it was, as intact as the rest of the basement.

Unlike the basement, though, the laboratory wall did not shine with magic. To human eyes, of course, it would simply look like a plain, white wall. Only the darkling could see the mass of tendrils it sent out to drain the magic from the neighbouring surfaces, even from the dust in the air, devouring every morsel.

Judging that she could more usefully tackle the laboratory as a human, she was about to take solid form again when a door slid open in the white wall. Her view into the laboratory was blocked by the two people who stepped out: a blonde woman built for battle and a dark-haired man whose shirt sleeves were neatly folded up to his elbows and his jacket grasped in one hand. Both were workadays.

"That went well," said the man as the door slid closed behind them. "Didn't even have to get my hands dirty." He rolled down his sleeves, buttoning the cuffs.

"Disappointing," said the woman with a yawn. "I thought he might put up a fight. I suppose we have the Auditor to thank for that. This latest model of the collar is a definite improvement on the last version."

The man opened out his jacket and the darkling caught sight of a number of internal pouches and pockets. It was only a glimpse, but she thought she recognised one of the items tucked into his jacket. The man carried Helios hunting flares and that could only mean one thing. His people knew about darklings and how to defeat them.

"I for one am happy to face brooding obedience over violence," said the man, slipping into his jacket. "It makes for an easy life."

"Easy life," snorted the woman. "This one is only easy because all we have to do is contain him. I doubt he'll answer our questions as quickly as the other one did."

"Hardly quickly," said the man. "That one likes the sound of their own voice, but they haven't given us anything useful so far."

"You don't call that device useful?"

"True. The boss did get his prize," said the man. "Two down."

"It's only a matter of time before they break," she said. "I can see it in their eyes."

As their voices tailed off into the next room, the darkling took solid form and stepped closer to the white laboratory wall. She stood three or four feet away but already she could feel the pull of whatever draining magic was imbued in the substance of the laboratory. She knew full well that, if she moved any closer, her very essence would be at threat. Darting away to a safe distance, she returned to shadow and flowed out of the room to catch up with the workadays.

Chapter Fifteen

"Steve, wake up."

"Just five minutes more, Mum." Steve pulled his quilt up to his chin. The quilt felt strangely furry.

"Steve, wake up!" Rough hands shook him by the shoulders. "They are here."

"What?" He blinked as the quilt was ripped out of his grasp. "Mum?"

"Do I look like your mother?" Ana scowled down at him, the fur that had covered Steve in her hands. Morning sunlight streamed through the open front door, layering a golden veil over the room. "Come on, get up."

"Sorry." Steve rubbed his eyes and sat up on the edge of the sofa he'd fallen asleep on the night before. "What's happening?"

"One of the Council is here with a contingent of Hidden. Selene has already taken Blessing deeper into the caves. You are to follow."

"Where's Hartley?" If being shaken awake hadn't already snapped Steve to attention, Ana's words had finished the job.

"I'm here." Hartley shouldered a battered knapsack. "I thought it best to gather supplies for our journey. Just in case."

"So we're just running away?" said Steve. "Aren't we going to face them? The sisters said we were safe here."

"Safe is one thing, my boy," said Hartley, taking Steve by the arm and pushing him towards yet another newly appeared door at the back of the room. "Being observed is quite another. Best to move on while we have the choice."

"Does Sanctuary have a back door?"

"Everywhere has a back door when I'm around," said Hartley with a grin. "Come on, come on."

"Where's Cate?" Steve dug in his heels, which barely stopped the speed with which Hartley pushed him across the room.

"Conversing with Jonah Ledwitch," said Hartley. "She'll give him short shrift and provide us with plenty of time to make our exit."

"Goodbye, Steve Haven." Ana was dressed for conflict again, her bow slung across her shoulders. "Try to keep the old fool safe."

"That almost sounds like affection, Ana," said Hartley as she headed to the door.

"You have your uses," she admitted. "That's all I'm saying." Then with a smile, she left.

"This doesn't seem right." Steve turned to face the shopkeeper as they reached the door. "The sisters have been so good to us and we're leaving them to face the Council without us."

"They've faced much worse and scarier before now," said Hartley. "Trust me. Dealing with the Council and the Hidden is no more alarming to Ana and Cate than batting away an annoying insect. If anything, it's a little light entertainment for them. Now, grab the lamp and keep your hand on the rope. Whatever you do, do not lose sight of the rope."

"Why?" said Steve, taking a storm lamp from the wall. The candle inside flickered into flame.

"The Sanctuary cave system is extensive," said Hartley. "I don't have time for us to get lost. Who knows where we'd come out?"

And with that, he pushed Steve through the doorway into the darkness beyond.

*

The further that Steve walked into the caves, the thinner the layer of whitewash on the walls became, until eventually he was surrounded by bare rock. In one hand he carried the storm lamp, raised to ward off the shadows that surrounded them. He trailed the other hand along a rope that was fixed to the wall of their route by worn, metal rings. The journey through twisting tunnels, with only the occasional glimmer of light through openings into what Steve assumed were the caves he wasn't supposed to visit, was accompanied by Hartley's incessant whistling.

"Do you whistle when you're nervous?" asked Steve.

"I'm not nervous," said Hartley. "I just don't want to surprise anyone who's in here with us. Best to let them know we're around."

"Why?" said Steve. "Who's in here?"

"Not so much who, as what," said Hartley. "Rats mostly. Dust imps. They're harmless enough."

"That's good."

"I tell you, we'd have to be atrociously unlucky to encounter a ghoul."

"A what?"

"Of course, all ghouls hate whistling. They won't come near the sound. Not unless they're particularly starved." Hartley returned to his whistling.

When the darkness of the cave system eventually receded, Steve stood at the end of the rope and at the entrance to a new, vast space.

The cave was as tall and long as the interior of the cathedral where his uncle's funeral had been held less than two months before. In place of stained-glass windows, three panes of water flowed from the roof of the cave. The water rippled in the sunlight that streamed from somewhere above, the play of light with water creating a relay of racing rainbows that darted around and among the falling cascades. The cave was filled with echoes of the sound of the water meeting the ground below where it swept away into a channel that flowed off through the back of the cave.

"You won't need the storm lamp in here," said Hartley, slapping a hand on Steve's shoulder. "Leave it on the hook." He released a satisfied sigh as he looked around. "I do love Sanctuary."

As Steve hooked the storm lamp at the end of the rope, the flame within guttered and died. Pebbles moved and crunched under his feet as he followed his friend into the cave, adding to the echoes that sang around them.

"Steve, you're here!" Blessing was suddenly at his side, grabbing his hand as his feet slipped on the pebbles. "Isn't this wonderful?" she said as Steve fought to keep his balance and his dignity. "I've something to show you," she said with the brightest of smiles as she pulled him to the centre of the cave where a raised area of rock stood a foot above the pebbled floor. "Look."

Carved into the smooth rock surface was a roughly circular pattern of lines. Steve crouched down and after a moment he realised what he was looking at.

"It's a maze," he said, tracing his hand along one of the paths.

"Selene calls it The Journeys. See this?" She ran a finger along one of the pathways to a dead-end that was marked by a simply-carved drawing of a door. "Each path leads to these doorways, and each doorway leads to another world. Worlds like ours, but not ours, if you see what I mean."

"And what about this?" Steve pointed to the centre of the maze where a picture of a tree had been carved into the stone. "Another world?"

"I don't know." Blessing frowned and shook her head. "She didn't mention that." She sat back on her heels, her smile suddenly gone.

"Are you all right?"

"Not really," she said in a voice that sounded close to breaking. "Selene and her sisters are kind, but I want to go home. Back to reading books at Hartley's kitchen table."

"You will," he said. "He'll sort this out and then we'll all go there for a bowl of burnt porridge and a mug of his horrible coffee."

"It is horrible, isn't it? I thought it was meant to taste like that." She laughed, just a little, but it brightened her face for a moment.

"So," said Steve, "what have you been doing back here?"

"Practicing," she said. "Selene taught me something new. I'll show you."

She lifted her hand to her lips, forming a circle with forefinger and thumb, then she cupped her hand around a breath. When she opened her fingers, a light orb sat on her palm.

"What does it feel like?" he said. "The orb. Is it like a soap bubble or glass or, I don't know, something else?"

"Not like any of those," she said. "It's difficult to explain. I just know it for what it is."

"Can I touch it?" He raised a finger. "Or will it pop?"

"Find out." She held her hand and the orb closer to him. "Go on."

"Okay." He tapped his finger as gently as he could manage on the top of the orb. It wasn't wet, or hard, or anything he had expected. Instead, there was simply a feeling of 'fizz'—that was the only way he could describe it—on his skin as it came into contact with the orb. "That's..." He searched for a word. "Odd," he eventually landed on.

"It's what it is," she said. "That isn't what I've been practicing though. Watch this." She brought her hand close to her mouth and gave a small, open-mouthed breath onto the orb. Almost immediately, the edges of the orb shimmered and then it began to grow.

"That's amazing," said Steve, retreating across the pebbled floor on his knees. He wasn't sure he wanted to be quite so close to an experimental orb.

"Come on, you two." Hartley beckoned to them. "We need to depart quick sharp."

Selene stood on the other side of the cave, with the white hound asleep at her feet. Leant against the cavern wall were five doors in various states of decay. One was missing a door handle, while its neighbour had lost a panel and provided a view of the cave wall it rested against.

"Will these do?" she said to Hartley. "I kept them from your last visit."

"I fear that you and I have weathered far better over those years than these contraptions." Hartley rapped his knuckles on one of the doors, but the wood buckled under the force and crumbled. "Do you have any more?"

"How about now?" she said.

"That's more like it." Hartley clapped his hands as the doors changed in a blink to what they must have been when new. "Selene, my dear, you are a goddess."

"Obviously," she said with a chuckle and a roll of her eyes. "You're such a flirt."

"I mean every word of it." He took her hand and gave it a noisy kiss. "As always, you have been a delightful host, but I'm afraid it's time we were off."

"You know you're always welcome in Sanctuary. All of you are," she said as she looked around at the three of them.

"Thank you, Selene." Blessing hugged the sister. "Especially for the food."

"You're welcome."

"Yeah, thanks," said Steve as Hartley ran his hands over one of the doors. "You're a life saver."

"It has been a pleasure to meet another member of the Haven family." As Blessing released her, Selene took Steve's hand. "You do your parents proud."

"Here we are." Beyond the door that Hartley held open, there was only darkness. "Shall we take a stroll?" he said.

"Take care of each other," said Selene as Hartley stepped through the open door, closely followed by Blessing. "We are always here, if you need us."

*

"This is rather cosy," Steve heard Hartley whisper. "Can anyone find the way out?"

Wherever the door had taken them to, it was completely dark and so small that Steve was pressed up against ribs and elbows. The musty smell of Hartley's jacket mingled with the scent of cleaning fluid and hot metal.

"Ow!" Something sharp jabbed Steve in the shin.

"Sorry, Steve. Did I stand on your toes?" That was Hartley. "What we need is a little light."

"I could create a light orb," said Blessing.

"No. We can't risk using magic," said Hartley. "We don't want to attract any more Hidden. Can anyone find a door handle? Any kind of exit?"

"Ow!" said Steve as the same sharp jab dug into his leg. "Something's poking me."

"What's going on?" The space flooded with light as a door slid aside. "Darn robots. Why aren't you…?"

"Thank you very much, my kind sir. Coming through." Hartley pushed Steve and Blessing ahead of him and out of what Steve could now see was a cupboard as the confused janitor stared at them.

"You aren't a robot," he said. "What…?"

"Lovely place you have here, my man," said Hartley, shaking the janitor's hand as two small cleaning robots followed them out and set off at speed. "Always a pleasure. Good day."

"Hang on. What were you doing in there?" the janitor called after them.

"Where are we?" asked Blessing with wide eyes as she took Steve's hand.

"Looks like an underground station," said Steve, staring up the set of commuter-laden escalators that the cupboard they had travelled to was fitted beneath.

The space was brightly lit by illuminated blue panels that ran across the high, domed ceiling and down the walls. The ceramic floor tiles and metal escalators reflected the blue light, adding to the effect of height and breadth. The space was filled with the hubbub of the people who rode the escalators and dispersed around Steve and his friends. A steady flow of mostly small robots—following, carrying, and taking instructions—accompanied their human owners.

"Grovewall, to be exact," said Hartley as he marched past the base of the escalators and took a sharp right into a narrow and less well-lit corridor. "I've travelled out of here via that cupboard door before now. I've never travelled back in, however. I had no idea it would be so inconvenient."

"Why are we back in the city?" said Steve. "Isn't it dangerous to be here?"

"It's a necessary means to an end," said Hartley as he took another sharp turn. "The end being that we find what we're looking for." The corridor finished abruptly at what looked like another cupboard door. "Or rather whom." Hartley reached into his sleeve and pulled out a security card. "I hope that fellow won't be too put out by my borrowing this, but needs must." He swiped the card across a panel on the wall and the door slid open.

Chapter Sixteen

"Where are we going?" asked Steve.

He and his friends walked along the unevenly-paved path that hugged the side of the river. A level above them, the city of Caercester shone in all its granite-and-glass glory in the afternoon light.

Hartley marched ahead of them all, with Blessing close behind. Steve came last and, from time to time, he would nervously look back to check that the Hidden hadn't found them.

"To drop in on an old acquaintance," said Hartley. "If anyone knows which direction to point us in, it's him."

"But if the Hidden can track you—"

"There's no 'if' about it," said Hartley.

"Does that mean they know where we are right now?"

"I only light up on their map when I'm using magic. At the moment, I should be as dull as…" Hartley sidestepped to dodge an old woman coming in the opposite direction. "Hello," he said with a smile as she scuttled by with a look of suspicion. "As dull as any workaday. No offence, Steve," he continued as he set off at a jaunt again. "If the Hidden are looking out for my travelling magic, it's a fair assumption to make that they'll have been able to track me to the door in the underground station that we just left."

"That's not good," said Steve.

"However, now we're on foot and a distance away, they likely have no idea where we are at all."

"Okay, that's better," said Steve but it didn't stop him from checking behind them again.

"Of course, the Council are bound to have—what does James call it?—eyes on the street. That's exactly why we're taking the river lane."

"I've never been down here before," said Steve. The river water looked different close-up, more brown than the blue-black ribbon viewed from the city up above.

"It's an efficient way to get where we're going," said Hartley. "Less Council eyes and city cameras to avoid."

Ahead of them loomed the West Temple Bridge. At city level, the bridge's white metal construct gleamed whether by day or night. Down here, so close to the river, the white gave way to brown stone blocks patched with moss and graffiti.

"Quick warning," said Hartley. "The entrance to my acquaintance's home can only be accessed by taking a narrow walkway over the water to a door within the bridge itself. Do you think you can manage that, Steve? Blessing?"

"Of course," said Blessing.

"I should think so," said Steve with a nod.

"That's the spirit. This way," he said, taking Blessing's hand and heading for the river's edge. "We'll be over it in no time at all."

*

With the door in the bridge closed behind them, Steve found himself in complete darkness. He shuffled forward a step and bumped into Blessing.

"Sorry." He moved back an inch. "I can't see anything."

"Easily remedied," said Hartley. Steve heard him rub his hands together, then stop. "Darn, almost forgot. We mustn't use magic. I was going to conjure a most marvellous light orb. I'll just have to use this instead."

There was a rusty click and a beam of light from an aged hand-torch illuminated the space ahead of them. The staircase was a jumble of the same stone blocks that the bridge's base was made from, interspersed with worn, red bricks. There was no banister.

"Careful as you go," said Hartley, looking back at them as he took the first step. "The stairs are badly worn in places."

"Doesn't your friend get many visitors?" said Steve.

"Oh, lots and lots of visitors," said Hartley. "Just with fifty years or a century in between each one."

"How long have they been down here?" Steve braced himself on the wall as he started after his friends.

"You know, I'm really not sure," Hartley called back. "I always think it's impolite to pry. Plus, he might hex me if I ask too many age-related questions."

"Friendly then," said Steve, trying not to scream as a spider ran over his hand.

"Of course," said Hartley. "As long as we bring him a sufficient offering. He likes youngsters, you know."

"Pardon?" said Steve. "You are joking, aren't you?" he called after his friend as the shopkeeper sped off down the steps. "What do you mean he likes youngsters? Hartley?"

*

"How far down are we?" Steve asked after a while. "It's getting cold."

"We're well beneath the surface of the river by now," said Hartley. "Probably down past the riverbed itself."

"This place looks old," said Steve as the edge of one of the brick steps crumbled under his foot. "And broken."

"Ancient," said Hartley. "It may look sparkling new up there, but that white monstrosity was constructed over the foundations of the original bridge. I daresay starting from scratch would have taken too much time."

"And your friend lives down here?" said Steve.

"What can I say? This," he said, flashing the torch around

the stairwell, "suits his purposes. Of course, he isn't alone down here. He's not *that* private a person. Anyway, here we are. Home sweet temple."

Hartley stopped as the stairs evened out onto a dusty landing. He shone his torch around a stone archway that was a couple of inches shorter than him. Carved into its surround, Steve could make out an interlinking pattern of roughly carved birds in flight.

"I'd forgotten how small this door is," said Hartley. "It might be best if you let me go first. The Augur can be rather suspicious of new faces."

"Fine by me," said Steve.

"Blessing, are you okay?"

"Just cold," she said.

"Cold can be fixed." Hartley took her hands and rubbed them between his own. "A nice cup of tea will put that right. I've brought provisions."

True to his word, Hartley was the first to pass through the archway, pulling Blessing behind him. Steve followed quickly, not wanting to lose sight of the others.

"Wow." His voice echoed around the vast chamber they found themselves in. "What is this place?"

"Keep your voice down, Steve," Hartley whispered. "It's disrespectful to shout."

"This is way bigger than Caercester Cathedral."

"This is the temple of the Augur," said Hartley. "It's been around for centuries longer than any boring, old cathedral."

Six thick, stone columns reached from the floor to the ceiling on each side of the temple. Light flickered from a series of burning torches mounted on the walls. Where Steve and the others had walked, their footprints revealed polished marble beneath a thick layer of dust.

Ahead of them, on a raised pedestal, towered a statue of a man, cloaked and bare foot. A stone eagle, long since missing the end of its beak, rested on the arm of the statue. A series of small stone birds waited at the statue's feet.

"Who's there?" a voice shrieked. "Who disturbs the Augur?"

A figure stepped out from behind the statue. Away from the light of the torches, Steve could only see its bulky outline.

"Do you bring me sacrifices?" called the same voice. "Is it the boy? I can smell boy. Juicy. Fresh."

"Hartley?" Steve stepped closer to his friend.

"No sacrifices, honoured oracle," said Hartley, bowing. "We bring something much more palatable." He reached into his jacket pocket and pulled out a small linen sack. "Tea."

"Is it Darjeeling?"

"Of course, my dear friend. Just as you like it," said Hartley.

The man stepped into the light and slowly blinked the one eye that sat in the middle of his forehead. He was easily a head taller than Hartley and wore a long, faded tunic that had seen better days. Leather belts crossed his chest and wrapped around his waist. Hairy calves ended in a pair of battered sandals that revealed equally hairy toes. His wiry, tangled mane was piled high on top of his head and secured with rope. A single earring that looked alarmingly like a bone, dangled from his right ear.

"Is that the Augur?" Steve whispered.

"No, that's a cyclops, obviously," said Hartley. "Now, do keep quiet, please."

"Let me see them," snapped the voice. "Hurry up, you big lug. Turn. Turn."

The cyclops did as he was instructed and turned around until he was facing the statue. Crouched on his back and secured in a sling was a small, old man. His skin was wrinkled and dark. His head was bald except for a tuft of dark hair above one ear. His legs dangled, their muscles wasted away.

"Is that you, Keg? Keg. Hartley Keg?" He lisped when he spoke, spit spraying from his toothless mouth.

"It is indeed, great Augur." Hartley bowed again, this time with a sweep of his hand.

"With a child of light. Light. Bright." The Augur squinted at

Blessing. "Did you bring me anything else beyond the tea?" The Augur looked at Steve as he spoke.

"As a matter of fact, I did." Hartley reached inside his jacket. "I think you'll like this."

"I'll be the judge of that," said the Augur, squinting at them.

"It's a little special." Hartley drew out a silver hand mirror. "I've been hanging onto this for just the right person." He held it out.

"Do you think me a fool?" the Augur snapped. "Do you think I want to be reminded of my age by a mirror? Of my ravaged face? Take it away."

"But it's not just any mirror." Hartley slowly walked towards the Augur, the mirror outheld. "It's enchanted. Part of a collection that once belonged to an Amazon queen. The others are smashed. Only this remains."

"Enchanted?" said the Augur. "To do what?"

"Why don't you see for yourself?"

The Augur snatched it from Hartley and held it close to his eyes. "It's me," he whispered, touching his free hand to his wizened face. "I'm so young. Young. Youthful."

"And handsome," said Hartley.

"I was handsome, wasn't I?" he said, admiring himself.

"And with this mirror, you can always be so."

"Handsome." A drip of spit ran down the Augur's chin as his lips cracked into a smile. "I told you I was handsome." He slapped the back of the cyclops who grunted in response. "What do you want?" he snapped at Hartley.

"I'm looking for a way out of the city that won't light up on the Hidden's radar, dear Augur. I believe, in your great wisdom and benevolence, you may be able to help me. Yes?"

"Perhaps," said the Augur, returning his eyes to the mirror. "Perhaps not. Not." He tucked the mirror into the sling. "Come along then and bring that tea with you. Quickly now. I don't have all day."

Chapter Seventeen

"Well, isn't this lovely?" said Hartley.

I think you mean cramped and pokey, Steve thought, but he didn't say anything.

Steve sat at a round card table, shoulder to shoulder with Hartley and the cyclops, in a room behind the statue in the temple. Blessing sat on the other side of Hartley, keeping close to the shopkeeper. The cyclops worked at a piece of paper, folding and creasing it continually, his big elbow knocking Steve into Hartley from time to time.

The room was a picture of comfort and decay. Gold and deep red flock wallpaper sat uncomfortably on the walls, with the occasional corner peeled back to reveal the stonework beneath. The wall to Steve's left was covered in old-fashioned postcards pinned in place by thumbtacks. The opposite wall housed four battered filing cabinets that sat a little indented into the ground. Behind the Augur, two tattered black velvet curtains hung a little distance apart from each other. Dripping white candles lit the space from five elaborate, tall candelabras. Steve could feel the chill of the stone floor through a threadbare carpet that must have at one point been patterned.

The Augur sat across from them, perched on a pile of cushions on a high back armchair, the sling now wrapped around him like a shroud. He poured from a tea pot into five delicate cups, humming to himself.

"Lemon juice?" he said, reaching for a small, ornate jug.

"That would be splendid," said Hartley.

"And the boy?"

"I'm fine. I don't—" Hartley nudged him. "Same, please."

"Me too," said Blessing. "Thank you, Augur."

The Augur poured a dash of lemon juice into all of the cups and then took a slurp from his own. "Perfect."

Steve sipped his tea and quickly put the cup back on the table, trying not to pull a face at the mossy taste. Hartley drank his down in one go and grinned widely at the Augur.

"More?"

"We wouldn't want to use up your precious resources," said Hartley. "The Darjeeling was, after all, a gift."

"Do you have to do that now?" The Augur scowled at the cyclops who simply shrugged, then returned to his paper folding. "Origami, you know?" The Augur rolled his eyes.

"What are you making?" asked Steve.

"Birds, it's always birds, birds," the Augur answered before the cyclops could make a sound. "No imagination."

"That's nice," said Steve, feeling a little sorry for the hulking creature.

"So, to what do I owe this intrusion?" The Augur took another slurp of tea staring expectantly at Hartley. "What do you want?" he snapped, slamming one of his shrivelled hands on the table.

"I'm going to lay my cards out, respected Augur," said Hartley. "The Council…" He stopped speaking as the Augur sucked in a breath of air with a hiss at the mention of the Council.

"Them," muttered the Augur. "I might have known."

"Indeed, dear Augur. Them. They want to strip Blessing of her magic and imprison her." He wrapped an arm around her shoulders. "I can't let them do that. I won't allow it."

"Why would they imprison the girl, girl, her?" said the Augur. "What has she done?"

"Well," said Hartley, looking at Blessing. "It's a long story."

"I have time, time, tick tock." said the Augur. "Spit it out."

"I suppose I should start at the beginning," said Hartley. "I think I may need another drink first. Do you mind?" He released

Blessing and pulled a hip flask from inside his coat. "Have you heard of the Haven Robotics Corporation?"

*

By the time Hartley had told the Augur most of what had happened to them over the last few weeks—Winters, the destruction of the Reactor, the intervention, and Blaike Harn's decision—the little old man's eyes appeared to have grown to twice their previous size. The Augur's mouth had dropped open and a faint line of spit traced a line from the corner of his mouth to his chin.

"And that is it," said Hartley finally. "You know the complete story now. I'm sure I don't have to point out that the Council's heavy-handed ruling is totally unfair and ludicrous."

The Augur's mouth snapped shut and he blinked. He poured himself a cup of tea and knocked it back in one gulp. "I see," was all he said.

"I could travel us out of the city, but the Hidden will be on the lookout for my magic, dear Augur," said Hartley. "They would descend on us in the proverbial instant. We need to put as much distance between ourselves and the Council as possible so we can decide on our next step."

The cyclops sniffed, then made a deep, guttural grunt.

"I'm perfectly aware of that," said the Augur. "Give me a chance."

The cyclops grunted again and returned to his paper folding.

"So you thought of me," said the Augur. "Understandable."

"I did, dear Augur. We need access to the Station," said Hartley. "And a ticket to travel."

"And how will you pay for your travel?" said the Augur. "With your paltry gifts? I'm not a charity, you know."

"My dear Augur," Hartley began.

The cyclops muttered something that Steve didn't recognise as any language he knew. The Augur squinted at the creature, puckering his mouth to a tightly pressed line.

"I'll tell them in my own good time," he said. "Let me have at least a little, small, tiny shred of fun."

The cyclops grunted and shrugged his heavy shoulders.

"Fine," snapped the Augur. "Fine, fine, fine. You can have your travel, on one condition."

"Thank you, Augur," said Hartley. "Your help, as always, is—"

"Yes, yes, yes. You haven't heard the condition yet." The Augur leant forward, bracing himself on the chair arms. "Keeltown."

"Keeltown?" said Hartley with a gulp.

It could have been the dim, candle-lit atmosphere, but Steve was sure he saw Hartley grow considerably paler.

"You can have your ticket to travel wherever you want, but first you will run an errand for me in Keeltown."

"Well, I haven't…" Hartley spluttered. "I mean, I'm not sure…" He pulled at his collar as if it were suddenly too tight. "Keeltown? Is it an absolute must, dear Augur?"

"Have I ruffled your fathers?" The Augur gave a toothless grin, eyes alight with amusement. "Any reason you wouldn't be welcome in Keeltown?"

"You know there is," said Hartley.

"No matter," said the Augur. "You need to get out of the city. I need a favour in return." He nodded to himself. "Keeltown."

"If that's what it takes," said Hartley with a sigh.

"It is," said the Augur. "Frankie Una. Yes?"

"Who's that?" said Steve.

"A long-time friend," said Hartley. "Will I find Frankie in Keeltown?"

"No, no, no. Frankie fell off every map I own about a month ago. That takes a lot of power, or friends, or both to do. Those in the know tell me that Frankie has been detained by parties who would like to get their hands on you-know-what."

"And how much faith do you place in the opinion of 'those in the know'?" asked Hartley.

"In this instance, a lot. I like to keep my ear to the ground," said the Augur pointing up. "And the rumours I hear ring with a knell of truth. If these 'parties' are after what Frankie carries, then it may be that they want the others too."

"Other what?" said Steve.

"You're a nosey one, aren't you?" said the Augur, squinting at Steve. "Does the boy know the full story?" he asked Hartley.

"He was there when Blaike Harn—"

"No, not that," snapped the Augur. "Does he know the origin of the Reactor and its fellow devices?"

"Well, no," said Hartley. "I didn't think it necessary to tell him that."

"Necessary to whom?" asked the Augur. "The boy should know what he's got himself into. Don't you think? Think?"

"Well, when you put it like that." Hartley shrugged. "I suppose it wouldn't do any harm to tell him some of the story."

"Some of the story?" The Augur's lips flattened into a line, and then he rolled his eyes with a tut. "I suppose that *some* of the story will have to suffice." The Augur rested his hands on the arms of his chair. "I hope you're sitting comfortably, Steve Haven, because this may take a while."

"I'm okay," said Steve, shuffling a little on his chair. "Go on."

"Shall I?" The Augur raised his eyebrows at Hartley, or rather the hairless band of skin where his eyebrows should have been.

"Go ahead," said the shopkeeper. "Your storytelling skills are far superior to my own, dear Augur."

"Such flattery," said the Augur. "Let me see. How to begin. Ah, yes. There once was a man—we won't mention his name— who created a device for nothing less than to mend his heart."

"That is one way of putting it," said Hartley. "However—"

"Quiet. *I'm* telling this story," said the Augur. "The device was an invention of grief-laden madness. Nobody knows how he discovered the method to create the device, only that he did. The man never gave the device a name, but in time it came to be known as the Path."

"Did it work?" said Steve. "Did it mend his heart?"

"It did not," said the Augur sadly. "Some people think he was tricked into creating the device. Personally, I believe that what happened when he turned it on was a mere accident. Accident. Unexpected."

"Why? What happened?" said Steve.

"I presume that event is outside the 'some' of the story I am allowed to tell you," said the Augur, scowling at Hartley. "I heard from reliable sources that once the device came alive, it changed. It drained. Absorbed. Soaked. It became imbued with powers and abilities the like of which this world had never seen. It became more. Whatever theory you adhere to about how the device came to be, the man decided that the Path should be split into its constituent parts and never used again." The Augur fell silent, his eyes closing.

Steve was about to ask Hartley if the Augur had fallen asleep, when the old man blinked his eyes open with a sharp intake of breath.

"Where was I?"

"The parts of the Path being split up," said Blessing.

"Exactly," said the Augur. "And that's where we came into it."

"We?" said Steve.

"Those that chose to help the man," said the Augur. "Some new to the man's homeland, some not. Seven in all."

The cyclops mumbled something under his breath.

"Yes, all right, you were there too," said the Augur. "But you don't count. Do something useful one day and then you might. Maybe. Perhaps."

The cyclops let out a sound that was halfway between a sigh and a moan, and seemed to deflate a little on his stool.

"The Path was divided. Its power source, the Reactor, was now too powerful and corrupting to be left in the hands of any human, so a golem was created to carry it and given a darkling companion. The timing element, the Chronometer, was given to a man called Robert Elian, and the controlling part, the Gyrodial, to Frankie Una. The—"

"Er, Augur?" Hartley raised his hand like a schoolboy.

"Too much?" said the Augur.

"I think so," said Hartley.

"If these parties are after the parts of the Path, then word must get out," said the Augur. "Yes? We must inform the device-bearers. The Reactor's bearer is gone, and hopefully that device too, too, as well. We must warn Robert Elian. Or to be precise, you," said the Augur as he jabbed a finger in Hartley's direction. "You, Hartley Keg, must warn him. That is my price for your ticket to travel."

"How do you know Robert is in Keeltown?" said Hartley. "The device bearers aren't supposed to make their whereabouts known; not to anyone."

"That is an easy question to answer. Well?" the Augur snapped at the cyclops. "Go on then. I haven't got all day. Night. Whatever."

The cyclops rolled its one eye, left its paper construction on the card table, and went to one of the filing cabinets. He pulled at a drawer and, when it didn't slide open, he gave it a quick kick. The filing cabinet juddered, and the drawer sprang out an inch.

"The last thing I received from Robert was by squirrel," said the Augur as the cyclops pulled a bulky, leather-bound book from the drawer.

"Squirrel?" said Steve.

"Of course, squirrel," snapped the Augur. "It's that or conveyance charm. How else do you think I get any post down here? We don't have a letterbox, you know."

"Right," said Steve, looking at Hartley to make sure this wasn't a joke.

"Not that I like the creatures," said the Augur. "Zipping in and out of existence with no kind of warning. They nibble the mail too, you know? Horrible little vermin."

The cyclops returned to the table, still grumbling, and knelt at the side of the Augur with the book outheld.

"Now then." The Augur flipped the book open, licked his thumb, and began to turn the pages. "Here we are," he said as he almost reached the end of the book. "The last correspondence I had from Robert was a request for funds. Funds. Cash." He squinted at the page. "There it is. He collected the payment last week in Keeltown."

"Of course, he did. Why am I surprised?" Hartley drained his teacup, delicately placing it back on its saucer. "Dear Augur, you have been most kind. Your hospitality as always is impeccable."

"Of course." The Augur preened the tuft of hair behind his ear. "I have always been an excellent host."

"You have indeed." Hartley stood up, drawing Steve and Blessing with him. "Keeltown it is then. May we have our ticket?"

"Here." The Augur drew his hand round in a circular pattern before pointing a finger as if he were bursting a bubble.

"Ow!" Hartley slapped a hand to his face. "A paper ticket would have sufficed, you know."

"What's that?" said Steve as the shopkeeper dropped his hand. Hartley's skin was red and puffy around what looked like a newly-inked tattoo: a double banded circle around a bird-shaped, black splodge.

"Our ticket," said Hartley. "Thank you, Augur. Could I trouble you for a workaday doorway so that we can get to the Station?"

"He'll show you out." The old man waved a hand at the cyclops who stood with a grunt. "As always, Hartley Keg, your visit has provided a distraction from my solitude. Goodbye. Bye. Be gone."

"Steve. Bag." Hartley nodded to the knapsack that still sat on the floor by the table.

"Why me?" Steve picked it up and slung it over his shoulder. "Why can't you carry it?"

"Because you are young and strong," said Hartley, patting him on the shoulder. "And I am wise and opportunistic. Come along."

"Such a flatterer…" the Augur muttered as he closed his eyes. "Always…" He let out a high-pitched, whistling snore and sank into his chair.

Steve expected the cyclops to show them back to the door they had entered through, but instead the creature drew aside one of the black curtains and beckoned them to follow him through the archway beyond.

"Just how big is it down here?" Steve asked as he walked behind the others along a thin, dusty corridor that sloped in a downward direction.

"Nobody really knows," said Hartley. "The temple was built to be easily defended, provide a hiding place and, as a final solution, allow its inhabitants to escape. The architect died thousands of years ago and took her knowledge of the full extent of the temple with her."

The cyclops grunted as they came to a dead end. He nodded to a huge doorway that was several feet taller than the cyclops himself. It was made of stone and carved with more of the birds they had seen around the smaller door they had entered the temple through.

"This is it?" asked Hartley as the cyclops stepped aside to give them access.

The cyclops grunted and nodded.

"Thank you," said Blessing. "You've been very kind."

The cyclops lowered his head, clamping a hand to his chest to signify his acceptance of her gratitude.

"'Bye, er…" Steve awkwardly realised that he didn't know the cyclops' name. "What do I call you?"

The cyclops shook his head.

"Cyclops in service are rarely named," said Hartley, pushing on the stone door. "I have it," he added as the door creaked open. "Come along."

"'Bye then," said Steve, backing towards the door. "And thank you."

The cyclops raised its hand to wave as Blessing took Steve's arm and pulled him through the door.

Chapter Eighteen

"Marvellous. We've arrived," Hartley finally said as they stepped through a stone archway from the roughly carved and barely-lit corridor they had followed for the last half an hour.

"This isn't Caercester Train Station," said Steve as he followed the shopkeeper out into a vast space that stank of oil and singed metal.

"Of course, it isn't Caercester Train Station. Whoever said we were going there?"

"You did."

"No, I said the Station. This," said Hartley spreading his arms wide, "is *the Station*." His voice echoed up to the high stone ceiling above. Hartley slapped his hands, rubbing them together with a grin as he looked around. "Now, we just need to find the Inspector."

The Station was an enormous cavern, its ceiling supported by heavy, stone pillars. One broad train track, or what Steve assumed to be a train track, carved the space in half. Just as you would find in a normal train station, the track was lower than the platforms that lined its length. Unlike any train station Steve had seen before, five short walkways jutted out from one side of the platform and five more from the opposite side, each extending a pace over the track.

On the other side of the cavern was an entrance matching the one they had just walked through. A steady line of mostly human-looking passengers filed through that door to fill a row of long wooden benches. Some of the passengers carried luggage. Others were followed obediently *by* their luggage. The occasional passenger had animals with them. One clasped what looked like a covered birdcage to his body. The birdcage rattled violently every few seconds, causing the carrier to look around in an embarrassed fashion as he repositioned his grasp. Each outburst cast feathers, straw, and seed to the ground.

"Are you as much in the dark as me?" said Steve as Blessing stood staring around the vast space.

"It isn't dark," she said. "I can see perfectly well."

"No, that isn't what I meant," he said as she followed Hartley. "I meant… Oh, never mind."

"Tickets?" said a female voice that sounded as if it would much rather not be there.

"Miss Inspector," said Hartley, engulfing the cloaked figure with the most heart-felt of hugs. "How are you, my dear lady?"

"Oh, you know," said the Inspector, disentangling herself from Hartley's embrace. "Best as can be expected."

"You're looking well," he said.

Well? thought Steve. *How can you tell?*

The Inspector was a little taller than Hartley and dressed in a head-to-toe hooded midnight-blue cloak. Perhaps 'dressed' was the wrong word because inside the hood there was no face and the only suggestion of anything alive inside the cloak were the white-gloved, outheld hands.

"Fare?" she said.

"Fair to middling," said Hartley. "Kind of you to ask."

"No. Fare," she said, waving her hand at him. "How are you going to pay?"

"Oh, that," said Hartley with a grin. "The Augur sent us." He tapped the tattoo on his face. "I take it this is good enough to get us to Keeltown?"

"It'll do," she said.

"While I'm here, Miss Inspector, I have just the thing to make your day." Hartley span Steve around and delved into the knapsack. "Here we are. Splendid."

"What's this?" sighed the Inspector as Hartley held out a small, round tin.

"Open it and see," said Hartley. "You'll like it. Trust me."

"I hate it when people say, 'trust me'." The Inspector slowly took the tin from Hartley's grasp. "It's always a disappointment."

As she opened the tin, a smattering of purple powder coughed out onto her gloves and there was a delicate floral scent.

"Lavender candy," she whispered. Even without a visible face, Steve could tell that she was pleased.

"Did I do good?" asked Hartley. "Yes?"

"It'll do." She snapped the tin shut and pushed it into her sleeve. "Any animals?" she said, looking Steve up and down.

"No. Just us," said Hartley. "Three people."

"I see," she said. "The next tram will be here momentarily. Thank you for using our service. Have a nice day." The Inspector gave a long, deflating sigh and walked off.

"That's settled then," said Hartley. "Stay close to me. We don't want to miss our ride."

As they lined up on one of the short walkways that jutted out over the track, Steve felt the floor beneath his feet begin to shake. A warm breeze blew across his face and, starting quietly but growing louder by the second, there was the sound of trundling wheels.

Five short, windowed carriages zipped into the Station at speed, each carriage stopping to perfectly align with a walkway. With a wheezing gasp, the doors on each side of the carriage slid open. Steve watched as the inhabitants of their carriage spilled out onto the platform opposite.

"Better be quick." Hartley trotted into the carriage. "The tram doesn't hang around for long," he said, beckoning to Blessing and Steve to follow. "Come along, come along."

The interior of the carriage was sparsely decorated. In fact, the term 'decorated' didn't really apply. There was a scuffed, riveted metal floor. The walls and low ceiling were made from equally scuffed timber. The only parts of the carriage that looked as if they had been at all maintained and cleaned were the windows on each side of the tram.

"I do love a tram ride." Hartley grasped one of the hanging straps that dangled down from the ceiling. Blessing tried to reach a strap but, being too short, she took Hartley's hand instead.

"Why aren't there any seats?" said Steve.

"It leaves more room for livestock and passengers," said Hartley. "The Tram service is rarely averse to increasing its chances of making a profit. Never mind though. The journey isn't long, and besides the view standing up is much superior."

The doors gasped shut again and Steve scrambled for a hanging strap as the tram set off at speed.

*

"So where exactly are we?" asked Steve.

The view from the window was initially no more interesting than as if they were travelling on the underground train system in Caercester: dark tunnel walls and their own reflections thrown back at them by the window glass. It hadn't stayed like that for long, though.

"We're on the way to Keeltown," said Hartley.

"I know where we're *going*," said Steve. "But where are we *now*?"

On the other side of the window, a swathe of calm sea tinted lilac and peach by a glorious sunset stretched out to what appeared to be the horizon. The occasional seagull flapped by, calmly going about its business. At random intervals, dolphins broke through the water and leapt into the air, before crashing playfully back into the sea. The tram track cut an ugly line through the serene seascape.

"This is the Crossing," said Hartley. "It's a protected area, like Darkacre. It acts as a short-cut for magicals who want to take a long journey quickly. This," Hartley swept his hand across the view through the window, "is an illusion to make the journey more enjoyable. It's not always the same. Sometimes it might seem that the tram is travelling under the ocean, or through a snow-laden mountain region. The Inspector has an exceptionally good eye for the architecture of nature."

"So you could use this to travel anywhere?" said Steve.

"Not anywhere," said Hartley. "Just within our own landmass. But there are a handful of tram circuits like this dotted around the world with other Inspectors. For those in the know, of course." He tapped the side of his nose.

"That's amazing," said Steve. "But why is the Inspector so… you know… down, if she can create all of this?"

"Because she never gets to see what she creates," said Hartley. "She's not allowed to ride the tram. It's quite tragic really."

"Does this tramline go straight to Keeltown?" Blessing stood at one of the windows, with her face pressed to the glass. "I hope it isn't too quick a journey. I want to see lots more of this, first."

"If we're lucky, we'll go straight there," said Hartley. "Or we may stop at another intersection, like the Station in Caercester, on the way. It all depends on who wants to join the tram and from where. Some stops have stations while others are just occasional doors. Speaking of which," he said as the tram juddered to a slower pace.

Ahead of the carriage, a black box popped into view, unfolding and growing until it was large enough for the tram to enter.

"Please be careful what you say, both of you." Hartley nodded to the door of the tram as the seascape was replaced in a blink by a smaller version of the station they had left behind in Caercester. "You never know who might get on."

When the tram came to a halt and the doors opened, Steve and his companions were quickly surrounded by a flood of children. Steve counted twelve in all and noticed that each of them had the same, glossy moustache: even the girls.

Following them with a look of breathless frustration was an elderly man who hobbled on a battered Zimmer frame. He, too, wore a moustache much like the children's; except his whiskers looked appropriate and less disconcerting.

"Now, young un's," he gasped over the children's babbling. "Don't crowd the other passengers. Jerry, don't do that to Agatha. She's likely to spark you. Mort, remember what I said. Keep your hands to yourself. No pilfering."

"Afternoon," said Hartley with a nod.

"Sorry," said the old man, fighting his way through the children to hold out a hand to Hartley. "Hope we're not too much of a burden. My lot can be noisy."

"Not at all." Hartley pumped the man's hand vigorously. "School outing?"

"Grand-babbies," said the old man. "Thought I'd give my daughter a rest for a few hours. Give her the time to get her hair done and beard trimmed."

"We're going to the seaside," said a spectacled girl with blonde bunches who couldn't have been more than four years old. She blinked up at Steve. "I like candyfloss."

"Remember what I told you, Lupin," said the old man. "Don't bother the other passengers."

"I was just sayin'." She stamped her foot and turned her back on them.

"Sorry. I'm Gabe, by the way."

"Henry," said Hartley. "And this is Sam and Mabel."

"Good to meet you and your grandchildren," said Gabe.

"Oh, we're…" Steve looked at Hartley and Blessing. "We're off to the seaside too."

"Do *you* like candyfloss?" Lupin pulled at Steve's trouser leg. "Can we share?"

"Oh, Lupin." Gabe strained over his Zimmer frame to pick up his granddaughter. She squirmed out of his arms and climbed onto his shoulders, her blonde head brushing against the ceiling of the carriage.

As the tram trundled out of the station, the scene outside flashed from dusty grey to a vibrant blue that forced all of the passengers to blink their eyes shut for a moment.

"Wow." Steve dangled from a hanging strap, doing his best not to knock into the children who jostled around him. "That's amazing."

Outside the tram, tall streamers of seaweed the thickness of a man's arm stirred from a bed of pale sand. Jewel-coloured fish, the size of the smallest children that watched from the tram, swam amongst the seaweed. A crab with claws that could easily have snapped Steve's leg in two scurried across the sand. From up above the view line of the tram, light filtered down through the water, creating shades of aqua and emerald.

"Look, young un's," said Gabe, hobbling on his Zimmer frame to the window. "Isn't it pretty?"

Steve spent the rest of their journey pressed against one window with Hartley and Blessing while the carriage turned into a playground for Gabe's grandchildren. Not that he minded, really: as an only child, he'd always been a little jealous of his friends who had siblings.

When the tram came to a halt for a second time and there was an uproar of "Are we there yet?" and "Aw, Grandad", Steve followed Hartley and Blessing off the tram onto a walkway.

"Enjoy your day," Gabe called after them with a wave.

"Where now?" Steve hoisted the bag onto his shoulder. "*Are we there yet?*"

"Almost, my dear boy, almost," said Hartley as he led them through the tram station. "Be patient for a few minutes more and all will be revealed."

This station was a smaller still version of the one they had encountered mid-journey, with just the one door. Unlike either of the two tram stations that Steve had seen so far, this one was empty except for a tall, long-faced man in a suit that had seen better decades.

"Usher, my dear gent. How are you?" Hartley grabbed the man's hand and pumped it vigorously.

"Ah, you know," said the man, his face warming with a wide,

friendly smile. "Life is what it is."

"Never a truer word spoken," said Hartley, nodding.

"Are you wanting passage to the top?" said the man.

"That would be marvellous," said Hartley. "I want to visit a friend in Keeltown. Is the old place as it was?"

"Well, it's a little less bright." The man retrieved his hand from Hartley's grasp to pull open the door behind him which folded away to a strip of metal. Beyond a dusty, tiled floor was revealed in the light cast by a small, frosted glass pane. "Since people left to go back to the land and the like. You'll see."

"I daresay I will. Always a pleasure, Usher."

"Likewise, Hartley. Stay safe."

"I'll do my utter best. Come on, you two. No loitering now," Hartley called back to Steve and Blessing as he stepped into the revealed space.

"Thanks," said Steve, catching Usher's eye as he followed.

"No problem," said Usher. "Mind the step as you exit."

Steve heard the squeal of heavy hinges as Hartley swung open the door ahead. He shivered as the temperature dropped and raised a hand against the sudden daylight.

"Here we are." Hartley sucked in a lungful of air as he stepped outside. "I've missed this place."

Chapter Nineteen

Steve and Blessing stood with their hands pressed to the glass of a floor-to-ceiling window that ran the length of the space they stood in. The vast view through the glass was of blue sky, deeper blue sea, and two fingers of green land that pinched in to form a narrow outlet to the ocean beyond.

"Good old Keeltown. Marvellous place," said Hartley. "Hardly looks any different than the last time I was here."

"Are we on a ship?" asked Blessing.

"More of a platform," said Hartley. "Keeltown is a series of water vessels all fixed together. We're currently on the viewing deck of an old leisure cruiser."

"And Keeltown is where exactly?" asked Steve.

"Scotland. They call this the Black Strait," said Hartley. "Now, if you two have finished with your gawping, we really need to get on."

"What's the plan?" asked Steve as Hartley wrenched open the heavy steel door they had stepped through only minutes before. "Do you know where to find Robert Elian?"

"Not a clue," said Hartley. "That's why our first stop will be the Sheriff. He keeps a keen track of every visitor to Keeltown."

"And he'll tell you?" asked Steve as he followed his friend onto the landing of a grimy, steel staircase.

"Of course, of course," said Hartley. "Well, he probably will. Blessing, are you joining us?" he called. "We're heading down, by the way."

"Down there?" asked Steve. The staircase descended into

grimy darkness and the distinct smell of machine oil wafted up to him.

"I'm here." Blessing was suddenly at Steve's side. "Isn't this wonderful?" she said with a smile. "I've never seen the sea. It's quite marvellous, isn't it?"

"Careful," said Steve as Hartley set off down the stairs, his footfalls clanking on the metal steps. "You're beginning to sound like Hartley."

*

As they walked up and down staircases, across walkways, through rooms of growling machinery and past clutches of people deep in dealings, Steve came to the conclusion that Keeltown was much more than 'a series of water vessels all fixed together'. It was a community, albeit an untrusting one by the looks that he and his companions received as they entered each vessel. Or maybe that was just in response to Hartley's noisy "Halloo" and beaming smiles.

"This place looks like it's been here forever," said Steve as they crossed a wobbly walkway between the decks of two boats.

"Not forever," said Hartley. "When the threat of rising sea levels drove the cities to build upwards, villages and small towns were left out of the equation for the most part. Rural and coastal residents were given the choice to move to the cities or find an alternative."

"And Keeltown was an alternative?" Steve jumped off the walkway, running a little to keep up with Hartley's speed.

"Not straightaway," said Hartley, looking around before leading Steve and Blessing up a messily constructed, creaky staircase. "At first, many of the locals who lived around the Black Strait took to boats. Boats they owned. Boats they bought for the purpose. Boats they found abandoned. Or stole," he said in a quieter voice. "It was quite a sight to see. A mismatched flotilla of hope, hardiness, and ingenuity. Over here." He started across a simple plank that appeared to be haphazardly nailed to the top of the staircase.

"Is that…?" Steve wanted to say 'safe', but he knew he wouldn't get a sensible answer. Instead, he tried not to cringe at the way the plank bounced as he followed his friend across it.

"In time," Hartley continued, "the decision was made to join the boats into what you see today. Of course, the problem never presented itself. This world found an answer to its environmental problems and the sea stayed where it was."

"So why is Keeltown still here?" said Steve. "I mean, couldn't they just go home?"

"Some did return to the land," said Hartley. "But for many, this place had *become* their home. So they stayed."

"Is it much further?" asked Blessing, rubbing her hands together. "I'm really cold."

"Not much further at all, dear girl. In fact, we have arrived," said the shopkeeper as they reached a shoulder height, wooden gateway that stood ajar. "I'd best go first. I'm not sure who the current Sheriff is, but I do know how to talk to Keeltowners."

The walkway on the other side of the gate was narrow, too narrow for more than one person, so they walked in a line with Steve at the back.

"Halloo, my boy," Steve heard Hartley call ahead of them. "Oo thee keepan?"

"Who you callin' a boy?" The 'boy' Hartley had spoken to stood up from the stool he'd been perched on. Though painfully thin, he easily matched the shopkeeper's height, with a mop of black hair pushed greasily off his face. "Do I look like a boy, old man?"

"Of course, you don't." Hartley held his ground with a wide smile. "It was merely a greeting. Is the Sheriff in attendance?" He nodded to the door at the guard's shoulder.

"Maybe he is, and maybe he is'nae." The guard crossed his arms. "Depends who's askin'."

"The name's Keg," said Hartley, his smile spreading as the

young man's eyes widened. "Tell him that."

The guard disappeared through the door with a nod of his head and a "Yes, sir". There was the sound of dashing feet and hurried words, and then the door slammed open again.

"We're in," said Hartley, beckoning to Blessing and Steve. "Best not keep them waiting."

*

"Hartley Keg, to what do I owe this honour?"

The Sheriff's words were welcoming, but his face told a different story. He sat behind a desk that had been cobbled together from scaffolding poles and tattered planks. His craggy face and patchily shaved head gave the impression of a man who had long since given up on first impressions.

"Sheriff Ross," said Hartley. "Good to see you again. How long has it been?"

"Not long enough," said the Sheriff. "Who's this?" He jerked his chin at Steve and Blessing. "Grand-bairns?"

"Do I look old enough for…?" Hartley frowned as the Sheriff raised his eyebrows. "No, not grand-bairns," said Hartley. "But I am responsible for them."

"Responsible," muttered the Sheriff. "That's debatable. I seem to remember that the last time you were here—"

"Let's not dwell on a past that neither of us can change," said Hartley, cutting off the Sheriff's words. "But rather look for a better way forwards. How does that sound?"

"What do you want?" The Sheriff leant back in his chair while pulling open the drawer in his desk. His hand remained in the drawer as he kept his eyes on Hartley. "Why are you here?"

"I'm looking for an old friend who I have been informed is, or was, in Keeltown. I wish to reconnect."

"Uh-huh?" said the Sheriff. "Name?"

"Robert Elian. Elderly gentleman. Well spoken. Dapper in appearance."

"I remember the one," said the Sheriff. "He's like you? Has the way?"

"Well, not quite like me," said Hartley with a grin. "But yes, I get your meaning, and yes, he does."

"Hamish?" The Sheriff clicked the fingers of his free hand at the young deputy who hovered at the back of the room. "Robert Elian. Details."

"Yes, Sheriff. Robert Elian. Came aboard couple weeks back. Lodged at the Tumbler. Hasnae applied for departure to date, sir."

"It seems that you are in luck," said the Sheriff. "This friend of yours is still with us."

"At the Tumbler, you say?" Hartley didn't look as if he felt 'in luck'. He pulled at his collar and swallowed awkwardly. "Good news," he croaked.

"Normally, I would ask visitors to Keeltown to leave their weapons with me." The Sheriff looked at Blessing and Steve. "I take it the bairns don't carry."

"They do not," said Hartley.

"And you?" said the Sheriff.

"Nothing to declare." Hartley raised his open hands and turned around in a circle. "As usual, I am merely armed with my wit and my charm."

"Fine." The Sheriff closed the drawer and folded his hands across his belly. "In that case, you'd best get out. Go. See to your dealings. I have no more time for you." He clicked his fingers again. "Hamish. Make sure they get where they're supposed to go. No detours."

"Yes, sir. Straight to it, Sheriff." Hamish gave Hartley a wide berth as he crossed the room. "Come with, please," he said. "The Sheriff is a very busy man."

"It's been a pleasure," said Hartley as the deputy held the door open.

"Come on." Steve tugged on Hartley's sleeve as the Sheriff turned away with a grunt. "I think we've been dismissed."

"I think you're right," said Hartley as he followed Steve and Blessing from the room. "Nice man, the Sheriff."

*

"Here we are." Hartley had lost his usual enthusiasm and stared despondently at the door before him. "The Leaping Tumbler."

All of the doors they had passed in their journey around Keeltown had been made of cast iron or plain, unpainted wood. The one that the deputy had left them at though was altogether different. Within a deep red, lacquered frame that held a matching doorknob, a pane of vibrant stained glass depicted a pale grey dolphin leaping into the sky over a wave-laden ocean. Above the door, a run of red neon letters spelt out the words, *'The Leaping Tumbler'.*

"What's a tumbler?" said Blessing.

"It's an old fishing term for dolphins and porpoises," said Hartley as he pushed the door open. "They used to have those around here, you know. Now, then. Am I presentable?"

"Presentable?" Steve shrugged. "Well, you're you."

"That will have to suffice." Hartley smoothed down his beard and ran a licked finger over his eyebrows. "Here we go."

At first sight, the room inside appeared small and dark but, as Steve's eyes became accustomed to the light, or lack of it, he began to see that behind what he had first taken to be wooden-panelled walls were further rooms, each accessed by small, swinging doors adorned with more stained-glass panels.

At the far end of the room a short wooden bar cropped off a corner of the space. Behind the bar, a security model robot like the ones that guarded Steve's school dried glasses with a cloth.

"Jem," the robot called out. "We've got company."

"Hold your horses," a voice called back as one of the side room doors swung open. "I've got my hands full in here."

The woman who walked out was a vision of colourful clash. Purple roses bloomed on a lime green dress. A necklace of vibrant yellow beads sat at her neck. Her lips were daubed with a shade of pink that was so bright it appeared to glow. Topping it all off was a fiery red jungle of hair that sprouted the occasional thin plait and was tied off with an orange, tulip-design scarf.

"Blimey, is that Hartley Keg?" she said, squinting at him.

"Jem, my darling woman, how are you?" Hartley rushed to her side and planted a noisy kiss on her cheek. "You look as beautiful as always."

"Well, I don't know if I should hug you or hit you," she said, backing off a step.

"I wouldn't say no to a hug," said Hartley, spreading his arms.

She slapped him across his face, the noise reverberating around the small room. Hartley staggered back a couple of steps with his hand clasped to his face.

"Where have you been all this time? One minute you're talking about putting down roots behind my bar, and the next you're away with the tide winds."

There was a crash from the room beside them as a second security model robot travelled through the swinging door at speed, dragging a struggling man by the foot.

"Geroff," the man slurred, kicking with his free foot. "I haven't finished." He held a half-full glass of ale in one hand, deftly avoiding any spillage despite his rough handling.

"Yes, you have, sir," said the second robot, releasing the drunk and moving away on its metallic limbs. "Jem called time."

Now that Steve had the time to look at it, he could see that the robot wasn't as standard as it had seemed at first glance. A square patch of metal on the robot's spherical, central processing core had been removed and then roughly soldered back into place. There was more solder on a couple of the robot's limbs too.

"That's right." Jem leant down and snatched the glass from the man's hand. "If you can't finish up during bar hours, your dregs are forfeit."

"I paid for that." He staggered to his feet, eyeing the drink as if it was the love of his life. "Not fair."

"I'll tell you what's not fair. You spendin' a pittance in my bar and then destroying one of my mirrors when we ask you to leave. Manny?"

"Yes, Jem?" said the robot.

"Escort this personage off the premises, if you don't mind."

"Of course, Jem."

"I can manage," The man protested as Manny the robot grabbed him by the arm.

"Of course, you can, sir," said Manny as it pulled the drunk to the door. "Time to go home now."

"Bernard, tidy up in the snug required," said Jem. "Broken mirror."

"Of course, Jem." Bernard, the robot behind the bar, grabbed a sweeping brush that was leant on the wall behind it.

Like its companion robot, Bernard showed signs of repair and alteration. Patches of solder were scattered across its central orb. One limb was obviously much newer than the others because it was a completely different shade of metallic grey.

"Should I add a new mirror to the shopping list?"

"No, don't bother," she said as Bernard disappeared through the swinging doors to the snug. "You won't find anything like that round here."

"We appear to have arrived at an eventful time, my dear," said Hartley. "Should we come back later?" he suggested with an eye on the door out of the bar.

"No, no," said Jem, taking the glass to the bar. "We've closed up now and besides." She pointed a finger at Hartley. "I want to know where you've been, and more important, why you're back."

"Ah," said Hartley. "Well, dearest Jem, that may take a while to explain."

"It always does with you," she said.

"But in the meantime." Hartley took Steve and Blessing by the shoulders, pushing them in front of him like shields. "I'd like you to meet my friends. This is Blessing and this is Steve."

"Hello," said Jem. "I hope this old fool has been takin' care of you both. You mustn't let him cajole you into doin' things, you know."

"We don't," said Blessing. "Do we Steve?"

"And who are *you* exactly, Steve?" Jem stepped closer, looking closely at his face. "You seem familiar. What's your surname, hun?"

"Haven," said Steve. "I'm Steve Haven."

"That explains it. Doesn't he look like Rex, Hartley? That's quite a resemblance."

"Did you know my uncle?" said Steve.

"I did," said Jem. "Goin' back a while."

"All done, Jem." Manny the robot returned, brushing two of its mechanical grippers together as if they were human hands.

"Thank you, Manny."

"Will that be all, Jem?" it asked.

"Well, seein' as we have guests, how's about you prepare some food? I'll leave it up to you what to make."

"Of course, Jem." Manny sped to a doorway at the back of the room that was covered by a colourful beaded curtain. "I have just the thing in mind."

"Manny is a tremendously good cook," Hartley told Steve. "I seem to remember a particularly tasty seafood gumbo he used to make."

"You'll be lucky," said Jem. "Supplies are runnin' down. Business is slow. Thank goodness for paying guests."

"Well, actual—" Hartley spluttered.

"Oh, don't you get your beard in a twist, Hartley Keg," said Jem. "I wasn't suggestin' anythin'. I know better than to expect cash from you. No, this might interest you: an old friend of ours is in Keeltown."

"Robert Elian?" said Blessing.

"How'd you know that?" said Jem. "Hartley, how'd she know that?"

"That's why we're here." Hartley pulled Steve out of the way as Bernard the robot backed through the swinging door with four of its limbs wrapped around the remains of a wooden-framed mirror.

"Sorry, coming through," said Bernard. "Sorry. Mind yourself."

"Take it to the tip, will you?" Jem nodded to the front door. "No use to be had from that old thing."

"As you wish, Jem," said Bernard, changing direction and taking a wide berth around the humans. "Sorry. Excuse me."

"We need to speak to Robert quite urgently," said Hartley. "Is he here? We have things to discuss."

"Oh, he's out right now," said Jem. "I tell you what, why don't we move upstairs and you can fill me in on everythin'?" It was a question, but it sounded more like a demand.

"We really do need to see Rob—" said Hartley.

"And you will," said Jem. "When he returns. Come on now." The bead curtain clacked and tinkled as she drew it open and held it there. "Guests first."

Chapter Twenty

"Manny, you have outdone yourself." Hartley slumped on his chair with his hands on his belly. He looked content enough to never move from that spot ever again.

"Thank you, Mr Keg," said Manny.

"As I have always told you, call me Hartley."

"Yes, you have, Mr Keg," said the robot as it cleared the table. Five arms carried out a variety of tasks—piling the plates, grouping the cutlery—while the three remaining limbs maintained Manny's balance.

The meal had been simple but filling. There had been a fish that Steve had never tasted before, its pink flesh almost melting in his mouth, buttery greens, and small round potatoes that were crisp and herby on the outside but soft and fluffy in the middle. Steve's stomach felt blissfully full.

"Will that be all for tonight?" Manny balanced the plates in three of his eight limbs, a fourth limb holding the swinging door to the kitchen open.

"Yes, thank you, Manny," said Jem. "You can go rest for the night. Leave the dishes until tomorrow."

"If that would be acceptable." Manny did a little bob before disappearing through the swinging doors.

"Hartley, are there any pastries left in your bag?" Blessing looked at him hopefully.

"Wasn't Manny's cookin' enough for you?" Jem crossed her arms. "Anyone would think you had a bottomless pit for a stomach."

"Sorry," said Blessing. "I'm just really hungry lately. I think it's all the running we've been doing. First, we had to—"

"It has certainly been an active few days." Hartley cut Blessing off before she could say more. "I'll give you that. And let's save our rations, just in case."

"Runnin', eh?" said Jem. "Sounds about right for keepin' Hartley Keg's company."

"What happened to your robots?" said Steve, trying to change the subject and the severe look that Jem had fixed Hartley with. "They look like they've been damaged."

"I suppose I shouldn't be surprised that Rex Haven's nephew would be canny about robots." She took a sip from a glass of something that smelled very alcoholic, swilling it around her mouth. "I'll let you into a secret, Steve. When I got my hands on Bernard and Manny, they were scheduled to be scrapped. Apparently, they were too old to be updated but they looked sound enough to me. So, I took them in and modded them. Work perfect well after that. Have done for almost two decades."

"Isn't modding illegal?" said Steve.

"No reason for it to be, other than the greed of the robotics industry," said Jem. "I removed Manny and Bernard's trackin' chips. That way the Haven Corporation couldn't find out that two missin' robots had turned up in Keeltown. Then, I had a little tinker with their innards. Good as new. In fact, better than new. They have personality now."

"I thought maybe you'd, you know."

"What do I know?"

"You know," said Steve. "Used magic on them."

"Jem is a workaday," said Hartley. "Like the rest of the Keeltowners."

"You know I hate that word." Jem took a bigger gulp of her drink. "Makes it sound like zero magic equals zero imagination. I've plenty of imagination."

"And you gave them names," said Steve. "Bernard and Manny?"

"Well, I couldn't keep callin' them SGM1 and XKP92. That would be silly."

"I like their names," said Blessing. "They look like a Bernard and a Manny to me."

"Thank you, Blessin'," said Jem. "I'm glad somebody sees things my way."

"I didn't see any other robots in Keeltown," said Steve.

"No, well, life here isn't exactly easy. There's not much spare wealth goin' round. Robots cost money to *officially* maintain and it doesn't help that the sea air plays havoc with their circuitry. Your uncle doesn't make it easy for normal folk to run a robot. Didn't," she added. "Can't say I agreed with Rex's view on life, but I was sad to hear of his death. I'm sure your parents must be very upset."

"My dad was away when it happened. Mum didn't say much about it so..." Steve shrugged. "She went off to find Dad so she could tell him."

"I see," said Jem. "And she left you with Hartley?"

"She left me at boarding school."

"Where she thought you'd be safe?" said Jem.

"That's right."

"And yet, here you are with this old rogue." She tutted as she slowly shook her head. "Best laid plans an' all that."

"He has me, too," said Blessing. "I'll keep him safe."

"I'm sure you will," said Jem with a chuckle. "Livin' up to your name, hun."

"Well, now that we have eaten this fine feast," said Hartley, stretching as he sat up straight, "why don't you tell us what Robert is up to, Jem? I haven't seen him in such a long time. I would be very interested in catching up with the old songsmith."

"Would you now?" said Jem. "And how exactly did you find out he was in Keeltown?"

"The Augur told us. To be truthful, Jem, he sent us here to check on Robert," said Hartley. "He fears that our friend may be in trouble."

"I never trusted that old tittle-tattle." Jem went to a battered old sideboard that ran the length of one end of the room and refilled her glass from an almost empty bottle. "But Robert does. What kind of trouble?"

"Frankie Una has gone missing, apparently," said Hartley. "The Augur believes that they have been taken captive so that their jailer may obtain what they carry."

"Those wretched devices," said Jem.

"The very same," said Hartley. "The Augur thinks that whoever took Frankie will come for Robert next."

"Hang on now." Jem returned to the table, bringing her glass and the bottle with her. "There've always been those of your kind after the devices. And that Frankie Una is elusive personified. I seem to remember the Augur havin' a tantrum last time Frankie 'disappeared'. What makes this time different? Hm? Tell me that."

"I agree with everything you have said wholeheartedly, dear Jem." Hartley eyed the bottle which Jem kept in her grasp. His own glass was drained. "But the Augur is usually right about these things. Either way, it won't do any harm to drop in on the old chap. Have a good chinwag."

"And what do you get out of this jaunt for the Augur?" said Jem. "What price is the Augur paying you?"

"Me? Well, I may require a ticket to travel on the Tram system," he said.

"But travellin' is what you do," said Jem. "What with your doors and such like. Why do you need a ticket?"

"Oh it's a long story, Jem. Suffice to say—"

"I'm not goin' anywhere 'til you explain." Jem fixed him with a stubborn stare. "Spill."

"You might as well tell her," said Steve.

"Very well." Hartley released a long, drawn-out sigh. "It started with the Haven Robotics Corporation."

*

"Well, what a complete palaver." Jem completed her eleventh circle of the table. Steve had been counting as she marched around the room. "Makes me glad I don't have magic. Means I don't have to listen to hoighty-toighty wazzocks like the Council."

"Here, here," said Hartley, banging his fist on the tabletop. "Hoighty-toighty. Quite right."

"As for this second party who are after Robert, are you sure they're not the Council? Sounds like the kind of thing those fools would do."

"To be honest, Jem, I'm not sure of anything," said Hartley. "But the Augur believes that the two are not the same. Whichever, or whoever, has set their sights on obtaining the Path devices, it is imperative that I warn Robert."

"Of course, of course, except…" Jem stopped with her marching and dropped onto her chair. "I don't know where he is."

"I thought you said he was your paying guest," said Hartley.

"He is. Paid me upfront. The room's kept for his return."

"Return from where?" said Steve.

"Let me show you somethin'." Jem pulled a wallet from her cleavage, opened it up and slipped out a rolled-up piece of paper. "Robert got this note a couple of days ago." She unrolled the paper, smoothing it open. "Pushed under his door here at the Tumbler after the place had closed up."

"Can I have a look?" Hartley held out a hand.

"See how ragged the edge of the paper is?" Jem handed it over, pointing to one of the corners.

"Teeth marks," said Hartley. He sniffed at the paper and gave it a tiny lick. "Squirrel mail?"

"That's what Robert said too. Not sure how you'd get a squirrel on Keeltown though. Plain weird, it is."

"Who's it from?" said Steve.

"Don't say. Just the words, a set of coordinates, and four

digits."

"Nereid 8 is a lie," Hartley read. "How bizarre."

"What's Nereid 8?" asked Blessing.

"The Nereid platforms are solar-power stations," said Steve, glad that he could finally add something useful to the conversation. "They're all out at sea, all over the world. They supply most of the global electricity. We learned about it at school," he told Blessing.

"Let me see." Jem snatched the note back and squinted at it for a moment. "Yes, that'd make sense."

"Can we look at the coordinates on a map?" said Steve.

"Give me a chance." She shoved the note back at Hartley and strode to the sideboard. "Now, where is it?" she muttered as she opened one of the cupboard doors. "Blummin' things," she snapped as a sea of papers and cards flooded out onto the floor. "Here it is."

She rescued a large, rolled-up tube of paper from the pile. Using their glasses to weigh down the corners, she unrolled it on the table, revealing a faded map of the world.

"Let me see those coordinates again," she said. "Right." She nodded as Hartley held out the note for her to read. "So if that is that…" She moved her hand across the map before stopping at a point with a jab of her finger. "And that is that…" She moved down the map, lips pursed in concentration. "There." She tapped on the map. "Near enough halfway between us and the Continent."

"Now, that is intriguing," said Hartley. "Nereid 8, lie or not, is in the middle of the North Sea."

"And that's where Robert went?" said Blessing.

"That's where he set off for," said Jem. "Hired a local and his boat to take him out there, four days back. He could've gone there and returned in two days easy."

"Robert does have a habit of investigating things to a ridiculous level of thoroughness," said Hartley, rubbing a hand across his beard. "That might explain the delay in his return."

"Or he could be in trouble," said Steve.

"The risk of the Hidden picking up on my magic this far from Caercester is negligible," said Hartley. "It would be more than worth the risk, if only I had visited Nereid 8 before. What we need is transport."

"Fine," said Jem, shooting to her feet. "You don't have to ask me twice."

"Ask what?" said Blessing.

"To use the Porpoise of course," said Jem. "The boys can look after this place while we're gone. Come along. I'll get her started up."

And with that, Jem drained her glass and marched out of the room.

*

"You're full of surprises, Jem," said Hartley. "When did you have all this fitted?"

They stood in front of a narrow door in the back of the kitchen. In comparison to the utilitarian room with its clean edges and nostril-pinching scent of cleaning fluid, the door was decorative and elegant. Its black, lacquered surfaces were patterned with gold wavy lines and the door had a glass handle which was moulded into the shape of a dolphin.

"Few years back," she said as she pulled the door open. "I've always said it's good to have options. Bernard!"

"Yes, Jem." The robot stood at her side, balanced on four limbs with the others poised in mid-air in readiness for instructions.

"I need you to open up the Porpoise and then get down to the helm. I'll be there in a moment."

"Yes, Jem. Right away."

A couple of steps in from the first door was a second. It was wide, heavy, and made of the kind of metal that rings when you knock on it with a knuckle. In the middle of the door was a polished metal wheel with five spokes.

"Let Bernard and me go in first," she said as the robot easily turned the wheel. "And when you *do* go in, stay in the first room." She thought for a second, then added in an abrupt tone, "And no investigatin'."

There was a clunk and then a squeak as Bernard pulled the door open.

"I'll keep them in line, Jem. Don't you worry," said Hartley, following her through the doorway. "Hurry up," he called back to the others, beckoning with an outheld hand.

"You're the one I'm worried about, Hartley Keg," she called back.

There was no sign of the robot in the room beyond, by the time Steve and his friends arrived. The room felt strangely off-balance. The floor space was limited but the ceiling height was lofty. Fixed to the opposite wall but at a seemingly unreachable height were what appeared to be four single beds, each fitted with a harness. In the floor beneath the beds, a narrower version of the door they had come through had been left open.

"This is…" Steve struggled for a suitable expression.

"Decidedly odd," said Hartley, staring up at the beds.

"This is the Porpoise," said Jem, unhooking a ladder from the wall. "My pride and joy."

"A ship?" said Hartley.

"Better," she said. "A submarine."

"What's a submarine?" said Blessing.

"It's a boat that goes underwater," said Steve.

"But I thought boats went on top of the water," she said. "Is it safe?"

"Of course it's safe. I built it." Jem fixed the ladder to the bottom of the first bed. "Steve, you go first."

"Go up there?" he asked.

"You all need to be secure," she said. "So up you climb and fasten yourself in."

"All of us?" said Hartley.

"All of you," said Jem. "We don't want any brains gettin'

mushed."

One by one, the three friends climbed the ladder and secured themselves to a bed, until finally only Jem remained unfettered.

"Bernard, are you finished?" she called down through the door in the floor.

"Here." The robot appeared almost immediately, its central orb poking up through the door like a head, quickly followed by its limbs.

"Now, I'm goin' to be gone for a bit. I'm relyin' on you and Manny to hold the fort in my absence."

"Of course, Jem," said the robot. "We can do that. Goodbye, Hartley, Steve, Blessing. Have a wonderful trip." Moving on all eight limbs, it darted through the door back to the kitchen and slammed it shut with a clunk.

"The launch is a bit swift, so best hold onto your stomachs." Jem nodded to Hartley, then dropped through the door in the floor.

"I wonder if this is really necessary." Hartley tugged at the halter that held him tightly to the bed.

"Jem thinks it is," said Blessing.

"That's what worries me," said Hartley as he took a firm grip of the sides of the bed.

With that, the Porpoise gave an almighty shake and began to fall.

*

The wall that the beds were fixed to was now the floor. The door they had entered through only a few minutes before sat in the ceiling above.

Steve lay on the bed, the halter now loose around his chest. His heart had only just begun to slow in its battering of his ribs. He was aware that his eyes were uncomfortably wide, so he blinked them a couple of times until they felt normal. He wanted to sit up, but he had serious doubts whether the meal

Jem had served them earlier would stay in his stomach. He felt like he had just experienced the worst rollercoaster ride ever.

Blessing had been the first to unfasten the halter that held her to the bed and stand up with an exclamation of, "Can we do that again?"

Hartley had been slower to react. He sat on the edge of the bed, head down and fingers digging into the bedding.

"Can someone please explain what just happened?" Steve's mouth felt dry when he spoke. He swallowed and slowly unfastened the harness.

"Exactly what should have happened." Jem stood in the open doorway that had previously been in the floor. "I released the Porpoise into the sea. We're free of Keeltown now and on the way to Nereid 8."

"Right." Steve waved his hand weakly. "That's okay then."

"You all survived, then?" she said, looking around.

"Of course," said Blessing. "That was fun."

"Some survived better than others," wheezed Hartley.

"I can see that," said Jem with a grin. "Bernard programmed in the coordinates. It'll be an overnight journey, so seeing as it's already after nine, you might as well bed down for the evenin'."

"I don't think I could sleep straightaway." Steve sat up, his hand on his stomach which thankfully didn't complain about the movement.

"Neither could I after so much excitement," said Hartley as he clambered to his feet. "How about a tour of the sub?"

"I'm not lettin' you get your hands on my Porpoise, Hartley Keg," she said. "No, you can make do with a visit to the helm, where I can keep an eye on you."

"That would be marvellous." Hartley was beginning to sound more like his old, enthusiastic self. "Wouldn't it, younglings?"

"Come on, Steve." Blessing pulled him to his feet. He held his stomach at the lurching movement just in case. "This is so exciting," she said.

"Exciting, intriguing, and curiously energising," said Hartley.

"Now then, Jem?"

"What?"

"Would you happen to have any food in the helm? I think I may need a little sustenance to settle my stomach."

Chapter Twenty-One

After a night of fitful sleep, Steve stood bleary-eyed in the helm of the Porpoise, with a biscuit in one hand and a mug of water in the other.

The problem with being underwater in a vessel whose only connection with the outside world were two eye-like windows at the front of the submarine and a bunch of electronic sensors, was that it was difficult to tell the hour.

The end of the helm that housed the switches and gauges, and where Jem stood peering out through one of two round portholes, hadn't been fitted out with comfort in mind. It was all hard edges and well-sealed joints with an array of pipes and hatches.

The other end of the room was a different story altogether. A raised bed ran across the back wall, fitted with an emerald-green, padded eiderdown and an array of pillows and cushions. Below and built into the polished wooden bedframe were a vast selection of drawers—some painted, some plain wood—each adorned with a brass handle. A blue and yellow step stool waited to one side.

Hartley looked as weary as Steve felt. The shopkeeper picked biscuit crumbs from his beard and his eyes kept drooping shut before blinking open a moment or two later. Even Blessing was full of yawns.

Jem, however, was as sprightly as if she'd slept a good few hours in the comfiest of beds, which made Steve think that she was probably one of those people who could sleep anywhere.

"Destination coordinates are in sight." Jem stood in the middle of the helm. Her colourful dress had been replaced by a plain white shirt and a pair of patched jeans faded so far as to almost match the colour of the shirt. Jem's vibrant red hair was scooped up into a polka-dot headscarf knotted on top of her head. "Anyone want to see?"

"Me," said Steve, raising his hand like he was in class at school.

"All righty." Jem went to one of the wheel-like controls on the side of the helm room and slowly turned it. There was a whirring, followed by the sound of something greased sliding on something else equally greased, and a stout, metal rod descended from the ceiling into the middle of the room.

"Here we are." She pulled two handles down from the rod, clicking them into place, and peered into the glass fronted window in the device. "You can have a look at Nereid 8 through the periscope."

"Brilliant." Steve handed his mug and the rest of his biscuit to Hartley. "I look in here?" He pointed to the window.

"That's right. It may take a moment for your eyes to adjust to the daylight."

"Okay." The view through the periscope was surprisingly crisp. Steve found himself blinking as the brightness of the day hurt his eyes at first but when that had passed, he took his first look at what they had come all this way to investigate. "Wow. It's huge."

Nereid 8 looked like an old fossil-fuel drilling rig. Its steel form appeared to sit on four bulky legs, but what set it apart from anything Steve had seen before though was the object that towered above the platform itself.

Reaching up from the centre of Nereid 8 was a construction of gleaming blue. Three spiral columns turned and danced around each other in constant action, their panelled surfaces glimmering in the sunlight.

"Could I take a look?" Steve felt a hand on his shoulder and heard Hartley's voice at his ear.

"Yeah, sure." Steve stood back to let his friend use the periscope.

Hartley let out a low whistle as he pressed his eyes to the viewing glass. "That is impressive."

Once Blessing had taken her turn too, Jem pushed the handles of the periscope back in with a click and it slid up out of view as she returned to the controls of the Porpoise.

"We're getting close," said Hartley with a smile. "I'm looking forward to this."

"Even though Robert may be in dire danger?" said Jem. "And we may be sailin' into that danger with no idea of how to defend ourselves?"

"Well, there is that, my dear Jem," he said. "But when have we ever let a little danger dissuade us from action?"

"Don't include me in your 'we'," she said. "I'd happily be dissuaded and turn this vessel round right now, if it wasn't for Robert."

"She's got a point," said Steve. "We don't know what's going on there."

"I didn't see anyone moving around on Nereid 8 through the perish-cope." Blessing took Hartley's arm. "I'm sure we can handle it."

"And there you have it." Hartley patted her hand. "Blessing says we can handle it. Now, we'd best gather our things ready for docking." With that, Hartley and Blessing dismissed Steve's worries and left the helm room at an excited pace.

"I'm with you," said Jem as Steve turned to her. "Fools rush in an' all that. One thing you've got to understand about Hartley Keg though."

"He's a fool?" said Steve.

"I knew I'd like you," she said with a grin. "Yes that, but this too. His enthusiasm is infectious. He has a habit of pulling people into his ventures without a thought for their safety. He doesn't mean to. There's no malice in him. It's just the way he is. You keep an eye out, Steve. Wariness around Hartley Keg is always the best way to survive."

*

"I'll go out first." Jem wore an oversized waterproof jacket in a startling shade of yellow as she fitted the ladder in place so they could reach the hatch in the ceiling of the rest quarters. "If there's any danger, I'll bob back in and lock the hatch behind me."

"I really do think I should head out first." Hartley hovered around her with one finger raised in the air. "What if there are guards?"

"What if there are?" said Jem as she placed a foot on the bottom rung. "I can handle myself, Hartley Keg." She scuttled up the ladder, turned the locking wheel above her head, and pushed the heavy hatch open with a grunt. "Besides, you don't have your sea legs yet. And I'm not divin' in the North Sea to rescue you."

"In that case, I think you should just take a brief peruse," said Hartley. "Then come back down and tell us what you see."

"Such a fuss," she muttered as she pulled herself through the hatch. "Anyone would think…"

Steve didn't hear the rest of her words as Blessing fell against him and began to retch. Hartley let out a pained "ooh" and grabbed the ladder, his ruddy face paling in a second.

"Jem!" Steve shouted up the ladder. "Jem, something's wrong."

"What's the palaver?" Jem's head popped through the hatch. "I hope she's not goin' to vomit in my sub. It'll reek for weeks."

"Close the hatch," Hartley moaned. "I feel…" He stumbled to his knees. "Wrong," he whimpered.

"Got it." Jem swung herself back inside and pulled the hatch door closed above her. With the air of a well-practiced move, she slid down the ladder and dropped onto the floor beside the now squirming Hartley Keg.

"Hartley." She grabbed his shoulders and shook him.

"Hartley, speak to me."

"That was horrendous." Hartley struggled to his feet with the support of Jem and the ladder. "I felt overwhelmingly sick and dizzy."

"All right?" Steve walked Blessing to one of the beds and slowly sat her down. "Do you feel any better?"

"A little." She nodded, hunkering forward with her hands on her knees. "I felt really tired and weak. It was like the collar all over again."

"The one the Council put on you?"

"Yes, like that. Only more."

"Hartley, is that how you felt too?" said Steve.

"Worse," said Hartley. "The collars prevented us from sourcing our magic, but this felt as if my magic was being drained away." He shook himself as if he could physically get rid of the feeling.

"That's downright odd." Jem shook her head. "I felt fine up there. It's a bit choppy, I'll give you that, but nothin' out of the ordinary. Steve, how about you?"

"I didn't feel any different," he said. "It must be to do with their magic."

"Makes sense, I suppose," said Jem. "If that's right, though, what about Robert?"

"I'm willing to give it another go." Hartley clumsily swung his foot onto the first rung. He was still pale and his hands trembled. "Blessing? Are you with me?"

"I'll try." She slowly stood up, then dropped back down onto the bed with a hand to her stomach. "In a minute."

"The two of you are goin' nowhere." Jem slapped Hartley's hands off the ladder and pushed him aside. "Neither of you are in any state to be useful."

"I find that a tad offensive," said Hartley. "And rather harsh."

"Don't you give me that." She leant back on the ladder with her arms crossed. "The best thing for you two to do is shut yourselves in the helm. With any luck, that'll lessen the effect when I open the hatch again. Steve, you're with me."

"Okay," he said. "But will the sub be all right without you?"

"We'll shut up the sub and park it." She pushed back one of her sleeves to reveal what looked like a wrap phone to Steve. "Remote control."

"Modded?" said Steve.

"You'd better believe it," she said. "Still looks like a phone-watch-thingummy but it does so much more."

"Cool," said Steve, both impressed at Jem's skills and amused at the thought of parking a submarine.

"Go on then," she said as Hartley opened his mouth to protest. "I'm not movin' until you and the girl are through that door and it's shut."

With a sigh and a muttered expression that sounded a lot like "charming", Hartley helped Blessing to her feet. By the time, the door closed behind them, Jem had equipped Steve with a jacket that matched her own. He tried not to breath in its stench of rotten fish and engine oil as he started up the ladder after her.

*

Standing on the ledge of the platform leg, Steve could now see how the Porpoise was constructed.

The door they had originally entered through was a horizontal hatch in the top of the submarine, about two thirds of the way towards the rear of the vessel. Below the hatch was the room with the beds. At the front of the submarine, the water level came halfway up each of the windows in the helm, which looked even more like eyes now the vessel had surfaced. If it hadn't been for the riveted, dark grey panels that made up its shell, the Porpoise could have almost been mistaken for a sea creature.

"We need to find a way up," said Jem. "I can see a door on the inward facing side of the opposite leg. Fingers crossed this leg is the same."

Steve watched the gap between the submarine and the platform leg widen a little as the sea pulled at the vessel.

"What about the submarine?" he asked. "Is it safe there?"

"It will be." She tapped the screen of the remote control gadget on her wrist and the Porpoise slowly sank under the waves. "Ready?" she asked.

No, he thought as his ride disappeared, but he nodded and said, "Okay. Let's go."

The walk around the ledge, with the sea splashing up onto Steve's feet every few minutes, seemed to take an eternity. He was thankful for the rail and grasped it tightly with both hands as he crept along. Jem might as well have been strolling along a wide, even travel-way on a sunny day for all the attention she gave to the narrowness of the ledge. The more time that passed, the further she marched ahead of him.

"Found it!" Steve eventually heard her call back to him, and then as he reached her, "That's not right."

The door was a sheet of steel, reinforced with an inlaid metal mesh. It was obviously meant to slide open. It was obvious because it was already a hand's width ajar.

"This should be shut," said Jem.

"Lucky for us, it isn't." Steve tried to sound cheerful as his teeth chattered from the cold that had crept up his legs from his damp shoes.

"You might have a point." Jem grabbed the heavy rail on the door and pulled. With a squeal of complaint, the door slid aside to reveal the interior of a lift, and the fact that the lift wasn't empty.

"Is that...?" said Steve as Jem knelt down beside the unconscious old man.

"Robert." She shook him by the shoulders. His head lolled about but he didn't open his eyes. "Robert." She patted his face, then grabbed his arm and peeled back the sleeve. "He's still with us," she said as she pressed her fingers to the inside of his wrist. "His pulse is weak, but at least he has one. We have to get him back to the Porpoise."

She hoisted Robert Elian up into a sitting position and

grabbed him under the arms, linking her fingers across his chest.

"We're carrying him?" said Steve. "Along that ledge?"

"Got another plan?" said Jem. "Feet first. That's the way."

*

Robert Elian sat on the stool in the helm with his head in his hands. He was a short, elderly, wiry man with a bald head, the barest traces of eyebrows, and a neatly trimmed white goatee. He wore a grey tweed suit, but in comparison to Hartley's own patched tweed jacket, Robert's attire was smart and well-tailored, if a little damp.

Jem fussed around him, one minute telling him off for being foolhardy, the next expressing how pleased she was to see him.

"At least you're in one piece," she said. "We can get back home now. You need a good night's sleep and a decent meal inside you. I'll have Bernard—"

"Stop telling me what to do," he said, cutting her off in her cossetting. "We can't go home yet."

"Oh yes, we can." Jem planted her hands on her hips and tapped her foot. "If we hadn't come after you, who knows what would've happened. You might have died."

"But I didn't." He slowly rose to his feet, swaying as he supported himself against the bedframe. "You saw to that and I'm grateful. But that out there..." He pointed to the ceiling. "That demands an investigation."

"Tough," she said. "Whatever 'that' is, it won't let you or them," she said, nodding to Hartley and Blessing, "to get anywhere close."

"You don't have to rub it in, Jem." Robert tugged at his beard as the remains of his eyebrows drew together. "I already feel useless."

"It does present a conundrum," said Hartley. "Nereid 8 could pose a serious threat to the magical community. I'd suggest reporting it to the Council, if we were on speaking terms with them."

"How do we know the Council aren't behind this?" Robert slowly began to pace up and down, steadying himself against the wall.

"Makes no difference to me," said Jem. "Let the Council sort it or leave it alone. I don't care. This is my sub, and I say we head back to Keeltown."

"But Jem, you don't see the big picture." Robert threw his hands up in the air as he spoke.

"I don't need to," she said. "I'm happy enough with the picture I've got."

"I could go," said Steve.

"You?" said Robert.

"Now, hang on," said Hartley.

"It didn't affect me. Or Jem. It only hurts magicals."

"And who are you?" said Robert.

"I'm Steve," said Steve.

"Haven," Hartley added. "He's with me."

"And me," said Blessing. She hadn't let go of Hartley's hand since Steve and Jem had returned with the unconscious Robert. "I'm Blessing."

"Of course, you are," said Robert. "And trust a Haven to be in the midst of drama. He looked around at them all. "Well," he eventually said. "It seems we have no alternative. Jem and Steve, you're up."

Chapter Twenty-Two

Viewed through the periscope, the towering, spiralling arms had appeared to float above Nereid 8 but now that he stood on the platform itself, Steve could see they were mounted on a silver-coloured, slowly-turning disc that formed the roof of a single storey building. Sunlight rippled across the blue solar panels that ran the length of each arm, giving the impression of writhing snakeskin.

"Jem, look at that," he said, pointing to the silver-roofed construction in the middle of the platform. "See the thing on top of it?"

Projecting from the roof, a golden orb, with three rings spinning around it on an ever-changing axis, shone in the morning light.

"What about it?" said Jem. She'd worn a petulant frown since Robert had persuaded her to investigate Nereid 8, matched only by the tone of her voice.

"When the Council tested Blessing's power, part of the testing machine looked just like that. Only smaller. But the Nereid stations are supposed to be scientific, not magical. So why is that here?"

"Maybe it's both," said Jem. "Seein' as it affected our friends so badly. I say that's answer enough for Robert. Let's get back to the Porpoise."

"Not yet," said Steve, running across the platform. "He'll want to know what's inside that building. I would."

"You folks are way too nosey," she muttered as she set off in pursuit. "Wait for me," she called, but Steve was already at the door.

Door handle, door handle. Where's the door handle? Steve ran his hands over the door to the platform building but found nothing he could get a grasp on. The door was as plain as the walls surrounding it. He pushed it to see if that would have an effect. Nothing.

"Open," he said. "Open door," he added. The door remained shut.

He ran his hands over the frame of the door but found nothing. He banged a fist on the wall to the right of the door out of pure temper. There was a click and a panel popped open.

"Got it," he said, pulling the panel fully open to reveal a button pad within. "Now I just need an entry code." At a whim, he punched in 1234. *Of course, that didn't work*, he thought. *It's never that easy.*

"What's the problem?" said Jem as she reached him.

"I need a code," he said. "I…" And then, he remembered the note. "Jem, what were the four numbers on the note with the coordinates."

"They were…" She squinted her eyes as she tried to remember. "58…"

"5874," he said. "That's it." *Or that might be it. Please let this work*, he thought as he punched in the numbers.

As the door slid open and Steve took a step towards the threshold, Jem grabbed him by the collar.

"Are you sure about this?" she said. "We don't know what's in there."

"Exactly," he said. "That's why we need to have a look. We don't have to stay long. Just a quick look and then back to the sub."

"Just a quick look," she said.

"That's all. Promise."

"I'll keep you to that." She set him free. "After you."

The minute that they stepped inside the small building, the

door slid shut behind them with a click. The outer wall, which had been solid and opaque only a moment before, blinked into grey-shaded glass and a runway of spotlights flooded into life in the ceiling above them. On the far side of the room was a door that was an identical match for the lift doors in the legs of Nereid 8, made of steel reinforced with an inlaid metal mesh.

In the centre of the crescent-shaped room was a sleek, grey console running up into the ceiling. It was split into three sections that stood side by side. Each section was covered in switches, dials, and gauges, but none of them were identical. The first carried a warning sign which declared *'Danger—High Voltage'*. The second featured a line of lights that flashed blue one after the other, giving the impression that the light was travelling across the console at speed. The third section featured three small screens.

"This must monitor what's happenin' up above," said Jem, examining them.

"I think you're right. Look," said Steve. "There are two different types of measurement. There's the solar power measured in kWh. That's obvious." He tapped the gauge beneath the first screen. The needle barely registered any current. "But this other measurement is O-M-N. Is that the measurement for magic?" he asked as he touched a finger to the second screen.

"Don't ask me," said Jem. "I don't do magic."

"The Council called the machine they used to measure Blessing's magic the Omnometer, so it would make sense." The needle of the gauge beneath the second screen was pressed hard against the top end of the meter. "But that would mean…"

"What is it?" said Jem. "What's afoot?"

"Nereid 8 is turning solar energy into electricity, like it's supposed to, but this Omn is being turned into electricity too. Loads of it."

"How many Nereid stations do you think there are?" said Jem.

"I don't know. A hundred? Maybe more."

"That's worrying."

She pressed a finger to the last screen which displayed two diagrams. The first was a pie chart that was mostly blue in colour. The second was a bar chart of what looked like a hundred, or more, bars. Most of them registered a low value, advancing no more than one or two blocks from the base axis. Only one bar shot up high above the others, almost touching the top of the diagram.

"Why is it worrying?" said Steve.

"Because if I'm reading this right," she said. "The only Nereid station creating any reasonable amount of electricity is this one. Nereid 8 is pract'cally powering the world. With magic."

*

"Let me get into the Porpoise first," said Jem as she jammed a hand onto a plain metal button by the door. "I'll call it back to the surface so it'll be waiting for us." She held her coat sleeve back as she tapped on the wrist-mounted remote control.

The door to the Nereid control room slid aside and Steve felt the chill, salty air on his face. Jem stepped out onto the platform, but before Steve could follow her a shadow fell across their path to the lift. Jem raised an arm to shelter her face as a strong wind pulled at her red hair and the scarf that bound it. Steve peered out and up.

Silhouetted against the sunlight, a large black helicopter hovered overhead, the noise from its rotors blocking out any other sound. Steve felt clanging vibrations in the floor under his feet as two massive security robots dropped onto the platform.

The downdraft ceased as the helicopter landed and its propellers slowed to a stop before folding away. Five men dressed in identical black flight suits spilled out.

Jem retreated a step, placing herself between Steve and the men with her fists raised. Steve had no idea what she would do next. Fight? Flee? Hopefully with him in tow. Instead, she spread her fingers wide and held up open hands as the men approached.

"Who are you?" demanded one of them, striding ahead of the others. His flight suit was identical to that worn by his companions, except for a yellow insignia on his shoulder. It was a single line spearing two triangles; a design Steve had seen only a couple of days before tattooed on the wrist of Elrick Olen. "How did you get here?" barked the man.

Jem moved to stand beside Steve and placed an arm around his shoulders. With a sideways glance, she gave him a sly wink and then her face crumpled into tears.

"Oh, I'm so glad you found us," she called out.

How does she do that? thought Steve as a flood of tears ran down her face and she began to sniffle.

"I said, who are you?" the man demanded. "Tell me your name."

"I'm Lily Hamlin," she said. "And this is my nephew, Simon. I thought we were goin' to die out here." She collapsed into noisy, blubbering sobs.

"All right, all right. There's no need for…" The man looked at Steve. His dominating expression had been replaced by embarrassed confusion. "Who brought you here, boy?"

"It was that wretched Kristofferson man," Jem wailed. "I told my sister her boy would be safe with me while she was away. Whatever will she think?"

"Kristofferson?" said the man. "Who is Kristofferson?"

"He's a pirate, that's who he is." There was snot running from Jem's nose now and her face was blotchy red. "He said he'd ferry us to my sister's but instead he stranded us here." She gave a big, nose-gurgling sniff that made Steve cringe. "I thought we were goin' to die."

"Lily Hamlin and Simon," said the man. "Soldier 43K."

One of the robots raised itself up onto two limbs in response to its name. "Yes, Major." Its voice was deep and synthesised, a bad copy of human tones." How may I assist?"

"Carry out a facial recognition scan on the civilians," said the

Major. "What are their names?"

A light ran across 43K's central processing orb as it shifted to take in first Jem and then Steve. After a couple of seconds, the light disappeared and the robot spoke. "Jemima Mott, proprietor of the Leaping Tumbler on Keeltown. Steven Haven, son of Elijah and Mary Haven, nephew of Rex Haven."

"You've been lying to us, Mrs Mott," said the Major.

"Miss, actually." Jem wiped the snot from her nose with her sleeve. Her hand went to the wrist that bore the remote control, passing her fingers over the device as she appeared to rub at her wrist. "Never married."

"And Master Haven. My superiors will be pleased to hear that we've found you. They were worried by your absence."

"Who are your superiors?" said Steve.

"There's plenty of time to explain," said the Major with the barest of smiles. "I assume that the other members of your party can be found in Keeltown. You can answer our questions on the way. Take them," he barked at his companions.

As two of the men stepped forward, Jem raised her eyebrows at Steve. He raised his eyebrows back. *What?* Jem rolled her eyes and pushed him back into the control room.

She slammed her hand onto the button by the door. As the men outside shouted and the door slid shut, Jem pulled a screwdriver from her coat pocket and prised the button panel open. With a grunt, she stabbed the screwdriver into the revealed circuit board. The walls returned to their opaque solidity and the lights went out.

"That'll keep them out for a bit," Steve heard Jem say. "For what good it'll do us. We're trapped in here. Where's Hartley Keg when you need his travelling malarkey?"

"We're not trapped." In the darkness it was impossible to see anything in the control room but judging from where he thought he was, Steve turned around and stumbled his way to the rear wall. "There's a door back here. It might be a way out."

"But there's nowhere to go," said Jem. "We're in the middle of the platform, so it can't connect with any of the lifts in the legs."

"It's here somewhere." Steve felt along the wall until his fingers found the gridded metal of the door. "Got it."

"Keep talkin' so I can find you." He heard Jem shuffle nearby.

"I'm here." Steve ran his hands over the surface of the door. His fingers found an indented slot. "Keep coming this way."

"Got you." Jem slapped a hand on his shoulder. "What've you discovered?"

"If this door slides like the lift door in the leg—"

There was a hammering on the walls of the building, followed by shouted orders from the Major. The hammering increased.

"No 'if' about it," said Jem, pushing him aside. "It's this way or no way."

Steve heard Jem grunt and the passing of metal on metal. There was a *blink-blink-ting* and light flooded out from the space beyond. The door may have been identical to the other lift doors on Nereid 8, but this lift's interior couldn't have been more different. In fact, it wasn't a lift at all.

Jem pushed Steve through into a circular room and pulled the door shut behind them. Steve shivered. It was colder in there, or rather draftier. He could feel a chill breeze wafting around his ankles.

"Well, there's a turn up for the holidays," said Jem.

Hung on the walls were a range of diving suits and an assortment of matching headgear, but the thing that Jem raced towards sat at the centre of the room.

"This is sleek," she said with a grin as she ran her hands over the dark grey walls of the mini submarine.

The submarine was the length of a medium car, but that was where the similarities ended. The whole vehicle was built around a central glass orb that Steve guessed was around seven feet tall. He had to guess because the submarine appeared to be sunk a few inches into the floor.

"Nifty." Jem leant against the sub with her face pressed to the glass. "Look at that interior. That's quality, that is."

"Will it get us out of here?" said Steve.

"Only one way to find out." Jem pulled open the hatch that sat on the top of the sub. "Let's take it for a drive."

Two minutes later, she was fastening Steve into one of the seats. The interior of the sub smelt of equal parts of stale air and cleaning fluid. There were no physical controls, no switches, and no levers for Jem to manipulate. Instead, three screens had illuminated in the glass itself as soon as the two of them had climbed inside. One screen displayed a diagram of the sub itself, accompanied by read-outs like 'Buoyancy' and 'Internal Temperature'. The second screen showed a gridded circle and the word 'Surroundview'. He assumed that was a sonar display. The third screen was what delighted Jem the most.

"These controls are so dinky," she said with a grin as her hands hovered over the virtual control levers and switches that were displayed in the glass. "I could do with this on the Porpoise. It would save so much room and palaver."

"Can you work it?" said Steve.

"Of course I can work it," she said, scrolling through the displays on the first screen. "Now then, if I'm reading this correct, we're more than set for oxygen. And the battery charge? My, that is impressive. Looks like we could make it all the way back to Keeltown if we had to."

"So how do we get out of here?" said Steve. "There's no way the sub will fit through the door."

"You're thinkin' too laterally," she said, touching a hand to the controls. "We don't need a door."

There was a *clunk-clunk-clunk* as she tapped on a control labelled *'Release'* and the submarine dropped, lurching Steve's stomach with it. The last thing he saw before he closed his eyes was the Major and his men spilling through the lift door.

Chapter Twenty-Three

The darkling had found it a simple task to tail the man and the woman whom she had discovered in the basement of the Haven Corporation building. Clinging to their individual shadows, she had joined them in their sleek, black vehicle as it sped across the city to a run-down neighbourhood of derelict terrace houses and boarded-up shopfronts.

The warehouse that she now found herself in had long since abandoned any thought of survival. The ground was scattered with the metal and tiles that had once been the roof. The afternoon light filtered down through a criss-cross of rusted rafters and roof beams. The walls were coated in decades of graffiti. The only items in the space that did not speak of decay were a barred, white cell, a desk, and a chair.

She waited in the shadows of a doorless threshold. Even from this distance, she sensed how the substance of the cell pulled at the magic in the air. She didn't know for sure, but she assumed that it was made from the same substance as Winters' laboratory in the basement of the Haven Corporation building.

The figure who was held in the cell sat slumped over, their face hidden by a veil of long, matted, dark hair. Their shirt cuffs were tattered, as were the cropped trousers they wore. Their feet were bare and dirty.

Two of the black, spherical, guard robots she had seen in the Haven building rolled around the warehouse interior. Every so often, they would stop and turn a full circle as they scanned the space. Then, they would return to their tumbling patrol.

Elrick Olen sat at the desk, looking as smart and professional as the last time the darkling had seen him. His colleagues, the man and woman, stood on either side of him. All three stared at their prisoner as they talked.

"Don't we have enough information to proceed?" said the woman. "I'm not sure they'll last much longer anyway."

"Patience, Andra. We'll be on the move soon enough," said Elrick. "I've given the orders for our colleagues to clear out of the Haven Corporation base."

"And the asset?" said the man.

"Coming with us," said Elrick.

"Is that wise? He's dangerous."

"He's controllable," said Elrick. "He will be, right up to when he serves his purpose. There's just one more piece that needs to fall into place." Elrick glanced at his wrap-phone as it emitted a low tone. "Speaking of which." He tapped the small screen on his wrist and nodded. "Excellent. That's it then. Job done."

"What now?" said the man.

"The usual, Will." Elrick stood up and retrieved his jacket from the back of his chair. "You and Andra get back to the Haven Corporation and tie up the loose ends. I'll finish up here." He pulled his jacket on and pushed his hands into his trouser pockets.

"What about the hounds?" Will nodded to the robots.

"Leave them with me," said Elrick. "I have a use for them."

"What about…?" Will nodded to the cell.

"That's what the hounds are for," said Elrick. "Off you go."

*

When the darkling entered the Haven Corporation building in the shadow of Elrick Olen's colleagues, the place was quieter than usual. The black robots who had guarded the lift doors were gone. In fact, the only sound was the voice of the receptionist robot who addressed the man and woman.

"Can I help you?" it asked.

Andra hung back as Will approached the reception desk, holding out a visitor pass. "Is Miss Palmer still in the building?"

"Unfortunately not, sir. Would you like an appointment?"

"That won't be necessary," he said. "We'll catch Miss Palmer another time."

"As you wish," said the robot. "If you need any further assistance, don't hesitate to ask."

"That's a shame," said Andra as they crossed the space. "It would have made things easier."

"Steady now." Will jabbed a finger on the lift button. "You know she isn't part of the clean-up."

"She should be. She's seen our faces."

"As have a large proportion of the Haven workforce," he said as the lift doors opened. "After you."

"Elrick is getting soft," she said as she stepped into the lift. "Or too confident."

"Or maybe he's just better at seeing the bigger picture." Will followed her in and pressed the basement button. "We're just here to do what we're told, remember?"

*

Just as in the reception area above, no sentry robots guarded the lift doors in the basement. As Andra marched out of the lift and Will followed her at a more relaxed pace, the darkling flowed into the shadows that hunkered along the base of the walls.

"Last thing to wrap up," Will called to Andra, who was already at the doorway out. "I'll be glad to leave this place."

"Itchy feet?" she called back.

"You know me too well."

As the darkling tailed them through the basement rooms and corridors, she noticed how the magic that had shone from the walls when she had last visited the basement had diminished. The barest strands waved from the walls like riverweed caught in the current, all pulled towards what lay at the deepest part of the basement.

A few rooms further still, and the darkling began to feel the pull herself. Maintaining her shadow form required more and more intention and will power with each threshold they passed through.

By the time they reached the room that contained the laboratory, the darkling battled to maintain her shadow form as its instinctual response urged her to flee.

"This really is a genius concept." Will ran his hand over the wall of the laboratory. Its door gaped open and the darkling could see that it was empty of both inhabitants and furniture. "Completely normal-looking to people like us, but so damaging to the magicals. You have to love Winters' way of thinking."

"Workadays," sneered Andra. "That's what they call us."

"I hear that this substance…" He rapped his knuckles on the wall. "That it works on anyone with magic. Any *thing*."

"It would be interesting to test that theory." Andra reached into her jacket.

The darkling was so intent on the woman and maintaining her form that close to the laboratory, that she didn't notice what the man did next. She didn't notice, that is, until with a *'crack'* the room was flooded with an intense, fierce light that dragged her from shadow and hemmed her solid form down to the ground.

"There you are," he said, a flaming wooden rod held in each hand. "I wondered if you'd make an entrance."

"Got you." The woman clamped a collar around the darkling's neck. The light of the Helios flares guttered out and the darkling released a breath. She held out her hands, willing them to return to shadow. "Clever things, these collars," said the woman, prowling around the edge of the room. "The Auditor has perfected them to work on specific types. Magicals. Wisps. Even darklings."

"No, you don't." The man barred the darkling's way as she made a lunge to escape. "We've only just met. Why the haste to leave?"

The darkling backed away as they advanced on her. Her mind felt foggy and unfocused. Step by step, she retreated towards the laboratory until she found herself on its threshold.

"That's it," said the man. "You've got the idea."

"I'm not going in there," snarled the darkling.

"There's nowhere else to go," said the woman.

"Make it easy on yourself." The man closed in on her. "It's this or…" He shrugged. "You decide."

The darkling ran at him with her hands clawed and her lips drawn back into a snarl. Instantly, a wave of pain ran through her body. She fell to her knees, pulling at the collar that encircled her neck.

"The collar won't let you harm a Parity operative," he said, dragging her to her feet. "The Auditor made sure of that. Get in there," he sneered as he pushed her into the laboratory.

"No!" She threw herself against the door as it silently closed, then jumped back with a gulped breath. She waited for the substance of the laboratory to pull at her magic, her very essence, but nothing happened. She looked at her hands, willing them to turn to shadow but they remained as they were.

It took a moment for her to realise what had happened, and when she did the reality was startling. The collar had turned her into a human. There was no magic for this place to drain.

"Let me out!"

She slammed a hand against the door, then listened for a response. Whether it was the construct of the laboratory, or that her captors had left, she did not know. But she heard nothing.

Slowly, she turned around. The white room was empty. She was the only thing it contained.

Chapter Twenty-Four

Steve had decided that travelling underwater was weird but wonderful. There was a muffled peace to be found in the mid-murk of the deep sea. The deeper that the mini sub travelled, the more intense the blue of the water became. Above the sub, Steve could see the mottled sunlight. Below, the blue of the sea stretched out into darkness. If it hadn't been for the fact that they were being pursued and in search of their friends, he could have spent hours just watching the North Sea go by.

"That's far enough. We can take a breather for a second." Jem brought the vehicle to a halt in the dim sea depths. "I sent the Porpoise off to Keeltown at a swift pace when we were accosted. Time to call it back."

"Jem, if those men managed to reach Nereid 8 that quick, how long do you think it'll take them to reach Keeltown?"

"No time at all," she said. "That heli-craft they were in? I've seen them before. Incredibly fast vehicles. Part helicopter, part jet plane. They could be in Keeltown already."

"Good thing our friends are safe on the Porpoise," said Steve. "It took hours to get to Nereid 8, so we've got lots of time."

"Hours," said Jem. "It *did* take hours, but that was at regular speed." She shrugged. "It would've taken no more than four hours if we were travelling at the rate I sent the Porpoise off at."

"How long has it been since you sent the Porpoise away?"

"An hour, I'd say. Still, I'm sure it'll be fine. Unless Hartley Keg has done something stupid, which is unlikely," she added as Steve's mind began to race through the multitude of stupid things

Hartley might do in their absence. "I'm sure they're perfectly safe, if a little perplexed. Of course, the thing that concerns me most is where those people came from. Their heli-craft may be fast but…" She shook her head. "Not that it matters. We'll be back on the Porpoise any time now, far away from the Major and his men. Nothing at all to worry about." She pulled back her coat sleeve and tapped at the remote control device on her wrist. "Any time now."

"What's wrong?" said Steve as the tapping continued and Jem's face descended into a scowl.

"The Porpoise isn't respondin'." She tugged her sleeve back down and tightened the scarf in her hair. "They must be out of range. Only one thing for it, we'll have to catch up."

"Can we do that in this sub? It's not very big."

"Size don't matter," she said, returning her hands to the virtual controls. "This baby is fast. Just you see. We'll head them off long before we reach Keeltown."

"That's good," he said.

"No worries at all," she muttered as the mini submarine set off again. "Nope. Not at all."

*

It was difficult to tell how much time had passed when a long, slender shape glided into view on the sub's sonar, and a couple of minutes later a shadowy form appeared in the sea ahead of them.

"Is that it?" said Steve. "Is that the Porpoise?"

"Looks like." She tapped the remote control device on her wrist. "It's still not respondin' though and we're well within signal range. Come on, Porpoise, my old love. Do what you're told."

"Can't you contact them? Ask them to stop the Porpoise?"

"No, and no," she said with a sigh. "I don't have the means to radio them and the controls of the Porpoise will only react to my voice and my codes. There's a to-do and a half."

"But if they make it back to Keeltown, the Major might be waiting for them. They could walk into a trap."

"You don't have to tell me that," said Jem, shrugging off her coat and elbowing Steve in the process. "Even if we could make ourselves known, there's no stoppin' the Porpoise without me on board." She bundled up the coat and tossed it in the small space behind their seats. "Any ideas?"

"We have to beat them back," he said. "Be there first so we can warn them."

"Great minds and all that." She flexed her fingers, clicked her neck, and returned her hands to the control panel. "I'm not sure how much faster this little darlin' can take us or whether the battery will hold up, but I'm willin' to give it a go. Ready?"

"Ready," he said with a nod.

"Glad one of us is," she replied. "Here's hopin'."

*

Approaching from sea level, Keeltown looked more like a fortified castle rising up out of the water than an amalgamation of individual boats and vessels. They surfaced in the shadow of the floating township and headed to a jetty.

"Fortrose, give us a hand!" Jem stood with her feet on the arms of the seat in the mini sub and her arms, head, and shoulders above the vehicle's open hatch.

"Yes, Jem." A young boy, maybe seven or eight years old and dressed in a well-patched sweater that reached past his knees, jumped up from an overturned bucket and raced over to help. "What's need?"

"The mooring rope, hun. Told you we'd make it back first," Jem called down to Steve as Fortrose ran to a coiled-up rope on the jetty. "Only just, mind you."

"Here's you go." Fortrose struggled to the mini sub, piled up with an armful of rope. "Ready?"

"Always ready," said Jem with a nod as the boy tossed the end of the rope to her. "Thank you kindly, Fortrose."

"You's welcome, Jem." Fortrose returned to his stool, pulled his legs up into his sweater, and wrapped his arms around himself.

"Tie the rope round your waist, Steve," she said as she fed it down into the mini sub.

"Wouldn't it be more sensible to tie it to the submarine?" he said. "So it doesn't float off?"

"I'm more concerned about you endin' up in the drink. The water's choppy and I don't have time to mess about rescuing you."

"Fine." He wrapped the rope around his waist and was attempting to knot it when a cry went up from the jetty.

"They're here," Jem called down. "Fortrose, go secure the Porpoise quick-like."

"Yes, Jem." The boy was off his stool in a moment and running to the end of the jetty.

Peering through the glass globe of the mini sub, Steve watched as the Porpoise glided to a halt and Fortrose leapt onto the submarine's dark-panelled top with another heavy rope in his grasp. Jem pushed herself up and out of the mini sub and pelted down the jetty after him.

"Forget this." Steve dropped the rope and pulled himself through the mini sub's hatch. *If a seven year old doesn't need a rope…* He left the thought unfinished as he leapt for the jetty.

*

This ship has a mind of its own. Waited for as long as we could. Gone back to Keeltown to arrange a rescue.

The flaming words hung in mid-air in the helm of the Porpoise. Other than that, there was no sign of Steve's magical friends.

"He just couldn't help himself," said Jem. "Bloody Hartley Keg."

"So where are they?" Steve had slipped off the coat Jem had

provided him with, but the fishy, oily smell of it still hung about his clothes. It didn't help that his feet were sopping wet. The jetty hadn't been as close to the mini sub as it looked.

"Well, there's no ruckus going on in Keeltown. Fortrose would have told us if the Sheriff had raised the alarm." Jem crossed her arms. "Which means that nobody knows they're back."

"If Hartley travelled them out of here, where's the first place he'd go on Keeltown?" said Steve. "The Sheriff's office?"

"No, not there," said Jem. "They'd head to the Tumbler first. Regroup. Talk to Bernard and Manny."

"Come on then," said Steve, heading for the door. "Let's go find them."

"Right you are." Jem touched a hand to the low ceiling of the helm room. "Good to have you back, old thing," she said. "Be back in a mo'."

*

By the time they reached the Leaping Tumbler, Steve was out of breath from keeping up with Jem's twisting route through Keeltown and his hand was pressed to a stitch in his side. Jem entered the bar with a shout of "Bernard. Manny. I'm back." before disappearing through the beaded curtain at the back of the room. Before he had time to follow her, there was a shout of "Steve! Get in here!"

Now what? He darted across the room ready for… Well, he wasn't sure what he needed to be ready for but 'being ready' was becoming a habit.

The kitchen was a picture of chaos. His feet crunched on broken glass and he was forced to pick a path between the pans and cutlery that were scattered across the floor. At one end of the kitchen, Jem's robots lay on the floor, their limbs unmoving and the lights that should have shone from their central orbs, dead.

In front of the door they had used to enter the Porpoise, Robert Elian sat with his head in his hands. Beside him, Hartley

Keg lay flat out with his eyes closed. Jem crouched over him, two fingers pressed to the side of his neck.

"He's still with us," she said. "Hartley, talk to me." She patted his face.

"What's happened?" said Steve.

"We won't know that until they wake up and tell us. Hartley!" she yelled into the shopkeeper's face.

"Onwards!" With that exclamation, Hartley sat straight up, opened his eyes, and then clamped his hands to his head.

"Where did she go?" Robert struggled to his feet, leaning heavily on the nearest counter.

"Who?" said Jem.

"The grayling."

"What's a grayling?" said Steve.

"That's what I want to know," said Jem. "That and why it had to nigh-on destroy the place."

"Who, not what," said Robert.

"Where's Blessing?" Steve looked around, half expecting her to walk into the room at any moment. "Did she go for help?"

"She…" Hartley released his head and looked around, blinking as if it was difficult to stay awake. "She was with us when we travelled out of the sub. She should…" He shook his head, then cried out and clamped one hand to his forehead. "Damn sleep powder."

"What are you talking about?" said Steve.

"The grayling felled us with sleeping powder." Robert clicked his neck and straightened his jacket. "Horrible stuff. Gives the most horrendous hangover." He reached for Hartley, hooking a hand around the shopkeeper's arm. "Come on, old friend. Up you get."

Steve rushed to help Robert drag Hartley to his feet, 'drag' being the operative word as the shopkeeper seemed to have no intention of leaving the floor.

"Unhand me. I am perfectly capable. I…" Hartley stood unaided for a moment before falling back onto the doorframe.

"Blessing." He staggered a step from the support of the door. "We have to find Blessing." Then with a hand slapped to his forehead, he toppled to his knees.

"You can't stay down there." Steve crouched down beside him, taking care not to cut himself on the shards of glass that were scattered on the floor.

"Why not?" Hartley grumped. "I'm obviously of no use to anyone. An absolute failure of a man. I promised to keep Blessing safe and…" His voice trailed off.

"Stop feeling sorry for yourself," said Steve. "That won't help—" He stopped as a green light blinked on underneath the kitchen cabinet at Hartley's feet. "What's that?"

"What's what?" said Hartley.

"There's something under here." Steve reached under the kitchen cabinet. His fingers closed around cold plastic.

"What is it?" said Hartley as Steve pulled out the small device. Shaped like a hand-grenade, the only details of any interest were a single red button and a metallic coil.

"I know exactly what it is." Jem backed away. "It's an EMP. No wonder my robots are in such a dire condition. Steve, get it out of my kitchen this minute."

"Okay." Holding the device at arm's length, he backed out of the kitchen as quickly as the glass-strewn floor would allow him.

*

Steve sat at a table in Jem's bar. Hartley sat opposite, shoulders hunched and eyes on the tabletop. Ever active, Robert paced up and down the room. Steve could hear Jem clattering around in the kitchen with an undercurrent of muttered curses and complaints.

"Tell me again," said Steve.

"We've already told you twice," said Robert. "What more is there to tell?"

"I travelled us here from the Porpoise." Hartley's usual energy was gone. He spoke in a monotone voice, not meeting Steve's eye. "I thought we would be safe. The grayling used sleep powder on us. We passed out. End of story."

"Not 'end of story'." Steve banged a fist on the table. "What about Blessing?"

"The grayling must have taken her," said Robert. "Obviously."

"You still haven't told me what a grayling is!"

"That's what I want to know." Jem barged through the beaded curtain. "Because whatever it is, I'd like to tan its hide after the state it left my kitchen in. Have you seen Bernard and Manny? Frazzled, they are."

"You can repair the robots and buy new pots and pans, Jem," said Hartley with a sigh. "Blessing isn't—"

"I know, I know," she said in a softer tone. "Answer the boy's question though."

"If you insist." Hartley nodded. "A grayling is half darkling and half something else that you really don't want to know about. They have certain camouflage skills which allow them to remain unseen."

"They can go invisible?" said Steve.

"No, not that. It's more of a perceptive camouflage. If you don't expect them to be there, they can effectively disappear."

"Graylings. Horrible things," said Robert. "Complete mercenaries. They work for whoever pays."

"And pays the most," said Hartley. "The Council could afford that kind of price."

"But how would the Council know where we are?" said Steve.

"Because I'm a stupid, careless man," said Hartley. "When I travelled us from the sub back to Keeltown, it would have shown up on their tracking if they've cast a sufficiently wide net." He leant over the table, cupping his head in his hands. "What have I done?"

"If I'm understanding how the Council work," said Jem. "Why send one of these graylings instead of the Hidden?"

"Maybe they were already on to Hartley and the children,"

said Robert. "Who knows how long the grayling has been stalking them."

"What about Parity?" said Steve.

"What about them?" said Robert. "They're the least of our worries right now."

"I think the men on Nereid 8 were Parity," said Steve. "One of them had the same emblem on his uniform as I saw tattooed on Elrick Olen's wrist."

"The boy's got a point," said Jem. "They worked out who we were and that I run this place. Their heli-craft could have got them back here in time to accost the three of you."

"But why take the girl?" said Robert, tugging at his beard. "And why use a grayling? Parity are workadays."

For the briefest of moments, nobody spoke. The only sounds were Hartley breathing into his hands, the tapping of Robert's footsteps on the floor, and the ticking of the clock over the bar.

The table between Steve and Hartley gave a tremorous shake. Hartley sat up, hands raised in the air. It rattled again. Steve darted to his feet as the floorboards vibrated too. There was a sweet, pungent stink and with a *'ping'* a red squirrel wearing a blue sash landed on the table.

The squirrel tilted its head and gave Steve a short, high-pitched chirp.

"What does it want?" said Steve.

"It's just saying 'hello'." Hartley leant forward and tapped his finger on the table close to the squirrel. "Who do you have a message for?" he asked in a raised voice as if the creature was a little deaf.

The squirrel pulled a roll of paper from a pocket in the sash it wore and offered it to Hartley with a chirp.

"What *is* this?" said Jem.

"It's a squirr—" Robert began.

"Yes, I can perfectly well see that it's a squirrel. But what is it doing in my bar and how did it get here?"

"It's a form of magical mail." Hartley gently took the paper from the squirrel. "Untraceable. One hundred percent successful in finding its target. The only real problem is the chewing. Squirrels can be nervous creatures. Nibbling at the edge of a rolled-up message calms them."

"Give me a conveyance charm any day," said Robert. "At least you know who you're talking to."

"Well?" said Hartley as the squirrel crept closer and raised a paw. "Oh, you want a tip." He reached into his pocket and pulled out a peanut. "This is all I have on me, I'm afraid."

The squirrel grabbed the nut and scurried back to the centre of the table. With a stamp of its foot and a *bark-bark-bark*, the furry messenger disappeared.

"Well, that's just peculiar," said Jem.

"What does it say?" asked Steve.

"It says." Hartley unrolled the message. "Oh dear, that isn't good."

"What isn't?"

"We have the girl," Hartley read. "Bring the Chronometer to Sanctuary if you want to see her again."

"It has to be the Council," said Robert. "First the grayling. Then the use of squirrel mail. And now the mention of Sanctuary and the Chronometer."

"The puzzle pieces do seem to fit." Hartley rolled up the message and dropped it into his pocket. "The question is, Robert, are you willing to help us?"

"Well…" Robert looked at each of them in turn: Hartley, Jem, and then Steve. "The Council have never shown an interest in the Chronometer before. Why start now?"

"There is one sure way to find out," said Hartley with a raised eyebrow.

"I know what my answer would be." Jem clamped her arms crossed. "It's the only honest thing to do when a young friend is at stake."

"But Hartley, what about the Path?" said Robert. "If they have the Chronometer, they could reconstruct it. We can't let the

Council get their hands on it after all these years."

"I don't care about the Path," said Steve, charging up to Robert. "Or any of these stupid magical devices."

"Steve—" Hartley began.

"I care about Blessing. I care about getting her back. She's a hundred times more important. If we hadn't gone to rescue you," he said, jabbing a finger at Robert, "Hartley wouldn't have used his magic to travel back to Keeltown, and the Council wouldn't have been able to track us here and take her. We rescued you. Now it's your turn to help us rescue Blessing."

Throughout Steve's outburst, Robert Elian's face had grown redder and redder, his eyes wider, and his mouth had dropped open. Now, he released a heavy sigh and pulled his cap from inside his jacket.

"Fine," he said. "When you put it like that, I don't have any other option. There's just one problem."

"Which is?" said Jem.

"I don't have the Chronometer on me." He fixed his cap on his bald head and buttoned his jacket. "We'll have to collect it. It's not nearby, but with our resident traveller on hand, that shouldn't be a problem."

"That all depends on where it is," said Hartley. "I'm not exactly prepared for action in my current condition."

"We should be safe if we arrive with gifts and our wits."

"I'm liking the sound of this less and less, Robert," said Hartley. "Exactly where did you hide the Chronometer?"

"Not so much hide as deposit." Robert clasped his hands behind his back with his eyes on the ground. "I left the device with Miss Farspringer."

"But why? Surely there are less perilous places to store a precious item?" Hartley shook his head. "She's hardly an easy individual to deal with on her best days. Not that there are many of those."

"It could be worse," said Steve.

"Worse? Have you met…? Oh." Hartley stopped. "You *have*

met Miss Farspringer."

"Yup," said Steve. "It wasn't so bad."

"Then you were lucky," said Hartley. "Or you have a knack for understatement. Miss Farspringer guards her collection like a…" He shrugged. "Well, she just guards it very well."

"Who's this Miss Farspringer?" said Jem. "Will she be a problem?"

"Not if we go prepared," said Robert. "We need to provide three gifts. Something special. Something to impress. Something worth handing over the Chronometer for."

Chapter Twenty-Five

"So I suppose this is it, then," said Jem. "Thanks for the entertainment and farewell."

The four of them stood at the entrance to the Leaping Tumbler. Steve carried a canvas shopping bag that held the three gifts for Miss Farspringer. He was getting used to being the luggage-boy.

"Not farewell, my dear," said Hartley. "That always sounds so final. How about 'until next time'? Hm?"

"I'm not sure I want there to be a next time." She crossed her arms and let out a huff. "Not after all the trouble you lot have put me through."

"Less of the hurt petulance, Jem." Robert reached up and planted a kiss on her cheek. "It's been an adventure, and I know how much you enjoy those."

"Well, I suppose you did pay for the room, Robert." Her arms loosened a little. "There's that."

"Thank you, Jem." Steve held out his hand to her. He wasn't sure if this was the right thing to do but her current mood looked too prickly for him to attempt a hug. "It was very nice to meet you. Thanks for the food."

"Ooh, aren't you all formal of a sudden?" she said, but she took his hand, giving it a couple of firm shakes. "Before I forget." She reached into the pocket of the vibrant, floral overalls she wore and pulled out the device that Steve had found in her kitchen. "Finders keepers an' all that. I don't know if it'll work again but you might have a use for it."

"Thanks." Remembering the damage the device had caused to the robots, Steve carefully took the EMP from Jem's grasp and slid it into his jacket pocket. It was a snug fit, and he wondered how Hartley managed to cram so much into the pockets of his old tweed jacket.

"That's very kind of you, Jem," said Hartley. "I do hope we haven't caused you too much disruption."

"Well, it's what you do, isn't it? Disruption," she said.

"I'm sorry, my dear. I never meant—"

"Come here." Jem engulfed Hartley in a heartfelt hug. "You take care of yourself, you silly oaf," she said, pushing him away again. "All of you. I'm far too busy to come to the rescue again."

"What will you do about Bernard and Manny?" said Steve. "Can you fix them?"

"Of course," she said. "I'll have them up and servin' customers in no time."

"Well," said Hartley with a sad shrug. "I suppose we'd best be off." He laid a hand on the door frame. "It's been a pleasure, Jem, as always." He opened the door, nodded to her, and then he stepped through with Robert at his heels.

"Steve." Jem called his name before he could follow the others. "Remember what I said about our friend there. He doesn't ever mean to drag people into his trouble. Be careful and don't forget to think for yourself." She tapped the side of her head. "Promise?"

"I promise," he said.

"Good boy. Well, off you go," she said as Steve heard his name called through the open door. "You don't want to lose those old fools. They'd never survive without you."

As his name was called for a second time, Steve tightened his hold on the canvas bag, and stepped over the threshold.

*

"It would have been far easier to travel us into Miss Farspringer's quarters," said Robert.

"Only if we wanted to surprise her into attacking us," Hartley countered. "Besides, who knows what alarm bells it would have set off with the Council. I'm still half expecting them to materialise anyway."

The entry hall of the Ministry of Yesterday was relatively empty. Besides the three of them, the only human inhabitants were an elderly couple carrying a plastic floral wreath and a rather official looking man who talked to them in hushed tones.

"Can you keep your voices down?" said Steve. "You'll attract the attention of—"

"Can I help you?" said a polite voice. The enquiry attendant floated a few inches above the floor as it waited for a response. A smiling emoji sat at human head height on the black stone obelisk. "What would you like to do today?"

"We would like—" Steve began.

"To be left alone," said Robert, advancing on the obelisk. "We don't need any help."

"Why not take advantage of this quiet period of the week by consulting—"

"That will be enough, attendant," said a voice that Steve recognised. "I will assist the visitors. Return to your station." Cassie Moran watched the attendant leave in silence and then she turned to Steve with a polite smile. "Special enquiries again?" she said.

"Yes, indeed," said Hartley. "Most definitely special."

"Don't I know you?" She lifted her thick, pink glasses a little to get a better look at Hartley.

"Probably," said Robert. "Most people do."

"My friend here jests," said Hartley with a broad smile. "I just have one of those faces."

"You do look familiar," said Cassie. "But maybe you're right. This way."

As had happened the first time Steve had met with Cassie, she led them to the sectioned-off area beside the entrance to the

Ministry of Yesterday. Pulling aside a pink-cushioned chair, she reached underneath the mirrored desk. The quiet tones of the man speaking to the elderly couple stopped in an instant.

"What can I help you with today?" She sat down at her desk, her hands folded on the polished desktop.

"We need to see Miss Farspringer again. We have gifts." Steve raised the canvas shopper.

"Always a good start," she said. "Hold on." She slipped off her chair and dipped down behind the desk. When she returned, she held a small chirruping box. "You know the drill," she said.

"I do." There was a sound of rapid scrabbling from inside the box as he took it from her. "Thanks."

"Good luck," she called after them as they headed for the stairs that led down out of sight. "You'll need it."

*

"This doesn't seem particularly prison-like," said Hartley as they walked between two floor-to-ceiling bookcases. "It's quite pleasant in here, if a tad dusty."

"Shush," said Robert. "She'll hear you."

"*She* has already heard you."

Miss Farspringer glided into view at the end of the corridor formed by the bookcases. She looked exactly as she had the first time Steve had seen her only a few weeks before. Her tall, willowy form was wrapped in a long black dress that trailed behind her. Her eyes were hidden behind large, black sunglasses that reminded Steve of old vintage movie stars. Her hair was equally hidden, wrapped up in an emerald green turban from which a snake brooch dropped onto her heavily made-up forehead.

"I smell a snack," she said in her deep, dry voice. "A live one."

"Here." Steve held up the box that Cassie had given to him. "Just as you like them," he said as he pushed between the two men.

"Good," she rasped as she lunged forward to snatch the box

from Steve's grasp. "It's a start." She sniffed at the box. "What do you want?" she asked.

"Miss Farspringer," said Hartley, stepping forward. "We—"

"Not you, old man!" she snapped, her head swaying from side to side. "I wasn't talking to you. I was asking the boy."

"We've come to make a withdrawal," said Steve, stepping in front of Hartley.

"Always with the withdrawals," she said. "Why does no one ever visit me simply to talk or to dance or to sing? Fine." She beckoned to them with a long, gloved finger. "This way."

"I don't like this," Robert muttered as Miss Farspringer turned on her heel and glided towards a table beyond the bookcases.

"It's a little late for worries, don't you think?" Hartley muttered back. "It was your choice to store the device here. Remember?"

"I know," said Robert. "I was just saying."

"Enough chatter. What gifts do you bring me?"

Miss Farspringer waited by the table. Beyond her, a statue of a short, fat man reached chubby, ring-clad hands towards her. The statue's face, sculpted into an expression of horror, looked worryingly familiar. In fact, it looked exactly like one of Braeden Kendra's thugs who had attacked Steve after his uncle's funeral.

"Is that new?" said Steve, keeping the table between himself and Miss Farspringer.

"Recent," she said. "This fool attempted to steal from me. Nobody steals from me."

"So you turned him into—"

"It seemed proportional to his crime. He had these." She pulled two vials from her sleeve. "I believe the plan was to throw them at me, but he never got that far." She held them up to the light cast by the lamp at the table. "Do you know what these are?"

"Miss Farspringer," said Hartley. "May I examine them?"

"You are the door man," she said.

"That's one way of putting it," said Robert.

"I am," said Hartley. "I believe I've encountered these vials before. May I?" He held out a hand as he edged towards her. "Please?"

"You may," she said. "But do not try to trick me."

"I wouldn't dream of it, my d… I mean, Miss Farspringer," he said with a smile as she handed the vials to him.

"Good. Because I only trust the boy," she said.

"Quite right," said Hartley, frowning at Steve. "Just one moment, please." He sniffed the vials, squinted into one, and gave the other a lick. "Just as I thought. Soul dust to conjure up a revenant."

"What is this revenant?" she asked.

"A monstrous tragedy," said Hartley. "A lost soul captured in dust form to be used as a cruel tormentor. Had this vial met its target, the revenant contained within would have wrapped you in its smoky embrace and tortured you with your deepest fears. You're lucky the blaggard didn't make his shot."

"Luck! Hah!" She snatched the vials from him and rolled them at speed down the table to Steve. "Boy, take these away. I have no use for dust."

"Right." Instinctively, Steve stopped the vials' roll as they reached him. Then his heart lurched into a thundering beat as he realised what he had in his grasp. *Not again*, he thought as he carefully tucked the vials into his jacket pocket.

"What gifts do you have for me?" She leant across the table with her head tilted to one side. "Show me."

"The gifts," said Steve. "Of course." He placed the canvas shopper on the table and reached inside.

"No tricks." Miss Farspringer recoiled with a dry rattling sound. "I have plenty of room for more statues."

"Right," said Steve. "No tricks." He pulled out the first of the presents, a small, white paper bag, and opened it. "Barley sugars. For your throat."

"You remembered," she said. "Clever boy. What else?"

"There's this." He pulled out a flat, padded box, which he opened to reveal a string of pearls. "They're pretty," he said, searching for a way to sell the gift to her.

"Pleasant," she agreed. "And pearls *do* remind me of the sea."

"We all like the seaside," said Hartley, before Robert nudged him to be quiet.

"What is my third gift?" she said. "I hope it is more impressive than its companions."

"I brought you this." Steve pulled out a tissue-wrapped parcel. "It's a silk shawl," he said. "It feels really good against your skin," he continued as Miss Farspringer failed to look impressed. "And look." He unwrapped the tissue and opened out the shawl. "It matches your turban."

For a long, awkward moment, Steve stood with the shawl outheld and his heart in his throat as Miss Farspringer stared at him in silence. He wondered if his eyes were actually as wide as they felt.

"It will suffice as a third gift," she finally said as she took the shawl from him and wrapped it around her shoulders with a flourish. "Depending on what you wish to withdraw."

"Miss Farspringer. May I speak?" said Robert.

"You may," she said.

"I deposited an item with you many years ago and I would like to withdraw it in return for these gifts."

"This shawl does feel good against my skin," she mused, touching the shawl to her face. "This was a worthy gift."

"Miss Farspringer?" said Robert.

"Yes, yes," she said. "You want to retrieve your item. Name it and I will decide."

"It is called the Chronometer," he said. "It's a timepiece, a fob watch."

"I know what the Chronometer is," she said. "I document every deposit that is left with me. I also know what it can do, Robert Elian." She smiled a wide, cruel smile that revealed her fangs. "I know what you can do too, sky-singer."

This doesn't sound good, thought Steve.

"Here is my proposal," she said. "The boy may take the

Chronometer but in exchange you, sky-singer, will remain with me. You will conjure me skies and sweet zephyrs to break the tedium of my imprisonment. You will amuse and entertain me."

"Until when?" said Robert.

"Who knows how soon I will tire of your songs," she said. "That is my deal. Take it or leave it."

"Robert, you don't have to do this," said Hartley. "We'll find another way."

"We both know that time is against us, old friend." Robert tugged on his beard for a moment and then he clapped his hands together once. "So be it," he said. "Miss Farspringer, you have a deal."

"You will keep him safe, won't you, Miss Farspringer?" said Steve, with his eyes on the statue. "You won't…"

"A sky-singer is a rare commodity," she said. "If he behaves, all will be well."

"I'll be fine, Steve," said Robert. "Now Miss Farspringer, about the Chronometer…"

Chapter Twenty-Six

"Is this it?" Steve held the old, ornate, gold fob watch up to the bare, electric light of Saint Mungo's Sanctuary for the Homeless.

The rainy early evening had filled St Mungo's to the brim. A chattering queue of locals, young and old, alone and in families, progressed along the food counters, receiving trays of food and quickly-pocketed bottles of water. Unlike the city streets, there were no robots to be seen, just human beings helping human beings.

"The Chronometer, yes," said Hartley. "I haven't seen this device for more decades than I'd like to consider, but that is most definitely it."

"It just looks like a normal, old watch," said Steve. "Nothing special at all."

"All elements of the Path were normal to begin with," said Hartley. "And the appearance of normality is an excellent method of concealment. Still, it might be best not flash it around in public."

"Here." Steve offered the device to Hartley. "Take it," he said, when Hartley tucked his hands under the tabletop.

"It would be best if you hang onto it," said Hartley. "I seem to have developed a habit of losing things lately." He released a heavy sigh. "It's safer with you. Put it away in your pocket."

"I can't," said Steve. "My jacket pockets are full and the pockets in my jeans are too small. I could have used the canvas bag if Miss Farspringer hadn't decided to keep it."

"That's unfortunate," said Hartley. He ran a hand over his beard. "But perhaps we can improve on the storage dilemma we find ourselves in."

"Here you go, lovely." A tall, curvy woman slapped two mugs of hot chocolate onto the table and wiped a hand across her forehead, pushing grey-streaked dark curls under her vibrantly coloured headscarf. "Can't have you wasting away over here, now can we?"

"Emmie, my dear." Hartley's usual smile returned. "How are you?"

"Good, good," she said. "What brings you in here?"

"Just dodging the rain showers," said Hartley. "And partaking of St Mungo's warm welcome."

"Hello," she said to Steve. "Haven't seen you in this one's wake before." She slapped a hand on Hartley's shoulder. "Hope he isn't getting you into any trouble."

"Only what you'd expect," Steve said with a smile.

"I'd best not ask then." She gave him a wink. "We're closing up the food soon, but there'll be hot drinks all night. Just in case you need a place." She patted Hartley's shoulder again and then moved onto the next table of visitors.

"She's nice," said Steve, wrapping his hands around the heat of the mug.

"Wonderful lady," said Hartley. "Emmie is a Darkacre local. Well, she was until her family passed away."

"What happened to them?"

"It was a few years back now. Maybe eleven or twelve. Her husband and son crossed swords with Maeve Kendra a little too publicly for the Council's liking. The Hidden imprisoned Andrew and Sam for supposedly endangering our community. It hit Emmie hard, especially so when you consider what she is."

"Why? What is she?" said Steve.

"Emmie is a guardian. She has immense powers of protection, both of people and places. Unfortunately, she wasn't around when the Hidden came for her family, so she couldn't do anything. She left Darkacre soon after. I suppose it was to escape the memories of her family, or the pity of the community." He shrugged. "Completely understandable, in my opinion."

"Is Maeve Kendra anything to do with Braeden Kendra?"

"His mother. Gone now." Hartley take a slurp of the hot chocolate, leaving a foamy film on his moustache. "She was the master—mistress?—mind of his criminal organisation. Meticulous. Cruel. Cunning."

"Is that where he got his powers from?"

"No, no, no. That was his father. No, his mother was a workaday. Dangerous woman. She had a knack at sourcing you-know-what items that required no you-know-what skills to use. She built an army of street youngsters, equally loyal and terrified of her. She taught Braeden everything he knows."

"A model mother then?" said Steve, breathing in the smell of the hot chocolate.

"Of course. That's it," said Hartley, splashing his mug down on the table.

"What's it?" said Steve.

"Just because you're a workaday doesn't mean that you can't take advantage of you-know-what items."

"Okay," said Steve. "And how does that help us exactly?"

"You'll see," said Hartley. "Come on. This calls for a shopping trip."

*

"It won't be open at this time of night," said Steve. "Besides, we don't have time for shopping. We need to get to Sanctuary."

They stood at the stone-pillared entrance to the Sebastian Green and Sons department store. The building within was in darkness, and the automated glass doors remained shut at their approach.

"It's only closed to some people," said Hartley. He leant against the glass with his face pressed up against it. "If I can just attract the attention of the evening-guard…" He shuffled along the window, his nose squeaking on the glass. "He must be in there somewhere."

"May I enquire as to your intentions, sir?" said the man who stepped out from behind one of the pillars. He was dressed in a regular suit topped off by a peaked cap which bore the insignia of the department store. Under the cap, the man was completely bald and his face looked strangely unfinished. There were no eyebrows, no stubble, and not a wrinkle or fold in sight. "Oh. It's you," he said.

"Mr Knight." Hartley grabbed the man's hand and pumped it vigorously. "How are you? How's the family?"

"The clan are well." Mr Knight extricated himself from Hartley's grasp, wiping his hand on the side of his jacket. "What do you want, Mr Keg?"

"Is the tailor around? I may have a rush job for him."

"As you know, sir, the tailor is always around." He turned to look at Steve and pointed. "Is that with you?" he whispered.

"That, I mean, *he* is most definitely with me," said Hartley, pulling Steve to his side. "This is Steve. He needs a little work, if you catch my meaning."

"He's one of *them*," said Mr Knight.

"One of them in the know," said Hartley. "He's perfectly safe. Doesn't even bite."

"I don't like *them*," said Mr Knight. "They smell odd."

"I'm sure you can make an exception in this case," said Hartley. "After all, he *is* with me. I can vouch for the boy."

"On your head be it, Mr Keg. This way."

"Steve, empty your pockets," said Hartley as they followed the guard. "Give the contents to me."

"Why?" said Steve.

"You'll see."

"I hate it when you do the mysterious thing," said Steve as he handed the EMP, the vials, and the Chronometer to Hartley.

Steve expected there to be a door in the stone pillar to explain the guard's sudden appearance, but there was nothing to be seen when they walked past. Mr Knight led them to a narrow wooden entrance in the side of the building. Above the door, a sign with gold-painted lettering read, *'Tailoring and Weaving—Like Magic'.*

The narrow door led to an equally narrow corridor, so narrow that Steve's shoulders brushed against the walls on either side. Hartley all but filled the space, and only progressed along the corridor by holding his elbows to his belly and bending a little to reduce his height.

A second narrow door opened onto a single room that, despite its size, hummed with the voices and actions of the busy workforce it contained.

"Hartley Keg, what brings you to my shop?" boomed a voice. "Bring it in, my friend. Bring it in."

"Hello Tiberius," wheezed Hartley as the owner of the voice, a short but overly-muscled man wrapped the shopkeeper in a tight embrace. The difference in height meant that the man's intricately tattoo-ed, bulging arms caught Hartley around his rotund middle.

"How are you, old friend," said Tiberius as he backed off. The man's black hair was shortly cropped but his moustache was waxed and bound into the most marvellous of curls that stood out on each side of his face like two springs. "It's been too long."

"It has been a while, indeed," said Hartley. "Tiberius, this is my young friend, Steve Haven. Steve, this is Tiberius: master tailor and weaver."

"Welcome, Steve. Welcome." Steve was relieved when the tailor took his hand to shake instead of hugging him. "Please be careful where you step. My assistants are feisty, but they have delicate bones."

"Right," said Steve. "Of course."

Tiberius sat back down at a wooden contraption that stretched up to the ceiling and almost filled the width of the room. A series of threads ran vertically from top to bottom and building up from the floor, a row at a time, a panel of fabric jiggled into sight as he watched.

The rest of the room was filled with a long table. At the table, eleven pixies the height of Steve's hand sat on tall stools and worked at rolls of fabric—cutting, measuring, sewing—surrounded by an assortment of buttons, sequins, and rolls of threads. Dressed in green, each pixie wore a pixie-sized apron and wore a tiny thimble on one thumb.

"I know what those are." Steve whispered to Hartley.

"Ru-ude!" snapped one of the pixies. "We are not 'whats'." He slapped a hand to the side of his head and stuck out his tongue at Steve.

"So how can I help?" asked Tiberius. "New jacket? Hat?" He pulled a handkerchief out of mid-air and wrapped it around his head. "Headscarf?"

"Alterations," said Hartley. "More specifically, pockets."

"Oh," said Tiberius, balling up the handkerchief and throwing it away. "A little special then?"

"Very special," said Hartley, pushing Steve in front of him. "I'd like you to work your tailoring expertise on the pockets of Steve's jacket."

"Let me see." Tiberius pulled a pair of round-framed spectacles out of the air and placed them on his nose. "Come closer, Steve."

"Go on." Hartley pushed Steve towards the tailor.

"It's a good sound garment," said Tiberius, grabbing Steve by the lapels of his jacket. "Turn," he said, twisting Steve around. "Yes, yes. Let me see." He pulled Steve round again to face him and bent to peer into one of the pockets in Steve's jacket. "Shouldn't be a problem. I take it you mean just like *your* pockets, old friend?"

"Absolutely," said Hartley. "We are in need of concealment, in a hurry, so we came to the best tailor in the city."

"Just the city?" said Tiberius, snatching away his spectacles and throwing them into mid-air where they disappeared.

"Well, I didn't want to embarrass you," said Hartley. "How

long will it take? We're on the clock, I'm afraid."

"You know me, Hartley," said Tiberius as he spun Steve around and pulled the jacket off him. "Speedy is my middle name, as long as you can afford me."

"I wouldn't expect anything less," said Hartley.

"Now, let me see. Two pockets…" Tiberius licked his finger and drew a line of digits in the air. "Two pockets, what with the weaving and the added extra, will take one day."

"One day?" said Steve. "We can't wait that long."

"What could you do in a half an hour?" asked Hartley. "Forty minutes, tops."

"Half an hour?" Tiberius repeated the air-calculation with his finger. "It would have to be an emergency fix. Sub-par material. Just the one pocket. I'm not sure how long it would last. Maybe only a day."

"One pocket and one day will be more than sufficient," said Hartley. "Shall we wait in the parlour?"

"On you go," said Tiberius. "I'll call you in when it's finished."

"Come on, Steve." As Hartley tugged Steve through the archway on the other side of the room, there was the alarming sound of ripping fabric.

*

Tiberius' parlour wasn't what Steve had expected when they stepped through the archway from the tailor's shop. He thought it would be a domestic room, like Frobisher's parlour or the lounge at his own home. He didn't expect it to be a tearoom.

Hartley and Steve sat at the only table in Tiberius' parlour. The table was covered in a white cloth that had been ironed to within an inch of its life. A shelf that ran around the room just below the ceiling carried a range of teapots in every design you could possibly imagine.

"So what will it be?" Mrs Knight licked the end of a pencil and waited expectantly with a small notepad in her hand. If it hadn't been for the lipstick and badly attached false eyelashes, Mrs Knight could have easily been mistaken for Mr Knight in a pinny.

"Just tea, please, Mrs Knight," said Hartley.

"No cakes?" she asked as if the suggestion of 'just tea' was a shocking statement.

"Just tea, please," said Hartley.

"Tea it is then." She tucked her pencil into the slightly aslant wig she wore, dropped the notepad into the large pocket on the front of her pinny, and marched from the room.

"I've got to ask," said Steve as soon as Mrs Knight had left the room. "Do the people who own the department store know about Tiberius, and the pixies?"

"Somebody high up must know," said Hartley. "But the general public have no idea. The external door we entered through is only visible to people whom Mr Knight allows access to. I've always had my suspicions, however, that the store takes full advantage of Tiberius' masterful weaving and tailoring skills in some capacity."

"Here you are." Mrs Knight returned with a silver tray loaded with a steaming teapot, jug, sugar bowl, and a pair of ornately painted cups and saucers. "Are you sure you don't want cake?" she asked as she laid the tray on the table.

"Absolutely sure," said Hartley with a beaming smile.

"Please yourself." And with that, she turned on her heel and left again.

"You still haven't explained why we're spending time on pockets instead of heading straight to Sanctuary," said Steve as Hartley poured tea into the two cups.

"Isn't it obvious?" said Hartley. "Milk?"

"Yes," said Steve. "Hang on. Stop distracting me. Why are we here?"

"Answer my questions and I'll answer yours." Hartley poured milk into the cups. "Sugar?"

"Is that one of the questions?" said Steve. "No," he said as

Hartley raised an eyebrow.

"Question number one," said Hartley, dropping a spoonful of sugar into his own teacup. "Do we know who has taken Blessing?"

"The Council," said Steve.

"Do we know that for sure?"

"Well, no."

"Question number two." Hartley took a slurp of tea. "Mrs Knight always makes a wonderful brew," he said with a satisfied grin.

"What's question number two?" said Steve.

"If we *are* facing the Council and they place those collars back on Blessing and me, how exactly are we expected to protect ourselves?"

"Won't the sisters help?" said Steve.

"Perhaps, but what if they can't? What then?"

Steve opened his mouth to reply, then closed it again as he realised that he had no answer to give. He was stumped.

"We have to be prepared," said Hartley, adding more sugar to his cup. "I'll do all I can, but we have to face facts. It may come down to you, Steve, to save us all."

Chapter Twenty-Seven

"How's the fit, young sir?" Tiberius tugged Steve's jacket closed at the front and smoothed the shoulders with a swift sweep of each hand. "Better? Yes?"

"Yes," said Steve. *Except it doesn't feel any different*, he thought, *but I don't want to upset him.* "It's a great fit, *now*."

"I'm more than glad to hear it," said Hartley, "but what about the other adaptation?"

"The pocket. Yes." Tiberius stood back with a frown. "I'm not one hundred percent happy with it. If I had more time—"

"We don't have more time," said Steve. "We really need to—"

"You underestimate your skills, Tiberius. I'm sure the adaptation is marvellous," said Hartley.

"I did my best," said the tailor. "The pocket is functional. Try not to overload it, though. It's the right-hand pocket, by the way."

"Okay," said Steve, opening the pocket with a finger. Besides a new lining, it didn't look any different. "Thanks."

"How much do I owe you?" said Hartley. "Or is this more of a favour trade?"

"Nothing," said Tiberius. "It's not my best work. Pay me by letting me know how it holds up to wear-and-tear."

"Well, if you're sure," said Hartley. "We'll be off. Thank you once again, my dear friend." He grabbed Tiberius' hand before the tailor could engulf him in another embrace. "Always a pleasure doing business."

"'Bye," said Steve, heading for the narrow door back to the

street.

"Wait!" came a high-pitched voice. One of the pixies stood on the table, her arms piled up with a rubber band. A second pixie held out a needle and a small spool of thread. "You'll need these," said the first pixie. "It's always wise to be prepared for a calamity."

"Er, thanks," said Steve, carefully taking the pixies' gifts.

"You're honoured," said Tiberius in a quiet voice as the pixies returned to their work. "They don't give gifts to every customer we have in here."

"The boy is one-in-a-million," said Hartley. "I've always said so."

"Have you?" said Steve as Hartley steered him back into the narrow corridor.

"Well, I've always *thought* it," said Hartley. "And that's just as good."

*

Back on the street, Hartley directed them to a bench situated under a city streetlight. Evening had descended fully, and the street was clear of pedestrians and their robot companions.

"Let's reassess, shall we?" said Hartley. "I'm sure you're wondering about our detour to the tailor."

"Just a bit," said Steve.

"I can probably best explain through a demonstration." Hartley reached into his jacket pocket and pulled out the items Steve had given to him earlier: the EMP, the vials, and the Chronometer. He laid them on the bench. Steve added the rubber band, needle, and thread. "Now, for the demonstration. You'll like this," said Hartley as he reached into his pocket, and then reached deeper, so deep in fact that his arm disappeared up the elbow. "Yes, this'll do it," he said.

Steve expected his friend to perhaps pull out a weapon or a book or anything really other than what Hartley presented to him next.

"Always good in a fight," said Hartley, brandishing the hockey stick. "Or for an impromptu game."

"How did you do that?" said Steve, taking the hockey stick and examining it. Scratched into the well-worn wood was a single word: *Jolly*.

"It's the pocket," said Hartley. "Tiberius isn't just an expert tailor. He's a magical one, too. As long as I can fit an item into the opening of my pocket, I can store it in there. Had you not wondered how I seem to have just the right thing available to me at all times?"

"A bit," said Steve. "But I never thought it was magic. Just clever lining."

"Now, you try." Hartley nodded to Steve's jacket. "Try putting the hockey stick in your new pocket."

"Okay." Steve held his pocket open with one hand and pushed the hockey stick in with the other. Inch by inch, the hockey stick slid impossibly into his pocket until it dropped from his grasp and disappeared within. "That's amazing. But how do I get it back? I can't see it in there."

"It's quite simple," said Hartley. "You just put your hand in and think of the item you wish to retrieve. Go on. Try it."

Steve did just that, slipping his hand into his pocket and thinking, 'hockey stick'. Immediately, he felt the item in his hand. He pulled it out and laid it across his lap.

"Only you can remove items from your pocket," said Hartley. "If we are searched, it will appear that your pockets are empty."

"So I can pull anything out of my pocket?"

"No, not anything. Only an item you have already deposited there, but as you can see that leaves a whole host of possibilities." Hartley's broad smile slowly dropped from his face, and he looked down at his hands. "I know that I have led you into a perilous situation, Steve. Again. I would completely understand if you decided to return to your school at this point."

"Return to school?" The idea struck him as severely as if

Hartley had punched him in the chest. "I can't go back to school. Blessing needs me. Us," he said. "Blessing needs us both to rescue her. I'd never forgive myself if, you know." He shrugged. "I have to go with you to Sanctuary. My mind's made up."

"Well, if you're sure?" Hartley's lips lifted a little into an almost smile. "I don't know what we're about to face, but I'm sure we can handle it."

"Onwards?" said Steve.

"Indeed," said Hartley. "Together."

*

"Marvellous! It worked." Hartley peered out from one of the doorframes that leant against the wall in the cavern in Sanctuary. "Come along."

"Why?" said Steve as he followed his friend. "Did you think it wouldn't work?"

"I wasn't entirely sure I would still be able to access this doorway," said Hartley. "I had a niggling doubt that we would find ourselves back in the forest."

"Which would have been a bad thing, why?"

"Because the Hidden would have accosted you the moment you arrived there." Cate stood a short distance away, her hands leant on the top of her staff. Moon the white hound waited at her side. "Hello Hartley. Hello Steve."

"I feared there would still be a Council presence here," said Hartley. "Profuse apologies, Cate."

"It is a mere distraction," she said with a shrug of her frail shoulders. "They can't penetrate our field. The only real nuisance is that those in need can't access Sanctuary either."

"I may be able to put an end to that nuisance," said Hartley. "We have something they want."

"And they have Blessing," said Steve.

"But I thought they *wanted* Blessing," said Cate. "What has changed?"

"So much," said Steve. "We went to the Augur, and he made us find Robert Elian in return for a ticket to travel, but then a grayling attacked them." The words rushed out of Steve's mouth as Cate listened with a raised eyebrow. "I wasn't there. I was with Jem. So we couldn't help. And the grayling took Blessing. And then there was a note to say—"

"I think that's enough for one outpouring." Hartley patted a hand on Steve's shoulder. "Suffice to say, Cate: our time since leaving Sanctuary has been eventful."

"So it seems," she said. "I think you'd best come into the house. You can tell the whole story to my sisters. Come."

Steve took a deep breath as the eldest sister left the cavern with the hound at her heels. *Almost there*, he thought as Hartley set off across the pebbled floor. *We'll have you home in no time, Blessing.* But he wondered who he was trying to reassure: his friend or himself.

*

"What happened to this place?" Steve stood in front of the sisters' home.

The huge full moon above illuminated a glass-like barrier that wrapped the circle of stones and the entrance to the sisters' cave-house within an orb of protection.

On the other side of the barrier, the trees, bushes, and grass were scorched black. Some branches still flickered with the embers of the fire that had stripped them of life. Jonah Ledwitch hunched forward with his hands on his thighs. For the first time since Steve had met him, the magical had lost his air of arrogance.

At his side, Naomi Onai watched as twenty or more Hidden hurled orbs of light and fire at the barrier.

"The Council," said Cate. "They said that if we didn't hand over Blessing to them, they would take her."

"And you didn't tell them that we'd already gone?"

"Of course not," she said with the hint of a smile. "It was much more entertaining to watch them exhaust themselves."

"When we told them 'no', Jonah Ledwitch said he would burn the place to the ground." Ana leant against the central standing stone, her arms loosely crossed. "Selene couldn't watch him damage our forest, so she stayed in the cave-house. I told her that the forest would grow back."

"Our sister can be overly sentimental at times," said Cate. "But her absence adds to the impression that we have visitors out of sight."

"Jonah Ledwitch did all of this?" said Steve. "On his own?"

"Pyros are amongst the strongest of magicals," said Hartley. "But if he can't break your barrier, Cate, then I think it's fair to say that we're safe in here. And look at him. He's drained himself for the time being."

As if they had received a shouted order, each of the Hidden ceased their attack and retreated to the scorched tree line.

"What's she doing?" said Steve as Naomi Onai stepped forward and raised her hands to the sky. "Is she a pyro too?"

"No, she is something else entirely different," said Hartley.

"Is it just me?" said Steve as his words hung in the air in a cloud of steam. "Or is it getting colder?"

"She's started," said Hartley. "You might find this interesting. Get ready."

Steve touched his face as something delicately landed on his cheek. When he lifted his hand, his fingers came away wet. "Snow?" he said. "If she's trying to freeze us out, it'll take a long time if this is all she's got."

A chill wind blew across his face. He shook snow from his hair and brushed wads of it from his shoulders.

"It's getting heavier," said Hartley. "She's really giving it some welly, isn't she?"

Snow piled up around their ankles, chilling their feet. Steve cupped his hands over his eyes to keep the snow from blinding him.

"Ow!" Something flint-hard and sharp bounced off his hand. "What was that?"

"Hailstones," said Cate as small pebbles of ice bounced off her head and shoulders. "I hate ice-casters. They always make my bones creak." She gave a curt nod of her head and the barrier that protected Sanctuary jumped forward, knocking Naomi Onai off her feet.

"It's stopped," said Steve as the downpour ceased and the hailstones melted away.

"For now," said Cate. "Let's see what else they think they can throw at us."

"But we have what they came for," said Steve. "Hartley, can't you talk to them?"

"Don't worry. Of course I'll talk to them," said the shopkeeper. "Once they give me the chance."

"But we can stop all of this right now. All we have to do is tell them we have the Chronometer, and we can get Blessing back."

"That's their demand?" asked Cate. "Do you not think it curious that the Council show an interest in the device after all these decades?"

"Perhaps," said Hartley. "But I was more concerned about freeing Blessing. The girl has been through all kinds of trials already. She deserves to go home."

"As you wish," she said. "We shall wait for them to approach."

"Speaking of which," said Ana as two more Hidden appeared with the head of the Council. Blaike Harn stood between them. Her face was as calm as ever, but her bunched hands and the rapid turn of her head told a different story.

As she proceeded towards the protective barrier, Jonah helped Naomi to her feet. The two of them retreated to the charred tree line.

"Keepers of Sanctuary." Blaike Harn took a moment to look at each of those gathered in the circle of stones before fixing her eyes on Cate. "It seems that you have been caught up in the battle of another. I apologise for the inconvenience Keg has placed at your door."

"The only inconvenience has been caused by your soldiers," said Cate, slowly walking forward to face Blaike. "It is you who have brought this battle to us. Not Hartley Keg."

"We only want the girl," said Blaike. "We will forget the deviant actions of her cohorts if she is handed over. Immediately."

"What are you talking about?" said Steve. "You have—"

"Steve. Hush." Hartley yanked him back a step. "Let Cate deal with the Council, for now."

"Hello, Steve." Blaike's full attention was on him now, looking him up and down. "You've been travelling. Why don't you tell me where you've been?"

"Well..." The longer she looked at him, the more he wanted to tell her about Keeltown. He could almost hear her voice in his head, speaking kind words of reassurance and welcome. What harm would it do to tell her? "We went to—"

"Stop it." Hartley's fingers pinched Steve's shoulder, painfully yanking him back to the now. "Leave him alone, Blaike. It's unfair to use your mind-flaying skills on a minor; and a workaday at that."

"Always the meddler, Hartley Keg." Any semblance of calm and pleasantry fell from the face of Blaike Harn. "Why do you people have to interfere with things that don't concern you?"

"Someone has to keep a check on the Council," said Cate. "And when were we ever 'people'?"

"Sorry, my boy," whispered Hartley as he released Steve. "I had to wake you from her influence. You'd have told her everything."

"That's okay." *Painful, but okay.* "Thanks."

"Give us the girl and we'll leave without further unpleasantry," demanded Blaike Harn.

"Curious," said Cate, turning to look at Hartley. When he shook his head, she turned back to the Council Leader and continued. "But your threats are of no concern to me, Blaike Harn."

"But those who are prevented from entering Sanctuary

during this impasse are," said Blaike.

"Then what do you suggest?" asked Cate.

"I request parley." Blaike's façade of calm returned. She smiled but her eyes remained intent on the eldest sister. "You may set the conditions, as this is your ground."

"How considerate of you," said Cate. She looked at her sister. Ana nodded and retrieved her bow from her back, quickly stringing an arrow. "Parley is granted. The conditions are that magic will not be used by any party within the circle of stones. It is not a request."

"Agreed," said Blaike.

"And the Hidden must be sent away. In return, we will hear what you have to say."

"The Hidden sent away?" said Blaike. She wasn't smiling anymore. "But they—"

"You said we could set the conditions. This is one."

"Very well," said Blaike. "Agreed."

"Brace yourself," Hartley whispered to Steve as, with another nod from Cate, the barrier disappeared. "This could become unpleasant."

Chapter Twenty-Eight

The three Council members—Blaike Harn, Jonah Ledwitch, and Naomi Onai—sat at a round stone table that had appeared within the circle of stones almost immediately that the protective barrier had been dropped. Cate, with Hartley and Steve on either side of her, sat facing the Council leader. Ana and the white hound stood a couple of paces away, between the table and the door to the cave-house.

"Now that you have us here," said Blaike, "I hope that we can end this unfortunate situation for good. All we ask is that we are allowed to take the girl. We will forego any judgement of Keg."

"Thank you for stating your intent, Blaike Harn," said Cate. "Hartley Keg, how would you like to respond?"

"With puzzlement," he said. "We were of the understanding that you, Blaike, already had Blessing in your clutches."

"What buffoonery is this?" snarled Jonah. "Why would we assault Sanctuary if we already had the brat?"

"A question I've mused myself," said Cate.

"Keg has misled you," said Naomi. "As he has misled us all. Our Hidden scouts reported that Blessing entered Sanctuary—"

"And left," said Cate. "With Hartley and the boy."

"We only have your word for that," said Jonah. "Let us search your home so we can verify your claim."

"My word has always been sufficient for the Council before now," said Cate. "You overstep yourself, Jonah Ledwitch. Remember where you are and who holds control in this place."

"Blaike, surely you will not stand for this defiance. Tell

them—"

"Stop!" Blaike Harn raised a hand to halt Jonah's protests. "This is a parley. Keep a civil tongue, Jonah."

"Apologies, Blaike." Jonah looked as if he wanted to say more, but instead he simply glowered at Cate in silence.

"Hartley, if you do not have Blessing with you, why are you here?" said Blaike. "Why not just run and hide?"

"Because of the note you sent to me," he said. "The one that instructed me to come here."

"Until now, I assumed you were in Sanctuary with the girl. I had no reason to send you a note or request your presence."

"You said you'd give Blessing back to us if we gave you the Chronometer." Steve tried to stand up as he spoke, but Cate grabbed his wrist and kept him seated. For an elderly woman, she was surprisingly strong. "Why are you going back on it now?" He plunged his free hand into his pocket, thought of the device, and suddenly it was in his hand. "See?" he said as he held the Chronometer up. "We kept up our side of the bargain."

"Where did you get that?" said Jonah.

"Steve, put it away," said Hartley.

"But—" Steve sputtered.

"Put it away," Hartley snapped.

"Okay." Steve did as he was told, dropping the device back into his pocket. "But this is all wrong. They're not playing fair."

"Fair," said Naomi. "Such a childish concept. This boy does not belong at the parley table."

"I disagree," said Cate, finally releasing his wrist. "I think he has a better perspective on the situation than many of the adults gathered here."

"May I see this note that I supposedly sent?" said Blaike, holding out her hand.

"You want proof? Very well." Hartley pulled out the note from his pocket and pushed the scrap of paper across the table. "It arrived by squirrel mail just after Blessing was abducted by a grayling who incapacitated us with sleep dust. All signs of a magical influence."

"So you told the truth." Blaike briefly read the note. "But I did not send this to you." She rolled up the paper and tossed it back across the table. "Which poses the question: where is Blessing?"

Cate opened her mouth to speak, then stopped with a sudden inhaled breath. Leaning on her staff, she rose to her feet and slowly looked around the circle of stones.

"You sense it too?" Ana was suddenly at her sister's shoulder, her bow and arrow strung but pointed at the ground.

"Sense what?" said Blaike.

"It appears that someone is listening to our conversation," said Cate, stepping back from the table and tightening her grip on her staff. "Someone who is able to conceal themselves."

"You brought a darkling spy, didn't you?" Jonah Ledwitch stood up so suddenly that his chair fell back onto the ground. "What? To assassinate us?" He clenched his hands into fists, each bursting into flame.

"We did nothing of the sort." Now Hartley was on his feet too. "I, for one, respect the rules of parley."

"Not a darkling," said Cate. "The energy is too heavy. Too malicious. There, Ana."

Cate pointed to what appeared to be an empty area of the stone circle and, in barely the breadth of a second, Steve heard the zip of Ana's arrow as it sped towards its target. In the matching blink of an eye, the arrow revealed its mark.

The woman squealed as she dropped to her knees, clutching at the arrow that protruded from her shoulder. Dressed as casually as any workaday Steve might have passed on a street in the city, the woman looked to be young but battle-worn, from the crosshatch of scars on her face.

"Gotcha." Her rasping voice was unpleasant to the ears, both deep and high at the same time as if two people spoke in unison.

With a grunt, she threw a cannister into the centre of the stone circle. It bounced once, then rolled towards the table, spouting smoke in its wake.

Steve covered his mouth and nose, but not before he had breathed in the fumes. He watched as Jonah Ledwitch staggered to the floor. Blaike Harn and Naomi Onai collapsed over the tabletop. He heard Hartley cough somewhere nearby. Steve's eyes fluttered shut as the smoke took effect. The last thing he was aware of before he passed out was the pain of his forehead connecting with the stone tabletop.

*

The world hurtled back into focus with an extremely large helping of pain. Steve's head hurt all over and now there was the added sting of somebody's hand slapping his face.

"Ouch! Stop!" He struggled against the tight grasp on his collar.

"Behave!" The woman who had slapped him awake pushed his face down against the tabletop. "Or I'll make you," she whispered close to his ear.

"Okay," he said. His head throbbed and everything looked a little blurred around the edges. "I'll behave."

When she released him, he stayed with his head on the tabletop for a moment, trying to blink the pain away and the world back into focus. From his limited viewpoint, he couldn't see any of his friends or the Council members. What he could see, however, was one large, black, spherical robot waiting on the other side of the table.

He sat up as slowly as he could, so as not to set his head throbbing again, and looked around. It took him a moment to realise exactly what he was seeing.

Hartley and the three Council members stood against the wall of the cave-house with their hands bound. Each of them wore a collar that was similar to the ones the Council had placed on Blessing and the shopkeeper. These collars, however, were compact and streamlined. Their polished surfaces gleamed in the moonlight.

Not far from the standing stones, the three sisters wore collars too. Their unconscious bodies lay on the ground, their hands tethered. There was no sign of the white hound. A second robot stood guard by the sisters' bodies, its stripe of blue light standing out in the moonlight.

"He won't be any trouble," the woman told her companions.

"Did you search him?"

"Of course. He's got nothing. Just like all the others."

Steve rubbed his eyes to clear his vision properly. When he looked at the woman and the two men again, he mentally kicked himself for not recognising them sooner. He could almost hear the penny dropping into the slot.

Elrick Olen talked with the man and the woman he had brought into the office of Eleanor Palmer when Steve had visited the Haven Robotics Corporation only a few days before. Back then, the three of them had dressed like corporate executives. Now, they wore dark combat suits.

Steve felt something stir by his feet. When he looked down, he was met with a pair of amber eyes staring back and a wet nose that nuzzled his hand. Steve instantly wanted to pet the dog to comfort them both, but he didn't.

"The hound won't leave your side." Elrick Olen called across to him. "We didn't have the heart to separate the two of you."

"Heart...?" A sarcastic comment charged into Steve's mind, but he stayed silent. He didn't fancy another slap.

"Steve? Are you all right?" That was Hartley, taking a step towards him, his bound hands outheld.

"I'm okay." Steve called back. *If captured by Parity and with a head that feels like it's about to explode is 'okay'.*

"Back against the wall, old man." Will advanced on the shopkeeper. "I won't tell you again."

"No, bring him to the table." Elrick Olen picked up a briefcase that sat at his feet as he beckoned to Will. "Let's have a chat, shall we?" He took a seat a couple of chairs away from

Steve and placed the briefcase on the tabletop. Up close, the lightweight headset that the Parity agent wore could be clearly seen. It was made of a substance that appeared to camouflage against the colour of Elrick's skin and hair and consisted of two seemingly unconnected earbuds. One earbud extended into what Steve took to be a microphone. "You can fill me in on what adventures you've been having since we last met."

Steve rested a hand on Moon as the hound growled and snapped at the Parity agent. At his touch, Moon's snarl quietened to a rumble and the dog pressed himself to Steve's side.

"There's no need for manhandling," Hartley complained as he was pulled to the table. "I'm hardly any danger with this contraption around my neck."

"Sit down, old man." Will shoved Hartley onto the seat beside Steve.

"I'm not *that* old," Hartley muttered.

"I don't think we've been introduced." Elrick offered Hartley a professional smile. "My name is—"

"Elrick Olen," said Hartley. "Yes, Steve filled me in. You're Parity."

"Well, that saves time." Elrick leant back in his chair and beckoned to Will. "Take the others inside," he said. "I want to talk in private."

"What about the sisters?"

"Leave them where they are. They won't be waking up any time soon. Now the introductions are over," said Elrick as his colleagues dragged the three Council members into the cave-house, "we can get down to business. Where is the Chronometer?"

"So it was you who sent the note, and not the Council." To anyone who didn't know Hartley, he probably looked well and normal, if a little tired. Even though Steve had only met the shopkeeper a few weeks before, he could see how the collar was affecting his friend. When Hartley spoke, his voice was strained as if he was doing his best to ignore pain. His usual enthusiasm had been replaced by a careful focus. When Hartley moved his hands within their binding, his fingers trembled.

"I confess," said Elrick Olen, looking as if he was having the most pleasant of conversations. "The note was from me. I couldn't sign it of course. We needed at least a small element of surprise."

"My understanding of Parity is that you are a workaday unit," said Hartley. "You have no magic."

"That's right," said Elrick. "Although I take slight offence at the term 'workaday'. Don't you think it seems a little superior?"

"And yet you sent your note by magical means and employed the use of a grayling mercenary."

"We may not personally have magic skills, but we're more than happy to commandeer the services of those who do," said Elrick. "I'm especially proud of our discovery of the grayling contingent. They really have no morals. They'll do almost anything for the right payment."

"And where is your grayling colleague right now?" said Hartley. "The one that gassed us."

"Andra dragged her body into the forest. We thought she might prove too much of a distraction. There are plenty more who will take up her reins."

"That's awful," said Steve. "She was on your side."

"Side?" Elrick chuckled. "That's such a relative concept. Don't you think, Hartley Keg?"

"Where's Blessing?" asked Steve. "I want to see her."

"All in good time." Elrick's smile slipped from his face. "Tell me where the Chronometer is first. We searched everybody here and it appears to be absent. Unless one of you has cleverly concealed it. Possibly with magic?" he said.

"Hartley?" said Steve.

"It's okay, Steve," said his friend. "Well, not okay by any means. But we don't have a choice. Go ahead."

As he had done before, Steve slipped his hand into his pocket. *Right. Chronometer*, he thought, and the device was suddenly in his grasp.

"Here," he said, placing it on the tabletop. "You've got what you want. Bring Blessing here now."

"Spirited." Elrick closed his fingers around the Chronometer. "Don't worry. You'll be reunited with the girl very soon."

"Now?" said Andra from the edge of the stone circle.

"Might as well." Elrick raised the Chronometer in the moonlight to see it better. "Bring the other as well."

"Other?" said Hartley.

It's the darkling, thought Steve, both disappointed and happy all bunded up into one mess of a feeling.

"I do like surprising people," said Elrick. "You'll see."

Chapter Twenty-Nine

Four masked figures, dressed identically to Elrick Olen and his colleagues, stepped out from the charred tree line. The first supported a shorter, slighter individual—Blessing. She half leant on her jailer and half pulled away, a Parity collar clasped around her neck. The collar was similar to that worn by the others, but augmented by a ring of blinking red lights running around it. Her breathing was laboured and, even in the moonlight, the deep shadows under her eyes were obvious, as was the pulsing network of black and blue veins that marked her skin where the collar touched her neck. She gasped as she saw Hartley and attempted a faltering step towards the table before she was yanked back by her guard.

The second masked figure walked alongside a muscular, heavily set man. The man's face was striped by the shadows of the overhead branches, the moonlight playing on something metallic around his head and revealing patches of shaved scalp.

As the man and his guard stepped into view, Steve felt as if someone had hit him in the chest with a sledgehammer. He couldn't get his breath. His throat felt tight to the point of pain.

It can't be, he thought. *You're dead.*

Thomas Winters stood at the edge of the stone circle. He was dressed in a straitjacket, his arms bound to his torso. His feet were shackled, causing him to walk in short, unbalanced paces. Only half of his face and his scalp were visible. The other half was concealed in a heavy metal mesh. His neck was clamped in one of the Parity collars. A red light blinked where the collar met the mesh.

"Hartley…" Steve looked to his friend, but the shopkeeper simply stared at Winters with his mouth ajar.

"Like I said: surprise." Elrick Olen watched Hartley and Steve's response to the shackled man. "As you can see, the girl is unharmed."

"Unharmed?" snapped Hartley. "That is hardly unharmed."

"The collar does appear to have affected her in a more extreme fashion than the rest of you. I'll give you that. But it was necessary to adapt it to her superior level of magic." Elrick beckoned to Blessing's guard. "However, the girl is important to us. Other than the collar, she has been treated well. Keep your distance from her," he warned. "Deadly serious now. I won't tolerate any heroics." He glanced over to Andra, who met his gaze and nodded in response.

"You're all right," Blessing said to Hartley as the guard held her in place on the other side of the table. "I saw you fall down in Jem's kitchen, and I thought…" She gave a breathless sob, one huge tear running down her face.

"I'm absolutely fine, my dear girl," said Hartley with a sad smile. "Don't you worry about me. Or Steve. We're both well."

"Yeah. Of course, we are," said Steve. "Are you?"

"This hurts." She pulled at the collar. "It's worse than when the Council…" She stopped and breathed in another sob. "He's here." She looked back at Winters who hadn't moved since entering the stone circle. "I'm sorry. I thought we destroyed the Reactor. Thought we stopped him." She shook her head. "I just made it worse."

"No need for tears," said Elrick. "I told you. We can put things right now."

"What does that mean?" said Steve. "From where I'm standing—well, sitting—this doesn't look like putting things right. I thought Parity were neutral. Why do you want the Chronometer?"

"For the same reason that I wanted the Reactor and this."

Elrick opened the briefcase and pulled out a device that bore a striking resemblance to both the central part of the Omnometer and what Steve had seen at Nereid 8. Laid out flat, the device was constructed of three metal rings, fixed together at the top and the bottom. Where this device differed from the others was the concoction of metal cogs and springs within the rings, surrounding a circular space in the middle. The space was just the right fit for the Reactor and the Chronometer.

"The Gyrodial," said Hartley. "Frankie Una would never have given it up unless…" His eyebrows knitted together as he shook his head. "You killed them."

"Look at it like this," said Elrick. "I released Frankie from a lifelong burden." He held the Gyrodial up to the moonlight. "It's quite beautiful in its own right, don't you think? I wonder how much better it will look when I reunite it with its companion devices?"

"You want to rebuild the Path," said Steve. "But why?"

"How much do you know about the Path?" Elrick placed the Gyrodial back into the briefcase, adding the Chronometer. "Has Hartley told you the full story about the Haven lineage?"

"Haven?" said Steve. "What's my family got to do with the Path?"

"He hasn't, has he? How interesting." Elrick sat back, crossing his legs at the ankle as if he was relaxing at home. "Where shall I begin?"

"The boy doesn't need to know," said Hartley. "Not from you. That's his family's responsibility."

"Know what?" said Steve. "What are you talking about?"

"How much *do* you know about the Path, Steve?" said Elrick.

"That it was created by a man who caused some kind of magical accident with it, and that he decided to break it down into its parts. Split it all up so it could never be used again."

"Just the basics then," said Elrick. "Did you know that the man was an ancestor of yours?" He didn't wait for an answer before continuing. "His name was Sebastian Haven. He believed, completely wrongly, that he had created a time-travelling device. The idea was to jump back and save his wife's life. Of course, the device didn't do that. Did it, Hartley?"

"Hartley?" said Steve. "Why didn't you tell me?"

"It wasn't my story to tell. Your family would have explained when you turned thirteen."

"I *am* thirteen," he said.

"Yes, but your parents are…" Hartley paused. "They're away. When they get back—"

"What does it do?" said Steve, turning back to Elrick.

"Something wonderful. It opens a portal to somewhere other than our world," said Elrick. He paused, waiting for a reaction, then frowned as Steve's face remained blank. "I thought that would be exciting for a young boy like you."

"You want to open a doorway to another world." Steve's face might have been blank, but his mind was turning somersaults as he tried to absorb what Elrick had told him. The Path. Sebastian Haven. Other worlds. "What do you need Blessing for?"

"The girl's task is to recover the Reactor for us." He nodded to Winters. "From him."

"I won't do it!" She pulled against the guard's grasp on her arms. "You can't make me."

"Of course I can make you." Elrick spoke in a calm, even tone. "I have your friends."

"Don't you hurt them!"

"I won't touch a hair on their heads if you do what I ask. Otherwise." He shrugged. "Your choice."

"I don't understand," said Steve. "What are you asking her to do?"

"Isn't it obvious?" said Elrick. "The Reactor merged with Winters during the explosion. Something to do with the containment magic and the material of his laboratory. Blessing has the power to separate the two of them again."

"That'll likely kill the man. You can't ask her to do that." Hartley banged a fist on the table. "She's just a child."

"As far as any of you knew, she already *had* killed him," said Elrick. "When she contained him within the Reactor blast."

"That was different," said Steve. "That was an accident. One I caused."

"This is taking too long. Blessing?" Elrick climbed to his feet. "You will remove the Reactor from Winters to save your friends' lives. The situation is as simple as that."

"Blessing, I can sort this out," said Hartley. "Leave this to m—"

"Shut up." Elrick pulled a handgun from a halter around his chest and pointed it at the magical. "I've heard enough of your banter, old man. Blessing, remove the Reactor from Winters or I'll kill your friends."

"I told you before," she said in a shaking voice. "I won't kill for you, not even someone as bad as Winters."

"I see. Well, if you won't kill for me, maybe you'll kill for them." Without any change in his expression, Elrick shot Hartley. As the shopkeeper toppled backwards off his stool, landing on the grass with a wheezing exhalation of breath, Elrick calmly replaced his gun into its halter. "Now, do you believe me?"

"Hartley!" Blessing struggled in the guard's grasp. "Hartley!"

"You shot him." Steve knelt down beside his friend who had curled his body into a ball on the grass, his hand clamped to his shoulder.

"It doesn't look fatal," said Elrick. "Next time, it will be. Well, Blessing?" He reached for the haltered handgun.

"Stop," she said. "I'll do it."

"Good girl," said Elrick. "I knew you'd see it our way in the end."

"But my friends have to go. I can't have them see what I do."

"Acceptable," said Elrick. "Take them inside."

"Blessing." Hartley cried out in pain and struggled as Will dragged him to his feet. "Listen to me!"

Andra removed the collar from Blessing's neck as one of the masked guards pulled Steve to his feet and hauled him towards the cave-house, with the white hound lurking after him. Two guards dragged Winters forward, kicking the back of his legs to force him to his knees.

The last thing Steve saw before he was pulled through the doorway was his friend placing her hands on either side of Winters' face. Then the door closed shut behind Steve and he heard Winters scream.

Chapter Thirty

The immense cavern behind the sisters' home was as impressive as the last time Steve had seen it. The three waterfalls continued to cascade from the roof, pooling below before flowing out into darkness, and across the space he could see the raised platform that bore the carving of the maze with all its doorways to other worlds.

This time around, though, the cave was illuminated in an altogether man-made manner. Freestanding lights were dotted around the perimeter, each with two or three lamps supported on garish yellow tripods. The doors that had leant against the back wall lay in a pile of smashed-up timber.

The Council members huddled together on one side of the cavern, guarded by two of Elrick's armed soldiers. Naomi Onai leant against Jonah Ledwitch, her eyes barely open. She seemed so drained of colour and fragile that it looked like she would fall to the ground if Jonah released her. Blaike Harn's knuckles were white as she clung onto the collar that hampered her magic, her face racked with pain and rage.

Steve and Hartley had been abandoned. They sat against the wall of the cavern, with the white hound close to Steve's side. From time to time, Hartley would moan and close his eyes. The hand pressed to the wound in his shoulder showed traces of blood seeping through the fabric of his jacket.

Besides Hartley's moans, the only sound in the cavern was that of the waterfalls and Steve's thoughts. *Useless*, said the voice in his head which sounded scarily like Miss Scritch at that moment. *What purpose do you serve other than to fail? Your parents would be so disappointed.*

Stop it, he thought back. *That isn't helping.*

"Yes, this will do nicely."

Steve was so wrapped up in his thoughts that he didn't hear Elrick enter the cave. Behind him, Andra carried Blessing over her shoulder. Will followed with the briefcase in his hand. The two black robots rolled into the cavern after them, relieving the human guards at the entrance. The guards joined their colleagues on the other side of the cave.

At the sight of Blessing, Steve felt such a surge of anger in his chest that, if he'd had his way, he would have attacked Elrick there and then. As it was, Hartley grabbed him by the arm with his free hand, fingers clamping painfully on Steve's skin.

"We can't win that way," Hartley whispered in his ear.

"Of course, it isn't the original portal site. The Council made sure that was hidden away from the world. But this will serve our purposes," said Elrick.

"And what are your purposes?" snarled Blaike Harn. "I take it from your theft of the devices that you intend to reunite the Path. To what ends?"

"I think it's fairly obvious, don't you?" he said.

"To open the portal."

"Got it in one."

"But why?"

"Why?" he said. "New horizons. New minerals. The possibility of new trading opportunities. What's not to like? The Auditor has plans for whatever we find on the other side."

"Then the Auditor is a fool," said Hartley. "There was an exceptionally good reason for leaving that world to come here. I'd wager that reason still exists."

"I hate to say this, but I agree with Hartley Keg," said Blaike. "Too few years have passed for the threat to have abated. If you open the portal, you'll damn this world and yourselves."

"Such drama," said Elrick. "And none of it useful. I have my orders. The portal *will* be opened."

"But you don't know what's on the other side," said Steve. "Hartley does. And if he says it's a bad idea, you should listen to him."

"The Auditor has prepared us for any circumstance," said Elrick. "Don't worry, Steve. I won't head off through the portal until I've tested the conditions on the other side first. That's what you're all here for. You and your friends are my lab rats. Useful, but ultimately expendable."

"You can't do that!" Blaike spat out the words as she clawed at the collar that restrained her magic. "We are the Council."

"I'm sure the magical community have plenty more to replace you and your colleagues," said Elrick with a smile. "But as you're so important, you can go through first."

"Don't worry," said Andra as she dropped Blessing onto the floor beside Steve. "The girl is just exhausted. She did good. We could use more like her."

"Blessing." Steve pushed the hair out of her face and patted her cheek. "Hartley, she's not responding. What do we do?"

"For once, I am completely out of ideas. My magic is hampered. All our magic is hampered. Even Moon seems at a loss." The white hound made a low 'gruff', seemingly in response. "At this moment in time, my main concern is this dear girl."

"Me too," said Steve. *But there has to be something we can do.* "Hartley, can I take it that your pockets work, even though you're hampered?"

"Of course," said Hartley. "What exactly are you planning?"

"No idea," said Steve as he watched Will open the briefcase and display its contents to Elrick. "But..." He left the statement unfinished.

"Sometimes 'no idea' is the best beginning to a most marvellous plan. Or do I mean 'unplan'? Anyway, you get the gist."

"Worryingly, I do," said Steve. "Unplan it is then."

*

"Like a glove." There was a resounding click as Elrick fitted the Reactor onto the back of the Chronometer. "Not the most sophisticated of devices," he said. "But then what can you expect from a reckless, crackpot inventor?"

"As long as it works." Andra removed the Gyrodial from the briefcase, balancing it flat across her hands. Elrick fitted the combined Reactor and Chronometer into the central space of the device and waited. "Should I put it down?" she said when nothing happened.

"That may be wise," he said with a nod. "But remember what I told you."

"I remember," she said. "If it all goes wrong, nobody gets out of here alive."

"That's the one," said Elrick with a nod. "And now, showtime."

Andra lay the reunited device on the gravelled floor and stepped back a pace. The moment that the Path left the Parity agent's hands, the device tipped itself upright. Its rings turned, spinning at different rates. The central cogs and springs blurred behind the speeding rings, and the reconstructed Path device lifted off the ground.

Elrick and his colleagues retreated to the robot guards. Naomi buried her face in Jonah's chest. Blaike Harn wrapped her arms around her head and turned away.

"Don't look." Hartley placed his free arm around Steve, drawing their heads together. "Close your eyes."

But Steve just couldn't. This dreadful, dangerous device and all that it could do was just too fascinating to let it out of his sight. He raised a hand to partly shield his eyes and squinted between his fingers.

The Path hovered at shoulder height. The spinning rings had reached such a speed that they blurred out of view. The central portion of the device glowed with a pulsing silver light, cogs whizzing, springs shaking. Rising in tone, a buzz that vibrated

Steve's ears filled the cavern.

As the buzz reached its final ear-piercing note, the Path threw out a glittering ball of energy that hit the cavern wall with a smash. Steve expected the wall to break, collapse, but impossibly that didn't happen.

Where the energy had collided with the wall, a wavering doorway showed a clear path out of the space. Beyond the threshold, writhing grey smoke obscured any view of where it led.

"It worked," said Will.

"The Auditor said it would." Elrick advanced on the doorway, peering into its depths. "Disappointingly non-conclusive, though. I expected at least a glimpse of our new frontier." He released a long sigh and nodded to Blaike Harn. "Bring her over here. Let's try this out."

"You can't do this!" Blaike shrieked as two of the guards grabbed her arms. "I'm the head of the Council."

"We'll send one of the hounds through with her," said Elrick. "We can afford to lose one robot. Will, can you set up the camera feed?"

I can't let this happen, Steve thought. *But there's seven of them—nine if you count the robots. Against four hampered magicals, one dog, an unconscious Blessing, and me. They've got guns and robots. What have we got? Think.*

"Leave her alone!" Hartley tried to clamber to his feet but fell back, grunting in pain. "You have no idea what you're doing."

Steve plunged his hand into his jacket and pictured the only answer he could imagine. The item he pulled out only just fitted through the opening of his pocket.

"You'll get your turn, Hartley," said Elrick as Blaike struggled against the guards who dragged her towards the portal.

Steve switched to a crouching position and pressed the EMP and soul dust vials that he had pictured bundled together with the rubber band and thread that the pixies had given him to his lips. He kissed each vial and drew his arm back as he straightened up. With an inhalation of breath and a last worry about whether his unplan was the right one, he pressed his thumb down on the button of the EMP and threw the bundle at Elrick Olen.

The first effect was immediate. The two robots stopped working. The blue light that ran a complete circuit of their black orbs died and each rolled away, one coming to rest against a wall and the other against the base of a lamp.

At the same time, each of the collars that restrained the magicals opened with a clunk. Hartley was the first to pull the collar from his neck and throw it away, closely followed by Jonah Ledwitch. As the Council member released Naomi from her collar, Blaike Harn dragged herself free of the guards' grasp and hauled the collar from her own neck.

The second effect took a moment more to present itself. With Will and Andra at his side, Elrick watched as the dust thrown from the smashed vials stirred and began to spin around his feet. As it rose to knee height, the dust gained substance, forming into tendrils that inch by inch wound themselves around the legs of Elrick and his colleagues. Then the world descended into noisy chaos.

Working together, Jonah and Naomi turned on the guards closest to them, fighting with flame and ice. One of the guards who had held Blaike in his grasp cried out, his hands pressed to his head as he stumbled to his knees. The fourth guard dashed for the doorway back to the cave-house but Hartley, suddenly armed with the hockey stick he had stored in his pocket, knocked the man's feet out from beneath him. Moon pounced on the fallen man, sinking his teeth into the guard's shoulder.

Elrick and Will struggled and screamed in the arms of the two revenants. Each fully-formed creature clung to their victim, arms wrapped around the writhing bodies. One revenant pressed its ugly head to Will's face, while the mouth of the other hung loose as it held Elrick in its embrace.

With a wide-eyed expression of disbelief, Andra backed away from her screaming colleagues , her hand sliding down to a padded halter that ran around her hips. In a well-practiced move, she pulled a handgun from the halter and raised it.

"Gun!" Hartley blurted. "Steve, stay down."

But Steve had other ideas. Grabbing the hockey stick, he charged towards Andra. With a switch of her head towards him, she let off a single shot, the sound of it reverberating around the cave.

In the chaos and uproar, Steve didn't notice Blessing wake up or the speed with which she reacted as Andra fired her gun. He didn't see what his friend was attempting to do until she had already leapt into the air.

The bullet meant for Steve smashed into the shield that Blessing had created in a second, embedding itself in the solidified air. With an almighty crack, the shield shattered and vanished.

In two long-legged strides, Jonah Ledwitch was at Blessing's side. Before Andra could shoot again, he flung a barrage of flames at her, one projectile after another striking the gun and her hands. With a cry of pain and anger, she dropped her weapon to the floor.

"Damn magicals," Andra snarled. She reached into a zipped section on the torso of her uniform and pulled out an item that fitted easily into her hand. A button clicked under her thumb, then she drew back her hand and threw the grenade.

Pushing Steve and Jonah Ledwitch aside, Blessing pointed a clawed hand at Andra. The woman jolted as she lifted a foot off the ground, and continued to twitch as she was rapidly drawn across the cavern towards Blessing and the arcing grenade. Blessing pointed to the grenade with her other hand, circling her finger until the grenade slowed and hung only inches between the girl and the still struggling Parity agent. The air around the two of them shimmered and dimmed as Blessing left the stone ground, her hair flying around her head and shoulders as if she was in water. The surface of the orb that she conjured solidified, reflecting the light cast by the lamps as if it was glass. For the briefest of moments, Blessing and Andra faced each other, floating on either side of the armed grenade.

The grenade exploded at an ear-splitting volume. The orb shook, filled with flame and smoke, and then it flew apart like shattering glass. The force of the explosion blew Steve flat on the ground, the back of his head connecting with the stone floor.

After what felt like only a second, Steve blinked open his eyes. At first, he thought someone was ringing a bell or sounding an alarm in the room, until he cupped his hands to his ears. The ringing remained the same. He flinched as something wet and warm touched his arm. Moon the white hound gave a quiet bark, or at least Steve's hearing told him it was quiet, before drenching his face in licks.

Steve slowly sat up. The world tilted a little—he supposed it was the after-effect of the blast on his brain—but his stomach thankfully didn't complain. A couple of feet away, Naomi leant over Hartley, tending to his wound.

In the centre of the cavern, the floor dipped in a circular scar where the grenade had exploded. Flung across the perimeter of the scar, Andra's charred body lay face down. Trails of smoke hung in the air above her.

"Where's Blessing?" Steve tried to stand, but this time his stomach did complain, as did his head. He slumped back onto the stone floor, miserably looking around the cavern for his friend.

She's not here. At first, Steve didn't register the words as being anything other than the internal voice that constantly niggled him. She's not here, said the voice again but this time he recognised it. Blaike Harn limped across the cavern, her arm clamped to her side. She stared at him as she moved closer but her usual calm superiority had been replaced by sorrow. This time, she spoke the words. "Blessing is gone."

Chapter Thirty-One

"I'm so sorry, Steve." Hartley sat with his back against one wall of the cavern. His voice was laced with pain. His tweed jacket had been draped around his shoulders over the treated bullet wound. Steve crouched beside him, his arms wrapped around his knees. Selene sat with them, tending to Steve's wounded face and head.

"I don't understand." Now that the tears had gone, Steve felt numb. There was no anger. He had exhausted his grief. The only thing he felt was lost. "Where did she go?"

"Go?" said Hartley. "I don't think she…" He paused with a sigh. "It all happened so tremendously quickly. There was no time for her to go anywhere."

"But there's no, you know," said Steve. "No trace of her."

"I can't explain it," said Hartley. He shifted uncomfortably, squinting at the pain in his shoulder. "She's gone."

Over the twenty minutes since the explosion, the cavern had been cleared of most of its inhabitants. The Hidden had answered Jonah Ledwitch's summons, dragging the four masked guards from the space and rolling the unresponsive robots out too. Freed from the effects of the Parity collars, the sisters had appeared in the cavern, Moon the white hound leaping around them like a puppy.

Now, the only trace that anything catastrophic had happened was the silent, open portal and the two men who slouched in the embrace of the revenants.

"You should have a healing cup of tea." Selene fussed at the bruises and grazes on Steve's face. "Come through to—"

"I'm not leaving. She might come back." He pushed Selene's hands away. "Stop acting like you're my mum!"

"If that's what you want." He recognised the look on Selene's face. It was the same expression that his real mum got when he was mean to her; an expression that spoke of love and hurt feelings. "Hartley, I'll be in the cave-house, if you need me."

"That was unkind." The eldest sister, Cate, appeared at Hartley's feet as Selene left the cave. "She cares for you. She was only tending to your wounds."

"Sorry," said Steve. "I'll tell her sorry too, but later. I need to be here. For when Blessing comes back."

"I think we have to face facts, Steve." Hartley's eyes were red and puffy. Steve hadn't seen his friend cry. He had been so wrapped up in his own thoughts, he realised, that he hadn't considered how upset Hartley would be. "That was a powerful explosion. Close up. She saved…" Hartley's voice failed. He shook his head, and then he coughed and took a deep breath that puffed out his chest. "I don't know about you, but I would very much appreciate a cup of tea. I think you would benefit from a little fresh air too."

"I don't…" For a moment, Steve resisted. He was staying. There was nothing they could say to make him leave. Then he saw the misery on his friend's face and the deflated slope of the shopkeeper's shoulders. "Okay." Steve nodded. Hartley was right, even if leaving the cavern felt like he was abandoning Blessing.

"Before you go." Cate nodded towards the Parity agents who hung in the revenants' clutches. "Don't you think you should do something about that?"

"Me?" said Steve. "What can I do? I don't have magic."

"Hartley, did you not instruct the boy on how to use the soul dust?"

"Not entirely." Hartley shrugged, then winced at the movement. "You might say that Steve learnt on the job."

"Typical." Cate rolled her eyes and drew Steve to his feet.

"Come with me."

Two Hidden whispered in a huddle a short distance from Elrick and Will. Even masked, it was clear that they were puzzled and at a loss as to what to do. They moved as one as Steve and Cate approached, standing to attention but not barring their way.

"Watch," she said as she released Steve's arm.

She stepped close to the revenants and their prisoners, raising her staff before her. The revenants stirred, partly unfurling themselves from the men's bodies. They opened ragged mouths to roar at the sister, jutting their ugly heads towards her.

When she stepped back, resting her staff at her side again, the revenants silently wrapped around their captives and were still once more.

"Now you," she told Steve.

"I can't," he said, drawing away.

"Steve Haven, pull yourself together and come here." Cate's voice was stern and strangely convincing. Steve felt himself move forward a pace.

"They won't listen to me," he said. "I'm just, well, me."

"There is no 'just' about it," she said. "When you kissed the vials, you instructed the revenants with your intent. Intent is powerful, sometimes more powerful than magic. You are the only one who can tell these poor souls what to do."

"What do I say to them?"

"That's up to you," she said. "You can tie them to you, as slaves, or you can set them free. It is as simple as that."

"Okay." Steve braced himself as he stepped closer to the revenants. He was ready to run. In fact, he expected to run. "Right."

The revenants stirred, turning their heads to look at Steve, but that was all they did. This close, he could see how their form still hovered on the verge of smoke.

"Hi," he said. *What do I want them to do?* "Hi," he said again. "It's all right. You've done your job. You can go now."

With a long, trembling sigh, the revenants unfurled themselves from the two men. The Parity agents slumped to the ground at Steve's feet, muttering to themselves. The substance of the revenants returned fully to smoke, but it was a paler substance than before. It was as if two clouds hovered in the air. Then with another sigh, the revenants melted away and were gone.

Cate drew Steve away as the Hidden rushed in to grab Elrick Olen and his colleague. "Nicely done," she said. "Those souls are at peace now. Good boy."

*

In comparison to the cave, the stone circle outside was noisy and filled with arguing voices. The three Council members and a contingent of Hidden stood on one side of the stone circle. Hartley, Steve and two of the sisters stood on the other. Hartley leant heavily on Steve's shoulder. The table magicked up for their parley had disappeared.

"The Parity agents are ours." Jonah Ledwitch banged his fist against his chest. "I must insist on this condition."

"You don't have the power to insist on anything while you are in Sanctuary!" Ana snapped back. "And must I remind you that those people brought their battle to *our* door, not yours? They threatened the safety of Sanctuary."

"I would counter that Hartley Keg brought the battle to your door, not the Parity agents. We have a longstanding agreement with the Auditor. It is imperative that—"

"Enough!" Cate's voice filled the space. "This discussion is at an end. You may take the interlopers." She raised a hand to silence her sister as Ana protested. "They are of no concern to Sanctuary."

"And what about the Path and the portal?" Blaike Harn had returned to her usual controlled demeanour. "They should be in Council hands."

"As I'm sure your Hidden will testify, the Path cannot be

found," said Cate. "I conclude that it was destroyed in the blast."

"And the portal?" said Blaike.

"Without the Path, it can hardly be moved," said Hartley. "Not even the Council has that kind of power at their disposal."

"Exactly," said Ana.

"Hartley and the boy will remain under the protection of Sanctuary, of course," said Cate. "For as long as they wish."

"The traveller and the Haven boy are of no consequence to the Council," said Blaike Harn. "We only ever wanted Blessing. Now that she is gone, we can refocus our efforts elsewhere. However, there is still a discussion to be had about the portal, once we have recovered."

With that, Blaike clicked her fingers and one of the Hidden placed their hand on her shoulder. Two more did the same to Jonah and Naomi. With a nod from Blaike, she, the other Council members, and all of the Hidden disappeared.

"I feel rather like I've been dismissed," said Hartley. "We are of 'no consequence'. Charming."

"You should be pleased," said Cate. "Blaike Harn can be vindictive when crossed. You all got off lightly."

"Not all of us," said Steve.

"I think it's time to go home, don't you?" said Hartley.

"Home? That's a laugh," said Steve. "I can't go to my real home because my parents are somewhere they didn't care to tell me about. School is a prison and I'm going to be in all kinds of trouble for 'absconding'. That's what Miss Scritch will call it. I can't stay here because it reminds me of..." He didn't finish that sentence. "I don't have a home."

"Yes, you do," said Hartley. "You have Keg's Emporium—Whatnots and Assortments."

"Darkacre," said Steve. "That would be good. For a bit."

"A bit it is," said Hartley with a grin. "Cate?"

"You need a door," she said. "Come inside. I'm sure we can accommodate you."

"Marvellous." Hartley took a deep breath, the smile fading

for a second. Then he looked at Steve and it was back. "I'll make coffee," he said, pulling Steve to the cave-house door. "And if you're very lucky, porridge. How does that sound?"

"Good," said Steve. And despite all the terrible things that had happened that day, he had to admit that the best place he could think of to be at that moment was Hartley's kitchen with a mug of excruciatingly strong coffee and a bowl of burnt porridge.

*

Back in the waterfall cavern, the sisters had worked their magic. The five shattered doors had been restored to their pristine condition. Leant against the cave wall, they waited in a row to be chosen. This time round their transformation didn't surprise Steve at all.

Maybe that's what being a teenager is, he thought with a shred of sadness. *No more wonder or excitement at the magic. Or maybe that's just how I am now.*

To the left of the doors, the portal waited just as expectantly as its neighbours. The view beyond its threshold was still blocked by a curtain of shifting, grey smoke.

"What will you do with it?" Steve asked.

"Guard it," said Ana.

"From the Council?"

"Them," she said. "The Auditor." The youngest sister looked as unaffected by her treatment at the hands of Parity as her older sisters. Her hair was still tightly drawn back into a plait without a hair out of place. One hand rested on the bow she carried at her shoulder and the other on the head of the white hound. "Anyone."

"I fear the greatest threat may not present itself on this side of the portal," said Hartley. "Have you considered that?"

"We have," said Cate. "And while it has been a long, long time since we faced that particular threat, we have not forgotten."

"Of course, you haven't." Hartley nodded. "I wouldn't expect any less from you, from you all," he added with a smile for Selene. "Yours are the best hands to leave this predicament in."

"Steve." The middle sister touched a careful hand to his arm. "I hope you know that we will also keep watch just in case…" She looked to the roughly circular clearing that the exploding grenade had made in the gravelled cavern floor. "Should she return."

"Thanks." He couldn't bring himself to look at the indentation. I'm sorry for before, Selene."

"No need for apologies. I understand." She waved away his words. "So, what's next for you?"

"Back to the shop," said Hartley. "Then back to school, methinks. Time for a rest and a little normality, Steve, yes?"

"Is that what the boy wants?" said Ana. "Normal?"

"I suppose so." Hartley frowned. "What *do* you want, Steve?"

Normal, Steve thought. *What is 'normal'? It's not what it was before I fell into all of this. Apart from…*

"I want to find Mum and Dad," he said.

"Right." Hartley, for once, seemed a little lost for words. "Good plan," he said. "I've no idea where to start on that one. Perhaps a brainstorm and a hot drink will help."

"That sounds good," said Steve.

"My dear ladies," Hartley began.

"Do get on with it," said Cate, her hands tightening their grasp on the pommel of her staff. "Choose a door and leave us in peace. Your visit has exhausted me, Hartley Keg." She tilted her head with the barest of smiles. "Even if it has been interesting."

"Ladies." Hartley attempted to bow. "It has been a pleasure to see you all, as usual. May our next meeting be less eventful."

As the shopkeeper perused the row of doors, one last question poked at Steve. "Hartley, where do you think the darkling is?"

"That I cannot say." Hartley opened the middle door. A dusty waft of warm air brushed Steve's face.

"Do you think we'll see her again?"

"Undoubtedly. In my reckoning, paths rarely cross without

a reason," said Hartley. "Now, do you want to say it or shall I?" Hartley raised an unkempt eyebrow.

"I will." Steve took one last look at the sisters and then stepping through the door he said, in a voice that was stronger than he felt, "Onwards."

TO BE CONTINUED…

Did You Enjoy This Book?

If so, you can make a HUGE difference.

For any author, the single most important way we have of getting our books noticed is a really simple one—and one which you can help with.

Yes, you.

Us indie authors and publishers don't have the financial muscle of the big guys to take out full-page ads in the newspaper or put posters on the subway.

But we do have something much more powerful and effective than that, and it's something that those big publishers would kill to get their hands on.

A committed and loyal bunch of readers.

Honest reviews of our books help bring them to the attention of other readers.

If you've enjoyed this book I would be really grateful if you could spend just a couple of minutes leaving a review (it can be as short as you like) on this book's page on your favourite store and website.

Acknowledgements

There are so many people I would like to thank who have had a hand in creating Magic Bound. Where do I begin?

Well of course, I begin with home and those folks who put up with my writerly ways and inspire me on a daily basis - my husband, my daughter, and my son. Even the dog has helped by nagging me into those morning walks that provide an excellent opportunity to think away from my desk.

Thank you to my parents for raising me in a house of books, telling me tales of their childhood, and encouraging me to read. Who next?

My publishers – the wonderful people at Burning Chair – for believing in me and the Haven Chronicles series, and for helping me to see my book with fresh eyes.

Thank you to my beta readers for taking the time to read my book and help shape it into its current form.

Thank you to the friends, both on- and off-line, who have kept me going through life's changeable weather. Some of you are writers. Some of you aren't. All of you are absolute stars.

And thank you to you, dear reader, for joining Steve on his journey into magic. Don't go away. The journey is far from finished.

About The Author

For many years Fi Phillips worked in an office environment until the arrival of her two children robbed her of her short-term memory and sent her hurtling down a new, bumpy, creative path. She finds that getting the words down on paper is the best way to keep the creative muse out of her shower.

Fi lives in the wilds of North Wales with her family, earning a living as a copywriter, playwright and fantasy novelist. Writing about magical possibilities is her passion.

You can follow her on Twitter - @FisWritingHaven

Or at **fiphillipswriter.com** – where you can also sign up for an exclusive short story from the universe of Haven Wakes – absolutely FREE!

About Burning Chair

Burning Chair is an independent publishing company based in the UK, but covering readers and authors around the globe. We are passionate about both writing and reading books and, at our core, we just want to get great books out to the world.

Our aim is to offer something exciting; something innovative; something that puts the author and their book first. From first class editing to cutting edge marketing and promotion, we provide the care and attention that makes sure every book fulfils its potential.

We are:
- Different
- Passionate
- Nimble and cutting edge
- Invested in our authors' success

If you're an author and would like to know more about our submissions requirements and receive our free guide to book publishing, visit:

www.burningchairpublishing.com

If you're a reader and are interested in hearing more about our books, being the first to hear about our new releases or great offers, or becoming a beta reader for us, again please visit:

www.burningchairpublishing.com

Other Books by Burning Chair Publishing

Haven Wakes, by Fi Phillips

Beyond, by Georgia Springate

10:59, by N R Baker

Burning Bridges, by Matthew Ross

Killer in the Crowd, by P N Johnson

Push Back, by James Marx

The Fall of the House of Thomas Weir, by Andrew Neil Macleod

By Richard Ayre:
Shadow of the Knife
Point of Contact
A Life Eternal

The Brodick Cold War Series, by John Fullerton
Spy Game
Spy Dragon

The Curse of Becton Manor, by Patricia Ayling

Near Death, by Richard Wall

Blue Bird, by Trish Finnegan

The Tom Novak series, by Neil Lancaster
Going Dark
Going Rogue
Going Back

Love Is Dead(ly), by Gene Kendall

Burning, An Anthology of Short Thrillers, edited by Simon Finnie and Peter Oxley

The Infernal Aether series, by Peter Oxley
The Infernal Aether
A Christmas Aether
The Demon Inside
Beyond the Aether
The Old Lady of the Skies: 1: Plague

The Wedding Speech Manual: The Complete Guide to Preparing, Writing and Performing Your Wedding Speech, by Peter Oxley

www.burningchairpublishing.com